Klanty's *Daughters*

Colin Thomson

Detselig Enterprises Ltd.
Calgary, Alberta

Klanty's Daughters

Canadian Cataloguing in Publication Data

Thomson, Colin A., 1938–
Klanty's daughters

ISBN 1-55059-065-0

I. Title.
PS8589.H65K6 1993 C813'.54 C93-091241-1
PR9199.3.T56K6 1993

Detselig Enterprises Ltd.
210, 1220 Kensington Road NW
Calgary, Alberta T2N 3P5

Printed in Canada SAN 115-0324

To Shirley and Rod

Contents

Acknowledgments:

The author is grateful to the many people who kindly offered assistance and advice during the preparation of this book. Very special efforts were made by Sherry Wilson, Managing Editor of Detselig Enterprises. Once again Ted Giles, President of Detselig, provided his quick and effective support.

Technical assistance was extended by Barb Krushel, Cindy Cole, Charlene Sawatsky and Michael Gillespie. Medical insights were given by Dr. Joseph Hope and Dr. Margaret Winzer. Further ideas and information were gratefully received from Don Posterski, Wally LaClaire, Fred Thomson, Leonard Watkinson, George Brown and Don Pilling.

Detselig Enterprises Ltd. appreciates the financial assistance for its 1993 publishing program from Canada Council and The Alberta Foundation for the Arts (a beneficiary of the Lottery Fund of the Government of Alberta).

Credits:

Map by Michael Gillespie.

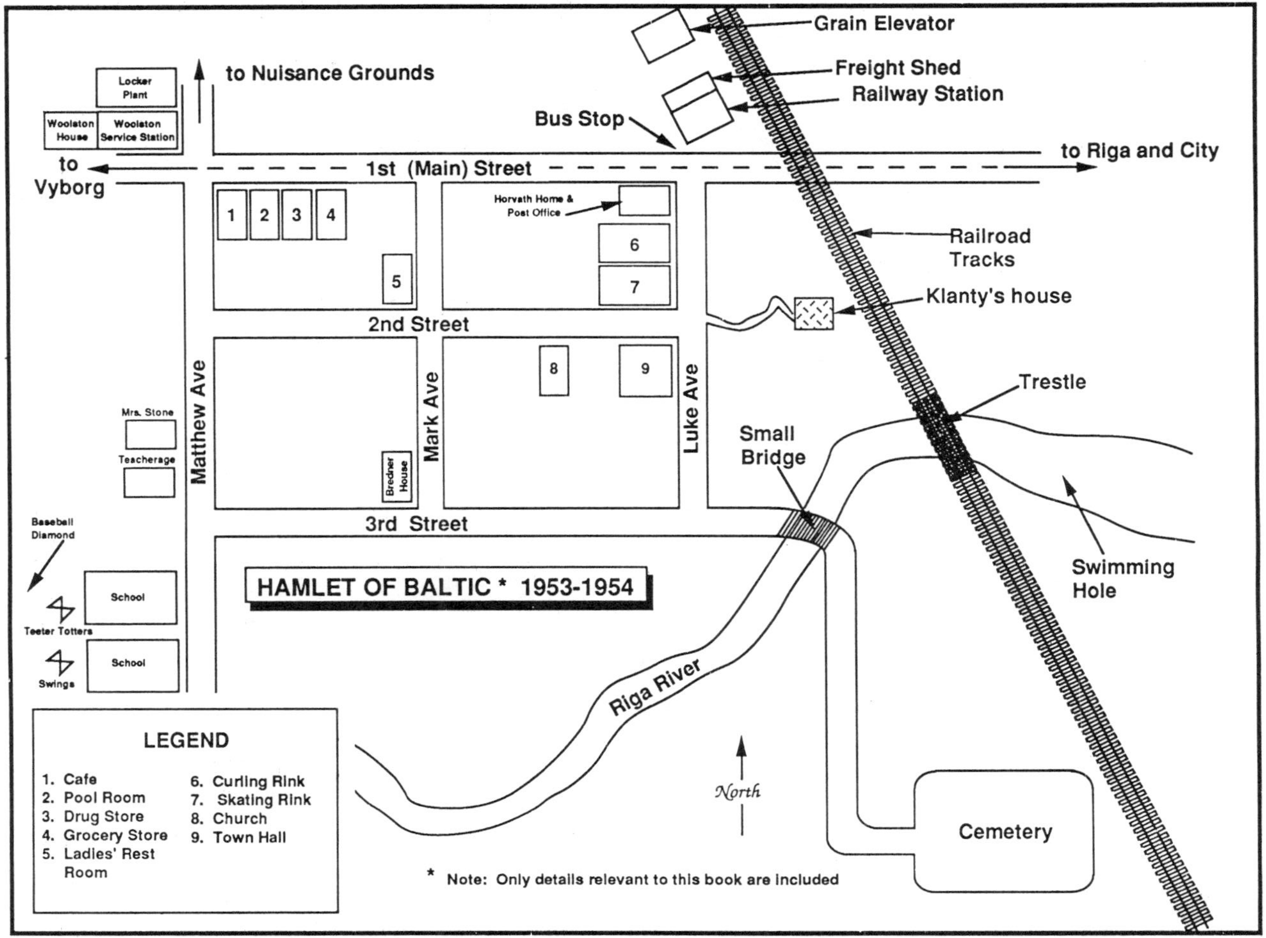
HAMLET OF BALTIC * 1953-1954
Grain Elevator
Freight Shed
Railway Station
Bus Stop
to Nuisance Grounds
Locker Plant
Woolston House
Woolston Service Station
to Vyborg
1st (Main) Street
to Riga and City
Horvath Home & Post Office
Railroad Tracks
Klanty's house
2nd Street
3rd Street
Matthew Ave
Mark Ave
Luke Ave
Bredner House
Mrs. Stone
Teacherage
Baseball Diamond
School
Teeter Totters
School
Swings
Trestle
Small Bridge
Swimming Hole
Riga River
North
Cemetery
LEGEND
1. Cafe
2. Pool Room
3. Drug Store
4. Grocery Store
5. Ladies' Rest Room
6. Curling Rink
7. Skating Rink
8. Church
9. Town Hall
* Note: Only details relevant to this book are included

1

Baltic

If you would be known, and not know, vegetate in a village; if you would know, and not be known, live in a city.
– Charles Caleb Colton 1780–1832

Spam, cold beans and lukewarm ginger ale purchased at *Woolston's Service Sentre – We Kater to all Your Motoring Needs* – filled the inner man. I promised myself to buy my next groceries elsewhere. A big promise, Woolston owned the only "store" in town. I unpacked my suitcase, and sat in the stuffed chair. "So this is Baltic," I said to the old kitchen stove which didn't manage a response.

A little earlier the service station owner and local school board chairman, Reg Woolston, had met the Riga train. We loaded my supplies, hot-plate and lumpy, stuffed chair in his truck, and rattled the fifteen miles to Baltic and my first teaching position. His large mongrel dog, King Rex, who had mange and bad breath, rode in the truck cab with us and graced me with his long jaw on my left knee. He yawned long and far too frequently.

It was late August and I had arrived a few days early to save Baltic and area children from the ravages of illiteracy. My comment about having the sharpest chalk in the west drew a dry grunt from Woolston. "Settle in, boy," he said, "'cause you are skitterish as a mare in rattler country." He wore a slight, hesitant, sad half-smile. The worst words I ever heard him say were "dangblast" and "pshaw" – he was one of those "come-over-

and-meet-the-missus" kind of guys. (I was to learn *that* wasn't a good idea.) I unloaded my things on the teacherage's front step, and Woolston quickly pulled away, leaving a blue haze from his truck's exhaust. It reminded me of the old story about the plumber's plumbing needing repair.

Woolston had forgotten to give me the damn school key, so I walked the two blocks back to get it from him. The front section of his establishment featured a counter and six Naugahyde-covered stools where customers could drink mugs of not-quite-hot coffee served with blue paper napkins meant to be saucers. Woolston was having some, "all saucered and blowed." Near an ancient cash register a sign advertised *Best Quality Grocs. Parts and Misc.* apparently all dispensed from the same counter. King Rex was asleep on a ratty, old wicker chair wide enough for two people placed by the door leading to the garage's shop area. The place was dirty but somehow friendly. Near the *Fresh Do-nuts and Koffee* sign a very successful, sticky yellow fly-catcher threatened the hair or hat of any tall, seated customer. Woolston offered to show me through his locker plant next door. Instead I returned to the teacherage immediately. The place, I swear, even smelled empty. No one had washed the dishes, apparently left by high school kids who had held a secret party there sometime over summer. I hadn't locked the outside door, nor would I for the rest of the year. The second bedroom door was locked.

Was my early arrival in Baltic a signal that as a first-year pedagogue I was dedicated, committed, and in search of excellence? Noooo. Simply stated, I was scared silly. If Woolston and especially the School Superintendent had known how little I knew, they would have tied me to the next train leaving town – backwards. I felt very small. I had signed my contract on May 29, 1953, the very day Edmund Hillary (a great name for a mountain climber) and Tenzing Norgay reached the top of Mt. Everest. Contrasts can be sobering. Everest vs. Baltic! A quick examination of my nearby classroom didn't change my mind, the blackboards still had last term's work displayed.

I decided to empty the cook stove's ashes, and go for a walk. Why do school work before seeing the hamlet? Such were the demands of dalliance and irritable restlessness. As I was dumping the second load of ashes behind the two-holer toilet, a tin voice said, "Don't waste them." A faint breeze had dusted my eyes with ashes so I couldn't clearly see the person speaking. With hands on her hips she stood between me and the bright sunset. "Why didn't you ask me if I wanted the ashes on my garden for next spring?" the voice demanded, imitating the sound of wrongly-angled chalk on a blackboard. As I wiped my teary eyes with a dirty knuckle she stepped closer, hugging her elbows, gave me a cursory examination, and in a toplofty way announced to the world, "I told them you'd be too young." As she spoke her curled forefinger thrust toward me as if she was tapping a cold window between us. Her breath smelled like yeast. My wheyfaced, fussily irritable, desiccated neighbor, who was at least five inches taller than I, was a sensible-brown-shoes-and-tweeds type of woman, all knees, knuckles and corners. A woman whose face was pinched with sorrow or anger or both? She smelled a little like Sloan's Liniment. Her hair bun looked like a large, frozen horse turd streaked with grey. Her nose was too high on her face, which wore an expression of sharp disapproval. The corners of her almost lipless mouth turned in a semi-permanent scowl. Her throat looked like the underside of a mushroom. She favored me with a glass smile above arctic grey eyes, exposing the smallest, whitest teeth I had ever seen in an adult. She turned on her heel and her long stick legs carried her to the house next door. That was my introduction to Mrs. Stone. I guessed that she wrung chicken necks for a living.

Dusk fell as I continued my walk, which took me past empty lots, empty buildings, and no people, dogs, cats or animal life of any kind. The churchyard's small, parched lawn had been taken over by dandelions and quack grass. The basement door around the side advertised last year's fowl supper, apparently held in the town hall. Dangling outside the church building was the exterior rope which was attached to the stubby steeple's bell. There another weathered sign proclaimed, *PULL ONLY IN EMERGENCY.* I doubted that riot or insurrection ever threatened Baltic. Obviously there was also an inside rope to the bell which weekly bonged the call-to-worship in the town's only church. It would be a shame to wake up the place! For no particular reason I entered the church with its hard but strangely comfortable pews. On the piano's cold keys I played (badly) the recent hit song, "Stranger in Paradise." "Now there's a laugh," I said to myself, thinking of Baltic. This town looked like a singularly boring place in which to live.

The next cultural highlight was the unpainted town hall. A faded and torn Union Jack sagged from the roof's flagpole, which jutted to the greatest height of anything in the hamlet other than the grain elevator. By then it was nearly dark, and it seemed necessary to relieve myself behind a large lilac which stood watch at the town hall's side door. Provided no doubt for country dances in full swing, when they open the side door to let in the fresh air and to provide fast exit. (Why do town halls have a ladies' toilet while the men, who drink most of the illegal beer, are forced to find dark places behind a car or tree?) I was nearly finished the process when a scratchy voice announced, "I know a guy on our ball team who peed up a wall eight and a half feet." I turned around and saw a young man standing there looking at me.

"My name is Stookie and you're the teechur," he said. (People in small communities know you're the new teacher even when they haven't seen you before. That newcomer is not a person but an event.) "Guess I'll join you," he added, and the hall's walls were further protected from drought.

"I sweep her out so let's go back in," my new acquaintance suggested. We went inside the town hall to share one-sixth of a dozen beer. Apparently Stookie had several "wet spots," as he called them. "Can't work dry," he said. Stookie was no heavy boozer, however. "Two a day is good," he informed me. During the coming months we were to have many a long one together in one of his secret "wet spots." I didn't tell Stookie that I was not yet twenty-one years old, and, therefore, couldn't drink legally – there or elsewhere.

Stookie turned the bulb to light the town hall's cramped kitchen which on a dance night would dispense strong, scalding coffee from copper boilers, plus an assortment of sandwiches which "sticks to your ribs." Stookie and I sat on the counter, dangled our feet, and with the modest light behind us we contemplated the near darkness and the dance floor before us. A large bunch of keys hung from his belt. He said that he had keys for all the "main" buildings in town except, he added, "the keys for them two school buildings and I ain't goin' to talk about schools right now." I decided it would be best not to ask him to explain that statement. Sewer and water had yet to grace Baltic. Only a few homes had pressure systems and septic tanks. Stookie was one "beneficiary" of the delay. He delivered coal and well water ("Adam's ale by the cream can" is how he described it) to most homes. He "minded and swept" the curling and skating rinks, and prepared the ice for both rinks. He also cleaned the Church, top and bottom; and, as noted, kept the cemetery neat and tidy. Stookie told me that he didn't "do the ladies rest room business" until very late in the evening "so there wouldn't be no ladies caught there." (I doubted if the place would be used, given the few people who ever came to Baltic.) I have no idea how much money Stookie earned, if any, for all those chores.

Stookie was a guy who removed beer caps with his back teeth. He reached for two bottles of warm beer and proceeded to decapitate them. He handed one to me while saying in one of his run-on sentences, "I catch where do you play?" (Apparently Reg, the garage owner-schoolboard chairman had mentioned to Stookie that I like sports, especially baseball.) My third baseman's answer seemed to satisfy him so we finished the illicit beer in silence. Just before we jumped down to the floor he looked sideways to me and said, "People who call me Wilbur or 'specially Adolph get their skull broke so you call me Stookie." He spoke in monotone, with as much lilt to his voice as a mallard. There was surely a child-like gravity to him. Was he simple-minded or merely guileless?

While in the faint light I took my first measure of W.A. Stook. He stood just over five feet. I saw that he had a big head, prognathous jaw, wide shoulders, and a great need for a bath.

"Mr. Stook, dare I say that the acidity of your armpits assaults my tender nostrils?"

"Yeah," said Stookie without hesitation, "I worked so I stink so let's go swimmin' down the crick."

After Stookie brought the flag down, carefully folded it, and placed it under the town hall's kitchen counter (Stookie raised and lowered the flag seven days a week), we headed through the darkening night for the swimming hole. The Riga River's swimming hole was just past the railway trestle that I had seen earlier from the gravelled highway. We stripped to mother nature's swimming apparel, and dived into the cool water. Stookie's beefy, broad, saurian body hit the surface first. Two fat mallards rose and squawked their way over the shallow river's tall banks and into the night. "Tomorrow they'll get twelve-gauge fever," said Stookie. Standing neck-deep in the water Stookie claimed that, "Kids don't go swimmin' here anymore 'cause they get their families to drive them to that cement pool they got there in Riga. Don't they figger this is good enough or something? Lotsa kids don't even know how to make grass whistles anymore." We finished our swim before the mosquitoes ate us alive and left for a good night's rest. In the full dark I slid down sleep's frictionless board a mini-second after I hit the pillow.

2

Stookie

If you want work well done, select a busy man, the other kind has no time. – Robert C. "Bob" Edwards: Annual

Next afternoon, Stookie, shotgun in hand, entered my then studentless schoolroom without the formality of knocking. "Let's get them ducks." Apparently my schoolwork could be delayed!

We walked to the swimming hole, and sure enough the two ducks or their cousins were there and within range. The mallards rose quickly, and Stookie waited and waited and waited, and then his twelve-gauge barked once. The two birds fell to the shore. We cleaned them immediately, not twenty-five yards from where we had belly-flopped into the shallow water the previous night.

"Spit-cooked duck breasts and spuds is good," said Stookie, opening his razor-sharp pocket knife. "I only shoot what's good to eat except rats and crows," my new friend added, "and crows is only for practice."

He had two large potatoes in his pants' pockets and salt in his shirt pocket. "Scrub the spuds down good in the crick," he said, "and I'll make the fire." I can't light kitchen matches with my thumb nail like Stookie did perfectly. You tended to do what Stookie suggested because his requests and pleasantries were so seamlessly joined. We washed the duck and potato meal down with creek water. He promised that next time we would "cook up a few prairie oysters" from Fred Kleiner's farm.

A few crows cornered a large owl in a poplar tree further up the creek. That strange, scary crow-call was answered, and from all directions hundreds of crows arrived – the poor owl had no chance at all. After 20 minutes or so, Stookie mercifully injected fever pills into the panic-stricken owl. Then I shot my first ever shikepoke and felt bad about my action. My new friend offered more insight. "Didja know that stupid birds like turkeys and prairie chickens is the ones that taste the best?"

Daylight wasn't kind to Wilbur Adolph Stook. Over out-of-season roast duck and greasy fingers, I counted many angry, ripe pimples on his cheeks, chin and forehead. Otherwise his soft, pasty face had a goat cheese complexion, pock-marked with the cicatrices of teenage acne. His low forehead sloped up to scurfy, burnt-toast brown hair. He had large, trusting, brown-marble eyes and scarcely any eyebrows or lashes. His hammer-blunt face, fat ears, and broadened nose belonged on a bar-brawler. I noted his thick, columnar neck and bunched, muscled wrestler's shoulders. Small feet anchored his bandied legs, and his hands were belt leather. Stookie was totally at ease within his hard, wide, deep and squat body. My ten month teachers' college training sometimes prevented me from seeing things as they really were and I wasn't yet sensitive enough to realize that in his own special way he was a master of clarity, articulation and gesture.

Stookie announced that "we should go back and git our baseball gloves and I'll hit you and throw you some." "If you play good," added Stookie, "I'll give you your uniform tomorrow." When we reached the ball diamond, he asked if I wanted him to get the little kids to go out in left field behind me. My 18-year-old pride said "no," so I took my third baseman's stance and waited for Stookie's best. He was terrible. A sweating clown. "What the hell kind of player and hitter is this guy?" I asked myself. I handled only two soft ground balls during my 10 minute trial run. Stookie simply could not toss a ball up and hit it. However, in a ball game he could hit line drives so hard that even the dead horse flinched. He was a superb athlete.

One baseball memory-snapshot of Stookie on the diamond was during a late September's afternoon game, when an opposing runner was at third base. The hitter sent a slow ground ball to our drawn-in shortstop, who fired a perfect strike to Stookie, our catcher. With his own right stanchion leg braced, Stookie met the tall, skinny runner. The beautiful throw was fractionally late yet the runner was called out. Out cold. Stookie carried him to his bench, poured two tin dippers of water over his face and head, and said, "You're okay now." Obviously the point was debatable. Stookie had a bullet throw to the bases. Thanks to Stookie's strong arm, in my first Baltic game I nailed three guys trying to steal third base. Stookie made his infielders look good, and clearly he was the fans' favorite player.

You never knew when Stookie was going to get a "kind stroke," as I called such incidents. In a league hockey game, for example, Stookie might fan on a weak shot from an opposition player who was in a deep scoring slump. "He needed one," our stalwart goalie would say. Wilbur Quickhands (as I called him in his absence) allowed pitches to get by his catcher's mitt, too. Those things happened only when Stookie felt that our team could afford such gestures. Sometimes those actions made me angry, damn angry. But then, I wasn't as wise as Wilbur A. Stook.

Stookie kept, sorted, and repaired our teams' uniforms and equipment. No one challenged or wanted that responsibility. We just knew that everything would be there when required. He was the unchosen captain-manager of our baseball and hockey teams. I don't remember a game that wasn't enjoyable, and the population in Baltic grew whenever we played a home game. The rural community appreciated our efforts, and we appreciated the community's support. Things had a habit of working well when Stookie was in charge in his determined but quiet and unfelt manner. He was the young man who without guile once told Wallace Talleck and me that "I only love people, thinkin' and things."

On our way back from the baseball diamond that first time, out-of-the-blue Stookie stopped me cold. "Ya know it was sure good that Joe DeMaggio married that Marilyn Monroe a while back 'cause they look so wonderful together and that's a fact." In any case, the unofficial coach, captain, manager, and owner of the Baltic Tigers then announced that I had made the team. Great was my joy. In a mere twenty-four hours I had reached the major leagues!

I wasn't sure, either, what he meant when Stookie said, "Come on and I'll show you the rest but we'll skidaddle 'round the empty parts." He led me to the hamlet's remaining grain elevator, and chose the correct key from his large collection. We entered "another of my places 'cause we can see the whole thing from here."

It was after hours, but that didn't matter to Stookie. Fearful of heights, I did not enjoy the long climb up the inside ladder, past the cleaner floor, to the top bin floor of the grain elevator. Stookie went first and uttered this advice, "Don't fall if you do most of your bones will get broke before you hit bottom 'cause people bounce all the way down." The climb was dark, dusty and musty, but we arrived safely at the top floor. Pigeons (is there a filthier bird?) cooed hello. A second, narrow wall-ladder led to the trap door which opened to a dazzling, blue sky. Beckoning me outside to the sloping roof, Stookie said, "Don't sit near the edge if you don't want to." More needless advice!

I sat on the roof and my scrotum tightened. My scalp felt cool and too small to stretch over my skull. Stookie said that "this is a good place 'cause nobody knows you are up here watchin' everybody." "Just a minute," Stookie added, as he disappeared with rubbery elasticity down the short, smaller ladder to another of his "wet spots." He was as quick and agile as an overgrown vervet monkey. We drank the warm beer in silence.

"I don't like guys who always pick the labels on beer bottles. You don't so I figure you're okay," said my personal town guide. A pigeon landed and pooped not 15 feet from me, quickly changed its mind about staying, and flew to another perch where love had to be in greater abundance. I really did hate those damn birds.

"Toldja this is a good place," Stookie said, as he started to point out the hamlet's highlights. He felt it was important to point a stubby finger at the things I was to see and know. He identified the various empty lots or properties which, in his boyhood, had contained a beauty parlour, town office, telephone exchange, barber shop, blacksmith shop, firehall "with a small jail cell in the rear," machinery and automobile agency, doctor's office, meat market, bank, two grain elevators, stockyards, lumber yard, jewelry and watch repair shop, two general stores, water tank "for the trains," two churches, Masonic Hall, town office, livery barn, hotel, and numerous houses. "Guess they're gone for good," he observed, "but Baltic used to be a real town." The trouble was that he would stand up with drill sergeant posture to do his pointing.

"Sit down Stookie; you're no sparrow," I said.

He looked at me calmly and reported, "I don't fall where I don't want to. Besides everybody has a time to die."

I supposed he was right. He seemed to have a blind, unreflective faith in himself. He said, "I peed from the edge the first time when I was ten." He patted the elevator's shingle roof like it was a breathing thing, and reported, "Yeah, I sweep her out." He also swept out the grain annex and any grain cars to be filled by the elevator agent, Jack Klackston. Stookie looked down on his town and told me that "I figure that some places aren't meant to be big and important just like some people. But ya know Baltic's story is enough to make the angels cry."

"Want to try out your pitchin' arm?" he asked. Then Stookie, blocky and square, stood with athletic casualness on the roof's apex and threw his empty beer bottle in a high arc into the stratosphere. It landed unbroken in the tall grass just past the railroad track. "Try yours," he said. I told him to forget it because there is no way I would stand on that sloping roof. (I was once told that people's eyes actually bulge when fear is extreme.) He stood and threw the dead soldier for me. We then slowly made our descent to safety, and we collected the unbroken bottles three feet apart.

A twist of Stookie's yellow key with the red head got us into the nearby, small, abandoned railway station. It was the first and only time my friendly tour guide was to show me the railway station. The building was special to him, I think. The tri-weekly "try-weakly, as the locals had called it" passenger, mail and freight services were withdrawn and the station's electrical services were disconnected. "Sometimes," said my new friend, "I liked the train's clang and sometimes I liked to hear her wheeze."

"I know, Stookie," I said, looking around the train station. "Ya sweep her out." A quick glance told me that one could have Christmas dinner in the place, it was immaculate. The waiting room's tall, big-bellied wood and coal stove was Bible black. The stove's nickel trim winked. The stove pipe, shovel and coal scuttle were also beautifully black. The benches were varnished and looked as if polish had recently been applied to them. Walls, window sills and frames, and two doors were painted with soft yellows and pale greens. Gladioli, forever the Roman swords, stood guard in a dull, green vase on the window sill. Perfect. A large, glass-covered, black and white photo of a cruise ship advertised the charms of the Greek isles. I admired the six-foot tall railway clock hanging on the far wall. Its pendulum, chains, weights, numerals and hinges were warmly brass to the touch. The pendulum swung to show the mechanism's life.

"I wind her," Stookie needlessly said. "When them railroad big shots closed this station down I came over to hide that clock 'cause it told the time to a lot of Baltic people for a long time so it belongs to people who like it." He paused. "Them big clocks sound soft when you're happy and real loud when you're unhappy." A faint but not unpleasant smell of metal polish seemed to emanate from the tall clock. Stookie claimed that he sometimes came over to the train station at night to do his "alone thinking."

"Yes," I replied solemnly, "there's too much traffic and noise in town for a fellow to find peace and quiet." He gave me one of his strange looks but said nothing. This was another of his "wet spots," but we didn't indulge. Apparently the office space behind the stand-up counter and half-grill was off limits for me. He added that "it used to be that trains used to tell people where they could go but now I can't go there anyways so now I only know Baltic real good."

"I get kinda sad sometimes," he added. There was, I believed, a somber solidity to Stookie, but there was also a shy warmth and an affecting candor.

It was only then that I noticed an old, tall radio, a battery-operated Stromberg Carlson, standing in the corner. Stookie noticed my glance and said that "I always listen to the news 'cause the world is bigger than Baltic ya know." He proudly showed me a very out-of-date globe which had gashes cut through Europe and holes punched in Africa, the Near East, and Central America. Red ink had been spilled over South East Asia. Original colors had faded. "Yeah," continued Stookie, "I follow the radio news on this old globe the school threw out but I guess they have invented new places now 'cause this globe sure don't show 'em. Didja know I even still got my mom's dictionary here?" He asked me not to tell anyone about "this school stuff I'm doin' here at the station shed 'cause most folks in Baltic think I don't know much which is kinda true." A strange young man! According to Stookie "this here is a great place to listen to the world series which is my favorite thing and if you wasn't too busy you could come here next month and listen with me. I figure the Yankees will win their fifth straight big one 'cause old Casey Stengel sure knows his baseball." I was beginning to think that Stookie talked longer about things he liked. Are we all that way?

He showed me the accompanying freight shed, where Stookie stored his five guns and ammunition, and all those wonderful tools, gadgets, wires, pails and equipment with which he served the denizens of Baltic. He kept our teams' equipment there, too. In that same shed Stookie kept "more wasp and hornet nests than anybody else has 'round Baltic (29) with my Indian arrow heads (approximately 275) and all my old blown birds' eggs I got when I was a kid." (I couldn't begin to guess their numbers.)

We went outside, where Stookie announced he had once placed his souvenir penny on the track, and the last passenger train flattened Stookie's precious penny perfectly. He drilled a hole in the flattened, copper coin, and carried it on his key chain ever since.

We left the station and walked across the weedy, pathless field to the road going past the nuisance grounds. A faint breeze drifted some bad smells our way. "We shoot rats here," said Stookie, "'cause there's nothing that needs more shootin' than rats. "Rats and flies is the only things I like to see dead," he added. "Nothin' is dirtier. That fella Noah shoulda kicked 'em off the boat."

More keys opened the Shanghai Cafe, Pool Room, Nyell Drugs, Baltic Mts. and Grocs. and H'dware, all empty and forlorn, sagging and tired. In the drug store's small dispensary I spied an ancient typewriter with *'C'* and *'D'* missing, an empty iodine bottle, and a clay mortar and cracked pestle. Dead centre in the hardware store was a box of 10 unused mouse traps and two full rolls of binder twine. I was immediately reminded of my own home town which also had too many empty monuments to more broken dreams, bad luck, poor planning and misguided optimism. Dying towns are sad places, indeed. The Baltic buildings had been seized for unpaid taxes, and the electricity had been turned off for years. Only a few of the buildings' dirty, partially-boarded windows had been cracked or broken by bad boys' stones. "I mind most of these buildings but don't always sweep 'em regular," allowed Stookie. He noted that these businesses were doing fine five or six years ago.

The second building, the nearly empty pool room, held the greatest interest for me, a pretty good player – sometimes. Apparently the former owner had sold four of his tables but was stuck with the one that greeted us. I removed its heavy blanket-like cover. One of those small, stiff pool-table brooms you can't buy anymore hung nearby on a nail. Two chipped, red balls and a good, heavy cue allowed me to show off my big city skills to my country cousin. My five-cushion bank shot worked perfectly, and I felt a bit smug. That's a damn tough shot, especially in the dim light of the pool hall. I glanced at Stookie for approval but all I got was one of those empty looks. I felt tired and a bit petulant as well as being very unhappy about my prospects in this dump called Baltic. At the end of a dark brown bench there was a spittoon with a 1948 girlie calendar hanging crookedly above it. Someone had given the scantily clad girl on the calendar a crude green moustache. My dark mood descended further as I pointed to the ancient brass spittoon, full of old butts, dead flies and worse, and asked, "Why haven't you cleaned that out yet?" Stookie's blank stare was direct but his eyes signalled no emotion. Stookie's stares and silences had a special flavor which often stung. Stubbornly, I asked him why he worked in all those buildings, empty or otherwise.

Stookie thought for a long time and then said, "If you don't do other people good then all you got to do is yourself. Hard work makes your heart open up more ya know." "Besides," he added, "if you do it right it's easy as poop through a goose."

"Guess I got time to take you to Mums," my new friend said. Again I wasn't sure of his meaning because he had told me that his mother died when he was twelve. We walked the short distance to the Baltic cemetery, identified by a rusty, wrought-iron entryway, and stopped by what I thought was a fresh grave. There was no headstone but the printing on the wooden cross said, *Elma Bea Stook, 1885-1942*.

"I make Mums a new cross every year," Stookie informed me. The dark brown loam rested loosely on a perfectly rectangular plot. Stookie said, "I been digging graves since I was twelve. Mum's too." A tiny weed grew in one corner and Stookie quickly plucked it. "No flowers, Stookie?" I asked. He replied in typical deadpan, "No. She had asthma." I pinched the back of my left hand to stop my smile from widening my mouth.

He told me something I had never even considered, "Christians are s'posed to bury their folks lyin' east-west ya know." As if anticipating my next question, he said that he had no father. "I guess I never needed one," he concluded. Stookie understood the stone-hard realities of his life.

I once read that some babies born of a mother near menopause have a quaint, old-fashioned solemnity about them. It surely describes Stookie, who said something I'll never forget, "When I pray real good sometimes I can hear Mums sing with the others."

Stookie, an only child, had been largely on his own since his mother's death. For a few years he lived with people who later moved to the city. After that the Horvath family, who ran the hamlet's post office, agreed "to take Wilbur Adolph Stook on." The youth was well cared for and loved by the Horvaths, an older, childless couple. Apparently he came and went as he saw fit. Indeed, very often his teachers would look up and find Stookie's desk empty. Authorities would return him, but his leaving ways would also return. Hooky Stookie!

The grade four "graduate" must have been the cause of real frustration to any well-meaning teachers. I later read the school records where one teacher commented, "Wilbur, age six, likely a brilliant boy, is unable to mesh his personality with the philosophy of the school system." The comment made me angry. What the hell does "mesh" mean? Shouldn't schools mesh with the world's six-year-old Stookies? He told me that at age twelve, he decided that "I knew enough already even though they nearly always failed me so I quit going to your school." (That statement was later carefully underlined in my diary.)

As we returned to the village from the cemetery we recrossed a little bridge over the small creek with the high banks, the "crick" we had visited the previous evening. He pointed to a small house a few hundred yards to the north, a house I had noticed en route to our duck banquet. I turned to Stookie and asked, "Do you sweep that house out too, Stookie?"

Another look, and another flat statement. "That's Sheba Faye Klanty's place her father is very bad ya know."

"Yeah," he said, "I'll have to tell her one of these days it's time for us to get married 'cause she's 17 now." Stookie then told me that he wasn't going to propose to Sheba Faye until the girl "got her Eight." He turned to me and asked, "Well teechur are you gonna pass her?" Apparently one Sheba Faye Klanty was going to be my Grade VIII student – and I was to decide her marital status.

Stookie and I parted just as the late day's first, faint coolness descended. Delicious. The tired sun was melting into the horizon, and the sunset began smearing reds, yellows, oranges, before splashing larger, darker colors. It wasn't until I got back to the teacherage that some questions popped into my brain. Did Stookie legally possess those keys he wore like a gunfighter? Was he paid for his "sweepin' and mindin'"? Was he trustworthy? Did he really know everything about this hamlet? Who was this Grade VIII kid, the would-be bride claimed by

Stookie? Did she share his bland assumption? And what about her "evil" father, Klanty?

I kicked off my shoes, put on an unneeded fire in the kitchen stove, and dragged my chair from the front room. Putting my feet in the yawning oven door, I shook off the weight of my small world. I was bushed. While I dined on an inch and a half of warm, nearly fizzless gingerale and more cold beans, I slowly realized that in two days I had spent perhaps seven hours with Stookie, and those hours had zipped by, despite my sometimes rotten attitude.

A few hours later I made a trip to the outhouse. At first it seemed I was the only thing that moved through the late summer night, listening to the thousands of mostly friendly night sounds. I liked the always-busy insect sounds, and it was a treat to hear a throaty robin or meadowlark at dusk. Those creatures know something special. Then I heard a noise in the back lane which definitely wasn't an animal of the night. An errant street light shone on Wilbur Adolph Stook, dressed in rubber boots, long rubber gloves, and heavy overalls. He opened our toilets' back trap and reached for the first pail which he dumped with a sound somewhere between "flooosh" and "splooch" into the back of a truck's large barrel. Stookie emptied the second pail into the "honey wagon," returned the pail, closed the trap door very quietly, started the motor, and rattled away in the truck towards the pit at the nuisance grounds.

I noticed that Mrs. Stone's light still shone. (A few months later she explained the reason. "When you're tired-old," she said, "Memory crowds out sleep.") With its belly likely full of warm baby mice, a coyote ("ki-yewt" to Stookie) east of the trestle and the graveyard yipped and spoke long notes to the beautiful night. The moon was a few days short of full. I was beginning to like the hamlet.

As I hit the sack a thought poked its way somewhere in behind my right ear. Stookie said that he had a girl. I had assumed there wasn't one eligible girl in Baltic for me, and the future in that area of research looked very grim, indeed. During recent years my pursuit had been diligent if seldom successful. The Sheba Fayes of my dreams were usually soft, warm girls with soft, warm lips who were, obviously, totally imaginary.

3

Wallace Talleck

You can grow corn or potatoes, but you cannot grow brains. Brains come hard and they come high. – William Osler, Canadian Club

Three days after my arrival in Baltic, Mr. Wallace Talleck arrived by car at the teacherage. A twist of his key unlocked his bedroom door, and he placed his suitcases in that room. After introductions and a brief conversation he unpacked his things, and then returned to the kitchen where I was slowly stirring can-brand hot soup on the stove. He was slightly behind me when he placed his right hand on my left shoulder, and said, "I'm a homosexual, you know."

My fist had a fast motor, and I aimed it at the tall man's Adam's apple. He went down like a poleaxed steer, and my guts turned to warm prune juice. He'd really been nailed. Surely he must have seen it coming, I thought. No, he'd been holding his glasses and cleaning tissue in his left hand. Had I hit a man who couldn't see the punch coming? Would it have been better if I had kicked him in the family jewels? I thought that he would choke to death or that his airpipe or something would be snapped shut. I could just see the headlines:

NEOPHYTE TEACHER KILLS MALE LOVER

I was petrified, so I put a cool, wet cloth on his forehead. Great thinking!

Wallace Talleck moved his length a bit, rubbed his injured chin, and carefully unwound himself from the kitchen floor. He was a gangly, tall, cadaverous, sharp-angled guy who looked powerful without being muscular.

"My neck is not hurt, idiot," he said in a surprisingly strong, rotund voice.

It was then that I noticed my third knuckle hurt. I poured some hot chicken-noodle soup (my Grandma's cure all for all ailments) and told my colleague to drink it. Thanks to his excellent first-baseman's aim, the soup industry's finest recipe was unceremoniously dumped on my head.

Wallace put on his glasses and threw me a towel. He apologized to me, or I think it was an apology – he used words I didn't quite understand.

"My anger is not always tethered by good intentions," he added, "so maybe you better tether yours. And for your own sake you better learn to control your splanchnic reactions to peoples' comments."

Who in hell talks like this guy? I asked myself, as I put the towel to work.

"Or do you want a mini-career picking up your teeth?" he asked, perhaps rhetorically. Yes, I sure understood those words. A tick convulsed his right cheek and his thick, rimless spectacles gave him a pop-eyed look of owlish erudition.

"You've got the brash convictions and the arrogance of the insecure, and you misunderstand my action and my words," he said. "You're like too many people – ignorant of the facts." Wallace stared at me calculatingly. "Don't be so busy flattering yourself, kid, and instead spend a little more time gaining maturity and compassion for both people and things you don't understand." He paused, then added, "I pray that you'll achieve those things."

"Do fairies really pray?" was my silly retort to my cool and self-possessed colleague.

Wallace pinched the bridge of his nose between forefinger and thumb as if he had a terrible headache. "I also expect you to share my confidence with no one," he said and walked stiffly to his bedroom.

I wasn't man enough to apologize. However, a mutual acceptance had been established, or at least begun. I considered his admission to have been a secret, and treated it that way. I assumed that the rest of the hamlet's residents did not know about his homosexuality.

Colleague "Tall Wall" (I was an incurable giver of nicknames) had taught in Baltic for the last two years. He was only 29 years old, but I thought I could see a hard-edged older man inside of him waiting to come out. His face was marked with hard-won knowledge, and he was often, but not always, laconic in speech. Wallace Talleck was a young man and an old one, especially in his eyes. I would learn much about his luminous intelligence and sometimes wry derision toward life.

A couple of weeks after meeting my colleague, we were teammates at a Sunday afternoon baseball practice. The sun was an imperfectly tarnished coin in a light blue September sky. Tall Wall on the diamond had the rangy, elastic strides, long reach, and quick hands needed by a good first baseman. A gristle and rope kind of guy. His arm was accurate and his speed deceptive because of his long, stilt legs. Wallace and I had planned to make a brief stop at the teacherage to clean up after practice and eat a bite or two before heading out.

The teacherage was really a transplanted ex-store on blocks whose high ceiling's fluorescent lights surely held the world's record for turning on slowly. Splat, a scabrous, tobacco-brown stray male cat who deserved that nickname, regularly brought very dead birds and rodents and left them under the teacherage. The cat played with his victims before killing them, of course, and then the hateful thing licked himself thoroughly.

Before Wall's arrival two years ago, carpenters with long spikes and thin lumber attempted to refurbish the structure. They divided the large store building into a kitchen, porch, two bedrooms, and a very large living room. The teacherage's big front plate-glass windows allowed us to enjoy visually the splendors of Baltic. I learned to both love and hate the dump/prison/den/library/music-room/poker-palace. We stored some of our private sports equipment in the small counter identified as "pens and stationery." In that counter, apparently not earlier opened by Wallace, I found an empty, finely-made wooden box on which was neatly printed *French Letters,* so I assumed the box belonged with the writing equipment. (As Tall Wall later explained, a French Letter is a term for a prophylactic.) There was a *Snellen's Eye Chart* hanging in the back porch and a frayed, fly-specked sheet announced *Gopher Tails 2 Cents*.

Wallace's bedroom was disgustingly tidy. You could bounce coins on his tight, chenille bedspread. Who else would have a green-felt blotter covering his bedside table? I knew that my dapper and meticulous colleague must train his shoes, socks, shirts and such to return neatly to their places. His slacks seldom needed pressing. Once when he was ironing his underwear and pyjamas I tossed him his Balbriggan socks and asked if he were going to iron them, too. His expensive foulard ties, fine shirts, eight or ten suits, slacks, and sport jackets were hung to perfection. He did his washing on early Monday mornings – just like most of the hamlet's housewives – and hung his wet items to dry on the clothesline which stretched from the porch to the outhouse. His fine shoes – half of them two-toned – always shone. He even polished his baseball cleats. He looked dressed up even when it was a day to relax. He wasn't fussy, just tidy with operatic thoroughness, and he carried out routine tasks with efficiency and quickness. It seemed to me that people's incompetence and lethargy were the two things that bothered him most. While Wallace appeared to have a fine store of calm and self-satisfaction, his laconism could not disguise his complex and perceptive intelligence.

While we changed and washed Wallace used the time to give me another of his lectures, this one on baseball history. He claimed that the first publicly televised sporting event was a Japanese baseball game on September 27, 1931. I wrote the date in my diary, and intended to put Wall in his place by proving him wrong (but never did). We had a quick meal and then "Bright Boy," Wall's sobriquet for me, and "the Fruit," as I (privately) called him, left to see the sights.

A slightly acid and hot fragrance lent itself to the late-summer smell of land, and there was a mustardly quality to the light. The casaba sun's late rays caught Wall's glasses as I looked up to the world's palest gray eyes a head higher in the stratosphere. His blond brushcut was a shade away from gray. His slightly askew, imperial beak stood watch over his nervous, simian mouth, sucked-in cheeks, and wedge of chin. Only infrequently did his face break into what passed for a nervous, quick smile. With a bent neck and head pecked forward like a tall bird, he was a curious study with a vulnerable look to him. He often smelled like hand lotion.

Most men, if they walk with fingers interlocked, place their hands behind them. Not Tall Wall, who laced his fingers in front of him, walking in a shambling, round-shouldered way that reminded me of a deacon. I was counting the planks in the wood (not "wooden" in Baltic) sidewalks. Under my breath I was saying over and over, while trying to get rid of the silly verse, *Step on a crack, break your mother's back, Step on a nail, put your father in jail.* I often felt that juvenile around Wallace Talleck.

Most times Tall Wall had a caved-in, unhappy, pecant look of failure, especially while he wore those old-fashioned, damn-fool glasses of his. When he removed his glasses for cleaning, a handsome, sentient face emerged, almost Byronesque, or more like a Lenin with pale blond hair. His cleverness often intimidated me. Wall was the kind of person you would choose to chair important meetings, a man who gave orders without raising his voice. Somewhere along the line tough experiences and pain had put a stillness and brooding intensity into Wall's eyes. My grandfather once told me that people with such eyes never find peace and tranquility. The great French thinker and scientist, Pascal, said that man is only a reed, the weakest in nature; but he is a thinking reed. That sure describes Tall Wall.

We were passing Mrs. Stone's front hedge, murmurous with bees. I hoped that we would get by her house without interruption. No such luck. Her humorless, see-all eyes spotted us. Mrs. Stone, that fine connoisseur of ashes, offered us lukewarm lemonade. She wore a long, shapeless yellow print dress, and when she bent to pour me a glass I saw down her flowery blouse. Her breasts were like my Grandpa's tobacco pouches. I remembered some high school boys referring to her as "old sag tits," and I hadn't been man enough to react. Those boys had been correct.

"There now," said the president of the local Women's Christian Temperance Union, "isn't that better than demon rum?" A damn tough question!

I learned two things about her – she had a daughter named Jenny, a student in London; and for some reason then unknown to me, she hated Wayne Klanty.

On the back wall of the veranda was a neatly lettered list of the seven deadly sins: *pride, wrath, envy, lust, gluttony, avarice* and *sloth.* On the front wall was a list of the seven virtues: *faith, hope, charity, prudence, justice, fortitude* and *temperance.* I asked Mrs. Stone which "team" would win a world series involving sinners. Tall Wall lightly kicked my ankle as our hostess shot me a hot glance.

I had to admit that no one grew flowers more beautiful. Mrs. Stone's prairie lilies, red-orange as hot coals, and her stately, proud gladioli, among other varieties, prove that sunshine, black loam and water know much about birthing beauty. In our neighbor's dining room and living room, many roses of all colors stood tall in their antique celadon vases. She had curtains of flowered chintz. Her end-tables and ledges held scores of glass knick-knacks, (Wall called them "cheap bibelots"), including at least two dozen of those useless crystal balls with snow flurries in them. All her heavy chairs and her large chesterfield were covered by what I quietly called "Aunty's awful antimacassars." (Wallace was unimpressed with my tortured alliteration.)

Mrs. Stone kept us late in her attempt to show us the right road of life, so we returned home, and spent the rest of that Sunday evening sampling Tall Wall's record collection and fine wines. He also introduced me to his library, and played the "newest sound" on his piano.

We discussed education, and Wall gave me one of his by now anticipated lectures. He believed that knowledge alone is not going to save the world, but with an imaginative use of that knowledge mankind might do it; intellectual courage must be the prime strength of the teaching profession; grinding anti-intellectualism and the fads of some university departments encourage learning but not understanding; only the best should become teachers, and they should be paid a king's ransom; teaching is an art and a science and a craft and the world honors and needs craftsmen of integrity; the best of the best teachers should be encouraged to teach the youngest of the young; teach students less but better; a little gumption would do a lot of teachers a lot of good; among all the animals, young people have a sense of awe, don't kill it. He had claimed that his hero, Oscar Wilde, was correct when he wrote that everybody who is incapable of learning has taken to teaching – that is really what our enthusiasm for education has come to. Was Wall referring to me?

Wall would dismiss any educator who did not love the intellectual and emotional sweetmeats of literacy and numeracy, the "Big Two." Kids must be drilled on occasion, he said; the progressive education movement was a disaster and teachers must encourage kids to work and to love the work. Wallace believed that there was nothing about a good learning situation that bureaucrats (he called them "the faceless and the chinless") couldn't spoil.

He also claimed that all young people should be humbled by having to experience such elemental power as cold, heat, flood, terror – and the unforgiving supremacy of nature. Getting their hands dirty with a little hard work and hard play would do students a lot of good. Coming as close to frivolity as he could, Wall patted the top of his head with one hand and stroked his stomach with the other while saying "keep children both lean and hard here and here because the mind and body are one and the same." Wallace believed that too many kids end up as adults with the necessary smiles and knee-jerk congeniality of a crooked used-car salesman, the chief purpose of which is to mask meaning. Schools, he suggested, produce too many people who confuse living standards with quality of life.

"With those big ideas why don't you move to the city and study for a university degree or two?" I asked Wall.

He favored me with one of his looks and said sharply, "I've read and digested more fine books than have any six of your Uni-Ed eggheads." Wall believed that Wilde was correct in his assessment of many professors' books, which show "a want of knowledge that must be the result of years of study." Wall also believed that too many unctuously political Education professors (he called them "troglodytes") taught methods, facts and knowledge, but not understanding, thoughtfulness and scholarship.

For an educator, Wall said, dullness was a sort of crime. Most of the education professors he had met had been neutered by compliance, he claimed, and many of them would eventually surrender themselves to cynicism – a short leap from idealism. Wall thought the best educators were people who loved the soil. He believed that if teachers lose contact with the soil they lose contact with our most definable reality. "That's why I teach in the sticks," he said, waving his hand vaguely towards the sleepy hamlet of Baltic.

"Scholarship," he added, "demands a lifetime commitment, not four or five years of intellectual games, beer contests and panty raids." I didn't dare tell him I didn't fully know about the last two items.

It had been a warm, special night, one that I enjoyed thoroughly, but I was yawning so vastly that I tottered, and I headed for bed. I recorded a few of Wall's views on education in my diary, and reflected on my own recent experiences at teachers' college. I had majored in *Skipping Classes 101*, as I received little scrutiny and even less instructional brilliance from many of our instructors. It must be said, however, that if my classmates brought as little to the endeavor as I did, the instructors faced the impossible task of turning young people into teachers. When I did attend classes, I found most of my instructors to be kindly, courteous, and full-of-human relations stuff, but also inept, poorly prepared, intellectually lazy and tired. That was the last year for the college, which "moved over" to the university that summer, where it should have been years ago. The three superb instructors who did meet with my royal approval fit in well at the university, but I haven't the faintest idea how the others could survive professionally there. The three instructors whose classes I never skipped were tough, demanding, encouraging, constructively critical, sometimes humorous, and consistently prepared – and they asked the damndest questions I ever heard. Thanks to them, I learned something of the pleasures and pains of heavy reading and disciplined physical activity.

It must also be said that much of what I did learn there came from the "courses" held in the library, gymnasium, and other sporting facilities; in various pool halls; and in the janitors' basement lounge – to loose that term loosely. There, beside the large furnaces, the head janitor taught me a bit about crib, poker and chess. Indeed, he is the only guy I ever knew who got two hands of 29 in cribbage. By spring I was winning my share in cribbage, but hadn't begun to reach his excellence in poker and chess. That lovely old man taught me something I'll never forget: for 26 years he held a railroad job which included mindless sweeping and repairing of the tracks at the busy city crossings. He said it was the best job a person like himself could have because it allowed his mind to go when and where it wanted to. "I used work, work didn't use me," was how he put it. During the work day he composed poetry in his head, and at night he returned home to write out those verses and read them to his wife and anyone else who would listen.

"You see, son," he said, "my railroad job added to my freedom. Most other jobs drain a person. You'll never find that kind of freedom when you start teaching school 'cause you'll be too busy in your head."

The most pleasant feature of that year had to be that the females outnumbered the males five to one. Not that the ratio granted me much success. I was good on the dance floor and on many back steps but that was about the extent of my success with the ladies. Only two of my male classmates owned automobiles and they claimed their "seduction rates" were very, very high.

I had the chance to see Wall put his theories into practice on many occasions. Wall taught grades I to IV and was terrific with his classes. He called every student, "hey kid," and got away with it. That September when some of the hamlet's children followed him home to the teacherage, he served them lemonade on our front lawn. (Was he aware of the town's attitude toward homosexuality?) At work with his students, that tall man would on occasion sit on the floor and help the youngsters at their desks. Even then his trousers refused to grow creases. After a day's work, his shirt and tie still looked fresh and sparkly. I could feel rumpled just by looking at him. In contrast to my lazy scrawl, Mr. Talleck's printing and writing on paper or blackboard were works of art.

I once told Wall that I could never match his ways with students, especially the younger ones. His response stung. "Like too many educators you are developing a pathological need to disprove your low and secret opinion of your teaching abilities."

I taught 16 grade V to VIII youngsters. My younger pupils' cheerful uncertainty made me feel old at 18. The high school students were bused into Riga – except Sheba Faye Klanty, who at age 17 was my oldest student.

School authorities took IQ tests seriously, and so did I. Marsha Fowler, my smallest student and a "future missionary," had a measured IQ of 178. It was exactly twice that of Sheba Faye Klanty. I didn't really know what Wallace meant when he said he loved children too much to give them IQ tests. When I asked him how else is one to separate the dull from the clever, his response was that they were "too separate" as it was.

My ignorance made me angry. I asked, "Then why don't you change your 'ways,' get married, and raise a few of your own children?"

Wall started to clean his glasses, as if such action would even make clear his next statement. "Mankind is already an island surrounded by a rising tide of blood, and I won't add to the total. But I will teach those who are already here." He asked with hard-jawed defiance, "Besides, who said I want or need to change my ways, kid?"

For Wallace the idea of loving and being loved was too much a burden to bear. He said that, given the world's unfailing perversity, he'd end up with a perfectly wonderful woman, and any man with sense, including himself, would forever feel undeserving or guilty, and would soon be ready for the funny farm.

"Anyhow, who would want a skinny streak like me?" he added. Then he quoted from Oscar Wilde. "Niagara Falls is the second disappointment in a bride's life."

I sometimes thought he used his self-mockery to disguise self-hatred.

I was not sufficiently clever or learned to understand many things that Wall had to say. Wall often made me "stop and think and be quiet," to use his words. It was getting through to me that Tall Wall liked quiet times, that he knew they were important parts of a good conversation. Certain silences, I think, have a feeling of their own.

Maybe all new, young teachers, especially cardboard wiseguys like myself, should spend a year or two with an educator like Wallace Talleck and his penetrating intellect, patrician feathers and all. But that description is not quite complete. Tall Wall was not patrician in all ways and in all circumstances. After all, he spent long hours at Klanty's place.

4

Insults

Of all the griefs that harass the distress'd,
Sure the most bitter is a scornful jest.
– Samuel Johnson

A few days after Stookie and I had enjoyed our duck and spuds banquet by the Riga River, I was again working in my classroom for the sake of my own survival. Mine was one of the two portable classrooms which had replaced the old two-storey Grade I to XII schoolhouse which had been demolished a few years before Wallace's arrival. The twin "portable blues," as I described them, were self-contained and comfortable. Oil heaters, identical to the one in our teacherage's front room, kept the classrooms if not the floors comfortable even during the coldest days. The large schoolyard, surrounded by an excellent fence, contained a terrific ball field and backstop, a small shed for Bill Bredner's janitorial supplies, the boys' and girls' outdoor toilets, two swings and a teeter-totter, a flagpole, high jump and running broad jump pits, the cement foundations of a forgotten school barn, lengths of untrimmed caragana hedges probably planted on Arbor Day many years earlier, and a low southwest corner which in the spring gave birth to a slough (sophisticated types would call it a pond) which provided fine rafting for the hamlet's youngsters.

There six years ago the wiry, sunburned war veteran, Bill Bredner, again proved his mettle. While doing his janitorial work he heard shouts from children who had upset their raft in the slough. All but one of the four youngsters clung to the edge of the soggy raft. "Casey's stuck to the bottom, Casey's stuck to the bottom!" one girl shouted – not totally impossible because when wet, the gumbo clay turned into a glue-like substance. The locally-born Bredner knew that danger, so he walked the tightwire fence to where the water was two to four feet deep and splashed through the dirty shallow water to the raft. Twice he dived under the muddy water's surface, near the raft, attempting to find Casey. Then he went under the eight-by-ten-foot raft and found the boy but not before a stray, sharp spike tore open Bill's forehead, left eye and cheek. When Bill rose to the surface his eye dangled like a mollusk down the side of his bleeding face. With blood streaming down his face, neck and upper chest, Bill threw the child on the raft, climbed aboard, pumped the boy's back, put his bloody mouth to Casey's, and blew air into the boy's lungs. Casey lived, and now attended high school in Riga.

Yes, Bill Bredner lost one eye. The injury left a wide, pink-white furrow starting at his hairline, continuing down his forehead, eyelid, cheek, and then turning left across his upper lip. The letter L grew no whiskers. There is a tuft of white hair where the scar begins above his forehead. No, his black, slightly skewed eyepatch and string did not make him look dashing or like a pirate. The stretchy string had made a permanent groove in his forehead. People tended to feel sorry for Bill.

School authorities told the war veteran he could keep the school janitor's job as long as he wanted it, as a reward. Our foul-mouthed pitcher, Jack Klackston, once referred to Bill Bredner as a seven-sided S.O.B. because a one-eyed person, Jack claimed, has an inside and an outside, a left side and a right side, a back side and a fore side, and a blind side. Bill decked Jack who then had an unplanned sleep on the floor of his country elevator.

I was working at my desk that late August morning, having already erased and washed the blackboards, and filled those blackboards with my questions and notes for my Grades V to VIII students. Come the first day of school, they'd be so busy they wouldn't have time to raise hell!

My handwriting was determined to slant downwards, no matter what. How do so many teachers write or print so well on the blackboard? I twirled the new globe on my desk and thought how little of the world I knew. It was 275 miles to my hometown. I admitted to myself that I wasn't really a city boy in spite of what I had told some people. When I had arrived in the city for the start of teachers' college a year ago, it was only the third time that I had ever visited a city.

I sat at my desk, and lonesomeness descended suddenly and heavily. A wasp landed on the globe's Baffin Island and I watched it walk (swim) to Portugal before it took off for another world. I didn't like this one much either. Likely the wasp had come through the front door or through one of the screenless windows I'd opened. The schoolhouse smelled of dust bane, varnish, carbolic soap and wax, thanks, no doubt, to Bill Bredner's efforts. The Department of Education, I was told at teachers' college, once legislated a certain ratio between floor size and window size – a ratio I couldn't remember. Because of the height of the open windows, from my desk I could hear but not see children playing tag or scrub or some other game in the schoolyard. Were some of the kids my students?

From one of the five windows to my right and to my students' left, I could see the ropes of the swings dangling from heavy crossbars which were supported by deeply-planted uprights. But now two ropes started to saw the air. Obviously someone below my line of vision was slowly swinging back and forth. It felt good to have another human being a dozen feet away, even if that person remained unknown and unseen. It was a little bit less lonely. I could hear a girl's soft humming coming from the direction of the swing.

Back to the tasks at hand. I scarcely noticed that the more distant youngsters' shouts and laughter had stopped, until I heard a boy's voice yell, "Hey, Sheep Face, Hey, Sheep Face, watcha doin' there on the swing? Lookin' for more green grass?" Laughter. The children had moved closer to the school's open door but were still out of sight.

Through the window I noticed that the swing had stopped. Another voice taunted, "When are they goin' to cut you up for mutton, Sheep Face?" More laughter. A girl's voice asked, "Why don't you sell all your wool, Sheep Face?" No reply. Then a mumble of young voices came through the open windows and front door. The kids left the school yard and I heard them run down the school hill past the teacherage. I guessed kids picked on each other just like those crows ganged up on the owl, the bird Stookie shot down by the crick.

I continued to busy myself in the classroom with warm gingerale. I washed down two spam and cheese sandwiches (prepared by my skilled hands) with warm gingerale, but everything hung heavily in my stomach. I thumbtacked a picture of the newly-crowned Queen above the front blackboard because it seemed the right thing to do.

According to "A Busy Educator's First Day" (page 4) from *Your Introduction to Worthy Teaching*, I should have been glad the rows of school desks were firmly attached to the floor because the kids would then learn or relearn the value of organization and place? What a bunch of crap! I decided to work the stuffing out of my students.

A little later I heard more soft humming. It sounded a little like "How Much is That Doggie in the Window," a recent hit song. The gingerale I'd drank demanded a visit to the boys' two-holer. On the way out, I noticed a few low, gray clouds.

For no special reason, unless the recent humming called me that way, I returned to work via the western side of the school. Ahead of me I saw a girl sitting on the school swings, her back to me. Her small frame slumped as her hands gripped the two vertical ropes. Coming behind her I twice said, "Hello," but she did not turn around. Was she deaf or was she like some children, in her own special world? She had to have been the target of the other youngsters' venom.

I touched the girl on her right shoulder, and she made a small, sharp cry of surprise. As I rounded the swing's uprights I looked casually at her and then almost said aloud, "You look like a sheep!"

The girl, at first glance, seemed to be about 12 years old. She had tightly curled hair, pointy ears and, forgive me, the demeanor and long, sad, facial features of that animal. Big gapped incisors pushed out her protruding lower lip which had a droop of fullness. Her upper lip was turned into faintly yellow-orange top teeth. Even her nose was a sheep's mournful nose which twitched slightly – a prehensile movement – as I approached. She was less excessively ugly than plain. Echo: *Hey, Sheep Face, Hey, Sheep Face, whatcha doin' there on the swing*? She had to be the target of the other youngsters' venom.

When she told me her name was Sheba Faye Klanty I knew she was not a child but rather the young woman Stookie had mentioned the previous day. It didn't take much imagination for kids to change "Sheba Faye" to "Sheep Face."

I sat on the other swing and chatted with her, actually because I was bored with my own company and my school work. As I glanced sideways at her I recognized the hints of womanhood under her shapeless light gray blouse and sweater, and heavy, long off-white skirt. Old running shoes (no socks) completed the picture. I thought that this was one ugly duckling – to confuse the metaphor – who would not turn into a beautiful swan. I immediately disliked myself for such a thought.

I decided to learn as much as I could about Sheba Faye. She would be the subject of my first parent-teacher interview.

5

Klanty

The ability to take a drink and let it alone takes constant practice.
- Robert C. (Bob) Edwards : Calgary Eye Opener.

Under its dormered and gambreled roof, the Wayne Klanty house slouched by itself on the east end of Baltic. Through summer weeds or winter snow, a narrow footpath was the house's frayed umbilical cord connecting it to the hamlet. Like a raised eyebrow, a height of land with clumps of wolfwillows and buck brush kept the Klanty place out of the villagers' sight, if not out of mind. Tall cottonwoods and maples partially defined the yard's perimeter. The medium-sized bungalow could have been attractive – with a paint job, minor repairs and a week or two of using a shovel and wheelbarrow, that is.

But now the house seemed ruefully uncaring and almost prepared to become a full-fledged dump. It was evolving into a tired monument to forlorn decrepitude. Six or seven bricks missing from the chimney were on the roof and the weed-infested front lawn. Obviously the storm windows had to fight the heat, cold and wet twelve months of the year; they received no rest in a quiet basement or shed. Beside the house's front entrance, untrimmed lilacs and caraganas reached for each other and up to the bent eavestroughs which ribboned the roof on all sides, and which provided a home to many brown-gray sparrows. A child's tricycle with one back wheel missing rested awkwardly near the rotting front step. At the rear of the property an ancient blue Packard lay on its side, showing its rusty underbelly. A resolutely dreary yard and house. A rather high but unfinished stone fence along the south side partially blocked one's view of the railroad trestle which spanned the Riga River's high banks, and wild cucumber vines tried unsuccessfully to climb the stone wall.

There was an ornate brass escutcheon around the doorknob. I knocked and heard someone say, "Come the hell in." My host's expression was flat and incurious as I entered. The living room was decorated in early threadbare. Its smells, reclamatory and pungent, were of tobacco, fly spray, old farts and spilled booze. The tall "throne chair," as I learned Klanty liked to call it, dominated the room from a corner position. A circular rug in a vomitous shade of yellow was placed under and in front of the chair. Paint and plaster curled from the ceiling and from what I could see of the walls. I was about to identify myself and the purpose of my visit – to obtain information about my troubled student, Sheba Faye – when Klanty smiled wickedly, coughed in a phlegmy way, cleared his throat, spat in his handkerchief.

"Gettin' much, kid?" As he spoke, on the heel of his hand he tapped out the dottle of the western world's worst smelling pipe.

Hadn't my teachers' college instructors emphasized the importance of making one's first parent-teacher interview a success? I was struck numb and dumb by his question. I found my way to a low, spavined, leather couch and faced the man I assumed was a bastion of neolithic thought. His prize fighter's face emanated a kind of glowering hostility, a remarkably abrasive personality, and a sense that he was musty, sour, and foul.

My manners returned. I stood up, walked across the worn linoleum, tripped lightly, and shook my rubicund host's hand. He remained sitting. Tufts of stiff hair, like miniature willows, sprouted from his bare shoulders. As I reached for his hand I saw that his knuckles, large with rheumatism, grew formidable crops of black hair. A ring with a dull, black stone cut deeply into the short, fat fourth finger of his right hand. I had wrongly anticipated a soft, sweaty handshake, but his hand was strong but cold like chicken skin. His fingernails, filed and freshly cleaned likely by the large, threatening jackknife resting on the arm of his chair, were glossy and somehow feminine. Did he actually buff the damn things? In contrast his bare feet were filthy, and his dirty toenails curled over his toes. (I don't know what clean hands and dirty feet together signify.) His shirt, the color of oatmeal, hung on the back of a chair and could double as a leaky tent.

"Just call me Klanty," my host said, frowning importantly and reproachfully. The whole of him smelled of sweat and whiskey.

Gesticulating with his large hands, he grinned at me. "Sit the hell down, 'cause you're up and down more often than a whore's panties." His laugh was a small seismic experience, his belly moving up and down. His heavily-lidded eyes saw everything. When I explained that Sheba Faye was my student, Klanty replied between loose, rubbery lips, "Don't waste your time with her."

Already I had suspected there was a solid, inner rottenness under his tremendous girth of outer rottenness. Beneath his partially bald, bullet head hung jowls large enough to make a bloodhound take notice, and multiple chins. To be consistent, perhaps, his suety stomach sagged hugely over a wide, black belt with silver belt buckle. Yet he had a certain thrusting, brawler's presence and a heavily-boned power. He looked strong and indomitable within his hairy carapace, and I thought that under that fat there was a lot of sheathed muscle and leathery toughness. His upper arms, which looked like something found on a butcher's block, featured a tattoo of a snake intertwined with the word *MOTHER*. One could image him looking down a gun sight. Klanty would be easy to dislike and tough to forget.

"Nice place you got here," I said facetiously.

Eyebrows like two wide caterpillars crawled up his forehead and then came down slowly, then spittle spray and his voice seemed to fill the room. "You're okay, boy," but there was something harder than amusement in his response. His short, lupine smile turned into narrow watchfulness. I could imagine his anger hitting my face.

Throughout our so-called interview, he would frequently raise one cheek to add more foulness to the mid-September air. After each minor explosion he'd shift his bulk, look vaguely upwards, and say, "Did I set on a fat frog?

He was a scratcher, too. His head, groin, chest and armpits seemed favorite targets for his crabbing fingers. I judged he was over sixty, yet in a certain light or with a twist of his large and somehow leonine head he looked forty or younger. I noticed that the lobe of his right ear was missing. A road map of capillaries wandered over his bulbous nose to each fat cheek, and his watery red eyes were rheumy from too much bottle time. A tic occasionally pulled the top of his right eyebrow. Klanty's suffused glances were seldom directed at me. When his eyes did meet mine, the look was vulpine.

He scratched the pallet of hair on his chest, muttered, "So you're a teacher."

Perhaps with more sarcasm than required, I replied, "If Sheba Faye is my student, then it follows that I am a teacher."

Drink had made him cotton-mouthed. There was an air of challenge to him as he efficiently circumcised a fat cigar with his snipper.

"I only get mad once a year but I make it last for twelve months, so watch out." He added, "You're a bit of a smart arse, so you are, boy. I was plantin' babies long before you were even a glint in your Daddy's eyes, so don't mix words with me."

Klanty went on to tell me he had married two widows – both dead now — each with a daughter. The older daughter was a high school teacher who had not taken the Klanty name. I already knew that the younger girl, my grade VIII student and Stookie's alleged bride-to-be, lived in Baltic with her stepfather. Klanty claimed that the girls showed no appreciation for the home he'd always provided for them.

He then waved his hand as if he were clearing the air of irrelevancies. "They're not blood, you know, and that's a fact." He smiled, wolfish and keen. "No, they're not even blood to each other." Then a strange sadness appeared on his face.

"Everything is cold when you move past the bounds of blood, and I've really got no family left." His face grew heavy and his sagging lids became almost reptilian. There was no further mention of the two deceased mothers.

I also learned that Klanty had been unemployed for some years now because of "a string of bad luck," and because "those damn girls take a lot of time and watchin', you know."

It wasn't difficult to determine that this thoroughly detestable man had constructed himself a character in his head, and then had spent years trying to play the part. How much of him was phony bravado? I could find nothing likeable in him but yet in a strange, perhaps perverse way, I was fascinated by his crudeness.

A Prince Albert tobacco can was tied to each arm of his throne, one for his tobacco supply and an empty one to use as a spittoon. (He was a superb shot.) Beside one of the cans on the arm rest was a heavy pocket watch and three fat cigars. I thought about the pool room's spittoon.

Klanty was a nose picker. Not infrequently he would send one of his wide index fingers to explore the archaeological mysteries and delights of his nostrils. The busy hand was covered by his second hand to avoid offense, of course.

During our 90-minute interview Klanty went through five beer and several shots of apricot brandy – "the ambrosia that keeps my bones bendy and warm." Every so often he dug out maraschino cherries and large black olives from two tall skinny bottles, pushing three or four of the mixed treats into his wide, wet mouth at one time.

As I was about to leave, he yelled through the thin walls, "Two beers!"

I hadn't heard Sheba Faye return home, but my student entered the living room and served Klanty and me with beer. She smiled my way, an engagingly shy and small smile. Klanty took his newspaper and playfully slapped her behind with it.

"Git now," he said. With a viperous smile, my host added, "When it comes to raising girls, fear is the basis of respect and obedience." Cherry juice escaped from one side of his mouth. "That damn girl can't hear much but when I roar she knows what I want – most of the time." I paid little significance to the statement as Klanty was getting quite drunk.

The homemade beer was excellent. Yeasty.

"Let's drink to rotted livers," he said by way of a toast, "because they're no worse than strokes and heart attacks and cancer."

After a long swig of his brandy, Klanty said with studied indifference, "It's okay if you want to visit again any time next week."

"I will probably come if I can bring Mr. Talleck with me," I said. (Wallace had never had the pleasure and I thought he might be of some use to me.) My teacher-parent interview seemed to have ended, with me only a little wiser about the problems and home life of Sheba Faye Klanty. Feeling nettled and unsure, I left the Klanty place.

Foolishly, perhaps out of boredom, I was to return often during the academic year. Klanty had the power to both attract and repel. I was to learn much about the man – but I didn't learn enough.

6

Maggie J

The two divinest things this world has got,
A lovely woman in a rural spot!
– Leigh Hunt: The Story of Remini

I was a few minutes late for church service, and took a seat in the back pew with Stookie. Wallace had driven to the city for the weekend and church service was something to do on that bright September morning.

At the midpoint of the service the minister, Reverend Framm (a transplanted Newfoundlander) introduced "our own Miss Margaret Jane Enders, home for the weekend, who will now favor us with her rendition of a popular song."

The minister told us that Stuart Hamblen, the cowboy-singer and songwriter, composed the song in 17 minutes, because, he claimed, God had helped him from becoming an alcoholic. Rev. Framm smiled his benediction to the faithful, and then motioned the singer to come to the front to sing "It is No Secret What God Can Do."

I sure found out what God can do – and I loved the results. As she walked to the raised platform near the pulpit, her skirt swung in a lithely feminine gesture. There was, I thought, a cool loveliness, an elegance, a sweet melancholy, rooted in inner beauty, inside her slenderness and smallness. Some women have the beauty of crystal but she had the soft loveliness of blossom. Her navy blue dress was perfect for her. She touched the top of her round blue box hat, perhaps in a nervous gesture, and stood prettily waiting for the pianist, Mrs. Stone, to begin. She was one of those singers who opens wide so the joy can be released. Her voice was true, and small like the singer herself. No one moved or shuffled while she sang. I stared and imagined my arms around her in a clean and decent way. The guest soloist finished her song and in silence turned to sit with the choir members, sitting with shoulders back, spine stiff, head high, and feet together, knees slightly turned to one side. She had small ankles and feet and impossibly beautiful legs. Placing her white-gloved hands on her lap, with a nod she acknowledged the compliments of the preacher.

Outside the church the ebullient, frothy, tubby, bespectacled minister, Mr. Framm, introduced Margaret Jane Enders to me. The bright sun and soft breeze played on Maggie J's coppery hair. Up close she looked even warmer and softer. She had deep-set blue eyes highlighted by dark, strongly announced eyebrows. Perhaps her eyes were slightly too large for her face. Those eyes, which in certain light flashed flecks of violet, were eyes that drew your eyes to hers. A leftover summer's tan gave her face and long neck a honeyed luminescence. She used little or no makeup but wore a perfume so discreet it was elegant. When she reached to shake the preacher's hand the top of her hat brushed the bottom of my chin. Margaret Jane Enders was a tiny, beautiful lady. I barely had time to impress her with my sappy, down-home smile. Pointing to the open church door I asked the minister to walk back inside "so this dream and I can get married right away." He laughed nervously, but Maggie J (as I immediately nicknamed her) chuckled deeply from her throat and said, "Don't you think we should shake hands first?"

Mrs. Stone appeared at the church door, and with frosty dignity announced to Miss Enders that it was time for them to go. Under my breath I said, "Damn you old lady, don't take her away." But she did, and I hadn't found out anything about Margaret Jane Enders. Who was she? Where did she live? When would we see each other again? I clumsily stitched a smile in place and said goodbye to the preacher.

Trust my homosexual roommate to have the answers. Tall Wall reported that Miss Enders was Klanty's stepdaughter and the stepsister of Sheba Faye. She was a high school teacher in Vyborg, an hour and a half drive to the west. She came only infrequently to Baltic for visits. Wall believed that she and Klanty didn't "hit if off" too well. However, Wall thought that the stepsisters were close and loving.

"Don't get too excited about anything, you're too young for Miss Enders." That made me angry, of course.

The choir members, bless their fervent hearts, planned for an October fowl supper to celebrate the end of the harvest. So two weeks later the town hall, carefully "swept and minded" by Stookie, was filled, the stage included, by table tops resting on saw horses. It seemed that the Saturday night crowd included every child and adult in the hamlet and district there to enjoy fine, home-cooked food, generous laughter, gossip, harvest news, and simple companionship. (Denominations seem to lose their significance when people are hungry.) Stookie had prepared a beautiful display of Mr. Horvath's pumpkins, carrots, parsnips, corn-on-the-cob, potatoes, onions, red and white radishes, beets and other vegetables. Rev. Framm, that rigorously decent man, gave the lengthy blessing (Mrs. Bredner's smallest kids had a screaming contest throughout the whole prayer) and announced, "the financial results of this great turnout will likely allow the congregation to finish paying for their organ, and start on the new choir gowns." He finished by saying, "Let's dig in," and we did. Most of the kids had already started. Delicious – and cheap!

My mouth was in overdrive when Margaret Jane Enders tapped my shoulder from behind. She asked in a low, warm tone just above radio-husky, "Ever bite off more than you can chew?"

"Maggie J!" I said, rising and trying to swallow a sizeable chunk of chicken breast.

"I think I like that nickname," she replied prettily. She smiled her genuine smile, but kept on going between tables up to the stage, where the choir and church committee members were enjoying their dinners. I should have anticipated that she would be home for the church's fowl supper.

Rev. Framm, that vigorous, elfin man, arrived at our table, damn it, as part of his good will tour of the hall. He cast his mild eyes on us, waved a languid hand, and burbled, "I hear you people ate the most." Pleased with his humor, he greeted Wallace with a pursed smile and that special heartiness a few clergymen reserve for infidels and the condemned. Do preachers have a special radar? He shook my hand, and asked when he could expect me to join the church choir. I'm sure he didn't hear my soft answer because his face continued to beam across the feast on the tables. Another thought entered his head, the smile on his round, innocent face snapped shut, and he said to no one in particular, "Oh dear, I hope the hall's septic tank won't overflow after all this." Then the minister moved on to the next table where he displayed his wit again. "I hear you people ate the most." I bet he had the line down pat by the end of the night. I wondered why individuals like Mr. Framm always addressed groups as "you people."

When it appeared that the stage's diners were nearly finished, I made my way to Maggie J Enders. Testosterone flowed. Excitement blossomed. I stopped on the stage and surreptitiously watched her as she chewed the last small, precise pieces of her meal with rather circular motions. She seemed to chew with the front of her mouth, which she touched with a paper napkin featuring last winter's Santa Claus. She wore a matching light blue sweater set of fine wool, a tartan skirt, and penny loafers. When it came to clothes she had an instinct for the appropriate. Again, she wore no makeup but she did compliment her lovely neck with a single strand of simulated pearls. Snobbishly I thought that Baltic certainly could not have taught her how to dress and eat so daintily. There was such a fine, unstudied grace about her. Maggie J, the tiny MJ of my recent dreams, looked a mere sixteen.

"Let's grab Rev. Framm and head for the church, and invite everyone here to our wedding," I said impulsively.

Again her light response, "Don't you think we should shake hands first?"

"Yes – at least." Fusty Mr. Framm overheard us, and gave me a look usually saved for the world's pagan sinners.

By 9 p.m. the tables were cleared, the paper plates burned in Stookie's stove, and the saw horses and table tops stacked under the stage. All the other chores were completed, and the citizens of Baltic and area had contentedly left for their homes. Baltic's luckiest citizen walked Maggie J. Enders home from the fowl supper. Who said romance is dead?

We slowly walked the wood sidewalks of Baltic around Horvath's corner, past the deserted stores and buildings Stookie had earlier shown me, and made two left turns which brought us back to the town hall, past the weed-filled, open-air skating rink, and finally to the rain-puddled, dirt path leading to the Klanty place.

I told Maggie J that I was 24 and had travelled widely and worked at several jobs for some years – necessary lies.

With a quick smile she said, "You hold your age well, old timer."

The hamlet's lights were slightly behind us and Klanty's place was in the darkness before us. With unspoken agreement we passed the house, walked the short distance to the railway tracks, and followed them to the centre of the unforgivingly high trestle. There was, I was to discover, a tomboyish daring under MJ's beauty and finesse. Meanwhile, heights continued to scare the hell out of me, and I asked myself what I was doing on the trestle. There was no moon, and the hamlet's lights to the west only hinted at the direction of the rails and railroad ties. I was vaguely aware of the distant susurration of the deep, early night. Shallow water waited a long distance below us.

MJ asked me for a coin. To impress her I gave her my lucky penny, which she took from my open hand. She said she was making a silent wish, and then tossed the coin through the railroad ties. It hit three beams before we heard a plop. Was that the time and place for me and my galloping acrophobia to be with a girl like Maggie J? I labelled us the "two terrifically tottering, tizzied, trestle tramps," and challenged Maggie J to repeat my silly alliteration. She did – first backward and then forward. "Now you do that," she challenged me. I could only say, "I'm too terribly, tortuously tizzied," and with MJ beside me, that statement was no lie.

The silence was almost a living thing. The air was very cool, the night was a coal bin, the spaces beyond and between the trestle ties were threatening. I had that terrible need to raise the water level of the sleepy creek below us.

Maggie J, with her special radar, led the way back to solid ground. You'd think she had memorized the route. Without touching we walked to her front step, partially defined by the now largely leafless, untrimmed shrubs. The house was in darkness, and I partially tripped on the front step. I managed to step lightly on her foot. That caused a lovely, deep chuckle from MJ. She reached in the pitch dark for my hand and shook it quickly and firmly before releasing it. That sweet, kissable girl softly said good night and slipped noiselessly through the front door.

I think I slept with a smile on my face that night. I thought that in so many ways she could gentle my arrogance.

Early next morning, swimming trunks and all, I was under the trestle looking for the lucky penny to which I attached some vague, talismanic significance. I knew the chances were slim that the coin was retrievable. Water that cold can change a bass to a soprano in a hurry, but fortunately I spotted the object in shallow water close to the shore. I told myself that the coin would remain unspent.

I changed clothes and rushed to church, anticipating that Maggie J would be in attendance. She was not. The preacher ranted about the ultimate perdition of all sinners, the choir seemed out of tune, the back pew shared with Stookie was hard, Mrs. Stone's organ music was too slow, I had a headache, and on and on, all because MJ was not there.

I suppose old Klanty or Sheba Faye could have told me when MJ would return again from her Vyborg teaching position. Either pride or embarrassment, I'm not sure which, made the inquiry impossible. Klanty likely would have responded with a leer and dirty words, while Sheba Faye would have given me that sheep-like look of hers – a look I still could not interpret.

7

Preacher

Do not, as some ungracious pastors do,
Show me the steep and thorny way to heaven.
– William Shakespeare: Hamlet

My experiences with men of the cloth did not always result in romantic introductions. One memorable Sunday a Methodist student-preacher – obviously a direct descendant of Chaucer's poor parson – knocked on our teacherage's door and said, "Good morning, gentlemen. I'm beginning services at the local school, so will please you come to church?" Apparently he had made arrangements with the School Superintendent in Riga.

I mumbled something about denominations. Tall Wall, however, shook the man's hand and said that we would be there shortly. Wall's eyes, judging and assessorial, told me I'd better co-operate. He always claimed that politeness came first. His moral sternness and urbane self-assurance could sometimes be infuriating.

So we were in my classroom a few minutes later for church service. Wallace played the school piano majestically. Meanwhile, Mrs. Bredner, the pregnant wife of the school janitor, and I constituted the total congregation. The sermon was forgettable but Wall's tenor was strong, and the preacher's baritone was soft during the singing of "The Old Rugged Cross" and "Shall We Gather at the River?" (my favorites, I must admit). I only mouthed the words.

Mrs. Bredner's soprano was loud and nasal and terrible. Mrs. Bredner, who still defined herself as "Baltic's English war-bride," told me that during the war she often sang for "our troops." No wonder the troops had morale problems, on occasion! She had an empty prettiness and a slight cast of piggishness to her mouth and nose.

The preacher had another service to give in a larger centre, so Wall invited him back to our place for Sunday supper. After our visitor left for his second sermon, I protested to Tall Wall, "Why do we want him here, anyway?" Immediately, it seemed, my colleague grew even taller while I shrunk. He removed his glasses, hesitated, and replaced them on his narrow face.

"The preacher is coming and that's final. It is the right thing to do." He spoke with such sureness and quiet authority that he carved out a moment of silence. He gazed my way witheringly, the way some people look at drunks or harmless idiots.

As usual, during the week I had experienced the soup-sandwich-jam-prepared-meats-cornflakes syndrome, but on Sundays Wall sometimes chose to wind up our old wood stove. He cooked, I served and washed the dishes. On that Sunday at early dusk the three of us sat down for Wall's roast chicken and all the fixings. The preacher, who had a habit of wringing his hands often, looked like he was fighting back tears.

Without Wall's knowledge, I had placed a fresh, uncooked egg inside the chicken's rear with the hot bread-and-onion dressing. Halfway through the meal I removed the egg with two fingers and a thumb, telling the preacher, "I pluck our chickens but I don't always gut them out before cooking them. I hope it's okay with you."

The man of the cloth smiled weakly and excused himself, but didn't quite make it to the outside privy. (Apparently Mrs. Stone heard him because the next day she handed me a card and said with a quiver in her voice, "I heard you being sick with John Barleycorn yesterday, and you couldn't even make it to the water closet, and you don't have any shame at all." Scrawled on the card was a quotation from Isaiah 5:22. *Woe to you that are mighty to drink wine, and stout men at drunkenness.*)

While the preacher had the heaves, Tall Wall took me by the full of my best shirt, and lifted me straight up past his height, where he held me for what seemed like a long, long time. His long, skinny arms were like steel cables under silk. He slammed me down hard. My heels and my insteps hurt for a week and to think I'd hit this guy!) Goose-flesh pimpled my arms and body. My precarious but precious ego suffered as well.

A thin, hard mask slid down Wallace Talleck's face. He mumbled something about social gaucherie.

"Grow up, japester," he said in a tone sinister in its evenness, "and dilute your bravado." His jaw muscles bunched and a second frisson of fear passed through me. In spite of this threat, I could not fight the temptation to ask, "Does this mean you didn't like my eggplant?"

A despairing noise came from deep within his throat. "More people are hurt by churlish blundering than by malice, Egghead."

Splat, the cat, (so named after I cleaned up the first of its many messes on the back porch linoleum floor) enjoyed the chicken bones. I don't know how the sinewy, whining, skinny, hateful beast got into his favorite dumping ground so frequently. I suppose I'll always hate cats.

The preacher did not return to Baltic. Wall later heard that he became a life insurance salesman. My flippant response was "That's what he was doing as a preacher, too."

One of the regulars for church services at Baltic's only church was Wilbur A. Stook. On Sundays he wore polished brown boots, baggy corduroy pants with green braces and a wide belt, and a white shirt buttoned tightly at the neck. He once told me that "I never learned why guys wear ties."

Apparently my friend had passed the church's collection plate for so long that no one else thought much about it. He always took the plate from one pew to another and then placed it beside Mrs. Stone who seemed to guard it with her life until counting time. When not playing the organ or the piano, Mrs. Stone "owned" the small left-front pew which during winter allowed her the first contact with the basement's furnace heat as it escaped up the large, cast-iron register. I was told that the only time Stookie did not sit dead centre in the back pew of the church was during his mother's funeral.

Stookie had a gift I don't understand. Although it appeared that he could scarcely read and his writing was labored and slow he seemed to know all the verses of all the popular hymns. Obviously he listened well and memorized the words. He not only knew the ten commandments, but could repeat the exact King James wording. When he was little his mother read and re-read the Bible to him, until he could correctly repeat the words. He claimed that "Timothy Eaton's finest" taught him how to read some of the big words. On one bitterly cold winter afternoon, Stookie recited by memory and in monotone large sections from Genesis and Exodus to a surprised pair of educators. With my colleague Wallace Talleck and I gathered before tors. With my colleague Wallace Talleck and I gathered before the kitchen stove, Stookie graced us with his gift. The phenomenal recall of the illiterate? Wallace sat in his straight kitchen chair and held the Bible while Stookie spoke. Stookie wouldn't "perform" at first, until I said that Mr. Talleck "would only be like a baseball umpire, and what the hell do they know?" The performer said he could also "do Matthew and a lot of them Revelations," but he didn't want Mr. Talleck to think that he was "gettin' tight britches." Even on the ball field Stookie always called my colleague "Mr. Talleck" because "he's a teechur ya know." However, Stookie did not find it necessary to be formal with me.

I simply didn't know how the grade IV graduate did many of the things he did exceedingly well. How did he measure the markings on the curling and skating rinks? Why were some of his sentences complete while others ran together like two colors of spilled paint? Often he dropped his "g's" or used double negatives. Educators really don't know a lot about such things. We can tell where and when and what but we don't know much about the why. We are busy spouting theories instead of searching for answers.

8

Grub

The appetite grows by eating. – François Rabelais: Gargantua

One pressing question that needed an immediate answer was "how to eat in style without really trying." It wasn't long before my laziness and ineptitude around the kitchen stove led me to investigate Stookie's claim that the grub where he lived "is always tastin' just right." I was tired of such masterpieces as fried eggs on spam with toast and honey – for supper. And who could eat as many carrot sticks as Wallace? Or would want to? I'm told that it is common that many people who choose to live alone are neat in their habits, and are good cooks. That adage was fifty percent wrong in the case of Wallace Talleck, whose cooking skills, although much better than mine, still left one reminiscing about mother's home-cooked meals. Tall Wall's tapioca pudding could graft large branches to tall trees.

Stookie reported that Mrs. Horvath might even let me peel the spuds. Great joy. So soon, most of my noon and evening meals (at a bargain price) were at the Horvaths', the couple who with fussy neatness ran the post office, and who had long cared for Stookie. Right away Mr. Horvath told me that "no bad words or dirty jokes are allowed in my wife's house."

Mrs. Horvath made the best meat pie in this or any other universe. Stookie was correct, the meals were truly, truly wonderful, with soups, vegetables, pigs' knuckles, gravies, pies, jams, cakes, oatmeal cookies, jellies, corn-on-the-cob, venison, wild fowl, cinnamon buns, mashed potatoes, steaks, roasts and more. She was a small, round, sun-browned woman with a quick, full smile on her kindly, well-worn face. She introduced me to the tasty tartness and loveliness of sauerkraut, relish, onions, garlic, mustards, curry, and spices I still can't spell or pronounce. To a hungry man nothing under God's blue sky matches the aroma of goose fat steaming under a roasting goose. I wanted to give Mrs. Horvath the Nobel Peace Prize for tarts and more tarts, an endless variety. When you bit into one of her dill pickles the snap could be heard in Riga. She taught me never to overcook the food or to underheat the liquids. She claimed that "coffees, teas, stews and soups are happiest when they can scald." The only thing she could not teach me to drink, let alone love, was buttermilk. The Horvaths seemed to drink buckets of the horrid stuff. She didn't have a refrigerator. She kept some foods in the crawl space under her kitchen floor, but she "rested her lovelies" in the deep vegetable cellar situated in her garden. Of course, she stored her meats and poultry at Woolston's locker plant, and of course, Tall Wall had another lecture for me about this. According to tradition, St. Elizabeth, of Mr. Horvath's Hungary, gave such great amounts of food to the poor that her own people did not eat well. Her husband, a suspicious man, demanded some answers upon seeing her leave with her apron full of food. God saved the woman by changing the food to roses. Mrs. Horvath's first name was Elizabeth, too.

During the hot summer months Mrs. Horvath stored her eggs, butter, lard, and such in large, husband-made, wood buckets which dangled low near the garden well's ice-cold water. I have never tasted water so cold and so good.

Mr. Horvath, well-known locally as a doddlebugger and expert dowser, knew exactly where his well should be dug. I believe in that process because I've seen him "divine" four district wells by using a forked willow branch. (My learned teachers' college instructors would scoff at that.) When I once teased him that he used his splendid handlebar moustache as an extra antennae, his laugh was as wide and deep as the Danube River Valley which taught him much about water and land. He had rosettes of white in his curly black hair. He was one of those men who didn't remove eye glasses while shaving with soap from a Yardley shaving cup, and an old-fashioned, leather-stropped straight razor, so he had a fair crop of black hair high on each cheek, just under the bottom rims of his glasses. I secretly wanted to shave him below his eye sockets.

Just as you might expect, he used rubbing alcohol as shaving lotion. He was an excellent gardener, and one of those people whose garden was a celebration of life. You'd think the man didn't have a first name: Baltic people, including his wife (in public, at least) always referred to him as "Mr. Horvath." It seemed to me that the Horvath's had secret sorrows.

As I'd guessed, Stookie's guns supplied the Horvaths with illegal venison ("Queen's mutton," he called it), upland game, ducks and geese. "Good huntin' ways," he said, "makes sure there will always be more good huntin." Stookie didn't believe in hunting licenses.

My 18-year old body, hardly forged and hardened to Grecian perfection, "lived " at the Horvaths. I'm almost embarrassed to admit that there I gained nearly two inches in height. (How can a guy be old enough to teach school but still young enough to grow?)

Tall Wall, of course, knew of the great grub at the Horvaths, but continued to eat alone in the teacherage, using linen serviettes during his bachelor meals. Tall Wall stood alone in more ways than one.

9

Scars

Experience is everything; it's hearin', and seein', and tryin'; and arter that, a feller must be a born fool if he don't know.
– T.C. Haliburton: Sam Slick

Tall Wall's excellent library, covering the three windowless walls of our living room, had impressed me on my first day in Baltic. Wallace had built the bookshelves himself. I wasn't allowed to remove the books (many of which were leather bound) from the teacherage, but I was allowed to read them. Wall's first "assignment" for me was Martin Heidegger's recent *Introduction to Metaphysics*.

He never disagreed with my comments but he always asked for clarification, and then for more clarification of that response, and so on. If my responses suited him he would choose the next volume for me. If not, I'd be on my own. Was this positive or negative reinforcement? Tall Wall read avidly and quickly, and began to teach me, already a fast reader, to do the same. "Concentration is boredom's nemesis," he often said.

Wall and his books taught me something of the beauty of language and the enticements of words. Words can give a person an intellectual and sensual pleasure, he believed. Words, he claimed, made one more persuasive, and persuasiveness led to a mastering of one's social environment.

I honored Wall's request that I not examine the books in his bedroom – I guessed that they dealt with homosexuality. Before leaving the teacherage he always locked his bedroom door.

Although he was generous in loaning his books, he showed inconsistency in loaning out his automobile. Not once would

Neo-Scrooge let me drive that black, powerful beauty, even though I grandly offered to pay for the gasoline. Moneybags told me that nothing would make me more vulnerable than my greed. Nuts!

"Materialism and permissiveness," he said, "will be our undoing. We chase the affluent life, not the better life. The fatuous pursuit of happiness is our society's goal." Who was he to talk?

During the year he drove us to three or four movies in Riga, but I didn't enjoy the Roy Rogers or Gene Autry cowboy thrillers. We went to a half dozen auction sales – Wall loved bargains! Once I told him that the car wouldn't have a heart attack if it went over 50 miles an hour.

"Try a Bennett Buggy if you don't like it," he said, his voice dusty in his throat.

I wondered how Tall Wall could afford his new car, beautiful piano (locked over the summer months), fine clothes, and terrific phonograph record collection – mostly Dixieland, Rhythm and Blues and some pretty wild interpretive Jazz. Apparently after each school year Wallace drove to the city "to roam through the stock market." With brilliance and intensity he studied the foibles of the stock market, emerging each summer with the means to finance in cash his car, books, clothes and so on. I once snooped in his wallet (a lousy thing to do), which he had left by his phonograph, and counted over $900 in big bills.

I supposed that when television hit the area, likely next spring, Wall would be one of the first buyers. Tall Wall had seen the 1951 introduction of color TV in the States, and the first televised hockey game in Canada, Montreal vs. Detroit, on October 11, 1952. It was hard to admit I'd never seen a television show of any kind. I didn't know how to answer Wall when he asked, "Do you think kids will continue to enjoy Howdy Doody?" Who the hell was Howdy Doody?

Yet Lord Bountiful (I didn't call him that to his face) was stingy in so many ways. In some respects Tall Wall seemed so damn tightfisted it made me boil. I once yelled at him after he refused to lend me his fancy car. He folded his arms like the twin blades of a jackknife and said, "Wealth alone is too low a peak for the thoughtful individual you ought to become." Yet in other respects he was one of the most generous people I've ever met. Perhaps we all have our peccadilloes.

I teased and criticized Wall about his luxuries but I wasn't too proud to use them myself, of course. As a nascent sybarite,

I especially loved one of his auction-sale acquisitions – the longest, highest, damn bathtub I'd ever seen. Wall had temporarily removed part of the back porch wall to get the lovely thing in place, his friendly brace and bit making the exit hole for the rubber drainpipe. Perfect. So when the sharp cold of our winter arrived, that tin monument-to-the-good-life often served this humble servant. It took almost two hours to heat the water, using both the school and our kitchen stoves. The open door to the kitchen made the back porch's temperature bearable. After a hot hour in the tub I'd sleep like a hammered hog. Tall Wall called it the "tub somnafacience." In my diary I defined these long soaks as "terminally narcissistic and selfishly hedonistic."

Quite petulantly, I once asked Wallace why he became a teacher if he loved the filthy lucre so much. He gave me a lucid lecture which I only half listened to. However, I remembered his first pronouncement.

"Among the professions the teaching profession must become first among equals." In our front room he had a wall plaque with Roger Bacon's statement: *Seek first the goods of the mind, and the rest shall be supplied, or no way prejudiced by their absence.*

For his birthday I bought Tall Wall one of those special prepared rubber stamps, and an ink pad. Partially in jest and partially in seriousness, I asked the dealer to imprint the stamp with five words in bold: *THE GOODS OF THE MIND*. To my surprise and pleasure, Wall used the stamp on a few of his books, the things he called a scholar's tools.

Some of Wall's attitudes towards money may have come out of his past. The Depression, drought and dust of his boyhood were part of his being. Wallace had learned from the land. His father, a small town merchant-gone-bankrupt, taught him love and respect for the land and for the elements, and an understanding of the unholy dollar bill's power. His mother, a teacher, taught him the love of learning and the need for compassion and forgiveness.

"We're all too poor at what we do, son," his mother would say. That was the reason that no one should judge others too harshly.

"Judgment," she said, "is God's job." She often told Wallace that friendship, love and generosity are the only things that grow when you spend them. His mother believed that "most people seldom show their hearts but if they do, you better listen." (It crossed my mind that Wall read people as easily as a fat bee finds a flower's juices in late summer.) She encouraged her son to increase his use of good language. One of his mother's favorite expressions was a quote from a 1720 letter written by Jonathan Swift to a young clergymen, where style is defined as using "proper words in proper places."

Wall claimed that his mother almost literally had a rod down her back. On her seventeenth birthday she was to begin her first teaching position in a country school. The chairman of the local school board met her train with his team and manure wagon, expecting her to ride with him. She had her pride and position, she chose to walk the three miles to her country school. She would not ride on that manure-carrying conveyance simply because she deserved better, and because she knew her students would scoff once they learned the story. However, to prove she wasn't "uppity," she chose to shovel out the man's pig barn the following Saturday, and her reputation spread accordingly.

I could tell when Tall Wall got angry because small red spots appeared on each cheek. The spots were there when he recalled how in the mid-thirties he had carried his aunt's three dozen eggs a mile to town to trade for one sewing needle, and then had to return home for six more eggs to cover the cost of the needle. His aunt sold butter for 11 cents a pound, while his uncle received 1 cent a pound live weight for his beef cattle. The freight cost more than the animals were worth. In 1932, Wallace's father lost his business to the banks. Wall pulled out other memories as stinking and rotten as a badly diseased tooth. Was that why Tall Wall sometimes seemed to be a tightwad?

Wall's mother had lovingly made him a shirt which was digested on her clothesline by sawflies. The year was 1935, the year her teacher's salary was $410.00 per annum, most of it uncollected – promissory notes instead! That year had the coldest and hottest spells on record. During the summer of 1935 there was a 41-day period when the temperature stayed between 90 and 105 degrees F. Wildlife largely disappeared, rivers and creeks dried up, gardens and crops perished, and even weeds died in the Dust Bowl. (Stookie told me that once in the thirties he could not see the Baltic grain elevators from the nearby railroad station for the dust. As a little boy, his job had been to pack the window sills with wet towels as a protection against dust storms.) On Wallace's birthday they had a stew made from stored Russian thistle, Jack Rabbit, and flour and water. His birthday treat was five jawbreakers which he made last a long, long time.

My roomie told me a depression story I had trouble believing. He said that his uncle once sold a load of "cement pigs" to an uninitiated stranger. The uncle had added portland cement to the pigs' final feeding. The cement added weight and blocked the animals' discharges. More profit than usual!

Wall's stories, and many my parents had told me, involved black blizzards, grasshoppers, crop failure, and despair. I knew the stories were true; they have been captured on film, in conversation, and on the printed page. I felt those stories. His depression stories and his anger helped me to understand my friend, and my own family's history. Nevertheless, his depression memories and war experiences surely stretched the decade or so which separated our ages. He was far more than a generation ahead of me in some ways. Even Stookie, only a few years older than myself, had been through experiences I could never equal. Those tough years made us decades apart. Yet Wallace was so damn delighted with his own boyhood, in spite of the many difficulties he remembered. He was so very proud of his parents. Likely it was his tough boyhood which gave that brilliant man his ability to make do, and to take most difficulties in stride.

In early December, an incident occurred to remind me of Wallace's origins. The snowplow had not yet arrived to clear the results of a doozer of a snowstorm which had struck the Baltic area. Most human traffic, except for hardy youngsters going to school, stopped dead. The school swings and teeter-totter were on the sheltered side of the school, so at recess some of the youngsters not playing "fox and goose" with Tall Wall made their own fun. As I walked around the corner of the school, near the swing, I heard a *thuk* and a soft scream. The seat of the moving swing had caught the little Bredner girl just above her eyes. (Her father, Bill Bredner, was our school janitor.) The girl bled badly, and the snow close to her head turned crimson.

I carried the little girl to my classroom, and immediately summoned her very pregnant mother, who came through snowbanks from her nearby home. All our students gathered to witness the excitement. Wallace and I managed to stop the bleeding with ice from the school's water cooler. Mrs. Bredner, big as a barrel, kept hollering "my poor little ducks will be scarred for life." I didn't doubt her – the flesh was parted over both her eyes like an angry, extra mouth.

Tall Wall put a little water in an empty coffee can and placed it on the school's oil stove to boil. He looked at the hysterical mother for a second and told her that he'd slap her hard if she didn't keep quiet. Then he turned to me. "Look after everything until I come back."

I considered putting my new tie in the screaming woman's mouth. In a few moments Mr. Talleck returned with what looked like strands of hair from a horse's tail and placed the long hair and a needle in the boiling hot water for a minute or so. With a look of concern that seemed to make his long face partially collapse, he sewed together the little girl's wound while three or four youngsters and myself held the patient down on my desk. Sheba Faye Klanty sat on my desk and placed the child's head on her lap. Tall Wall's hands were quick and soft as flying moths. What Wall had done was to take the thread from the old horse-hair cushion he had recently purchased at an auction sale. When we returned to the teacherage, the cut from his knife to the heavy leather cover grinned back at us. After supper, Wall used more horse-hair and a needle to make the leather grin largely disappear. He "made do," just as he had during the dirty thirties.

As an aside, Wallace told me "it looks like a boy for Mrs. Bredner." I just shook my head in bewilderment. How could he know such things ahead of time?

Later that night Wall was at his Socratic best discussing Thomas Hobbes' *Leviathan*, when there was heavy pounding on our front door. It seemed that the day's excitement had been too much for the pregnant Mrs. Bredner. The roads were blocked with snow, so she told her husband Bill to contact Mr. Talleck, who had been a medic in the war. I wasn't sure what Bill meant when he told us "her water just broke," but Tall Wall did.

That night was more special than I can say. With my mouth tasting like dry plaster, I must have said seven dozen times, "Take it easy, everything's okay," to a woman whose mouth was distended in that singular female pain beyond articulation. I wasn't much good to anybody. Yet the night was wonderful and unbelievable. No one had ever told Bright Boy about the magic of birth or the newly-born, or of the scary strength of a mature woman. Now that is special! I'll never forget that swollen, short, wide, screaming, sweating, blowsy creature with great pillow breasts which moved back and forth and upwards and downwards all at the same time under her half-opened pajama top.

For a while, she even smelled like milk. (Her house usually smelled of wet laundry, disinfectant, stewed tomatoes and boiled cabbage.) Her bed sheet was soaked with the liquids and exudations of her sweat. Wall tried to shave her with Bill's straight razor. No time – the great gush of life came, and as it happened I was stationed to catch the "missile" – a bellowing, wet, red, bloody, slippery, slimy, seven-pound mystery called a baby. Bill Bredner had taken his other kids to a neighbor's home, and returned only after the baby was born. "I started it," said Bill, "and you guys finished the job." Bill's idea of humor.

I felt diminished by the evening. Here I was a teacher, but I didn't know beans about birth, life and death. Meanwhile, the cool and seemingly detached Wallace had known what to do. Or should I simply say he knew how to make do?

Somewhere in the evening was an answer for the ambient mystery of creation, but I couldn't see or grasp it. That birth-night made me doubt if young men and women of my age and experience should really be placed in charge of educating youngsters. I asked myself if I could ever equal Wall's sympathy, courage, sense of justice, and blunt common sense. But, of course, I couldn't bring myself to tell Tall Wall that.

Two days later the snow-blocked roads were cleared, and the Riga doctor pronounced Mrs. Bredner, her injured daughter and new son as fit as three fiddles. At the teacherage Bill Bredner, Stookie, Tall Wall and I smoked Bill's strong, rotten cigars, and poured too much of his home brew, all in honor of baby Wallace William Bredner. Moonshine in canning jars! Bill explained how "a guy don't make whiskey but he 'runs' it, and he needs to give it four months to get good color."

The first shot was like swallowing barbed wire. The second didn't get any better, and incinerated my adenoids. No sweet, smooth, soft-sippin' whiskey in that batch! I never did see Tall Wall stagger, become obnoxious, fall asleep, slur his speech, talk loudly or become morose, even after a significant number of stiff drinks.

When Bill and Stookie left the room, Tall Wall took a long drag on his cigar and seemed to feel the need to lecture me. "Do you know what the word 'kinnikinnik' means?"

"I sure do," I replied, pulling on my cigar. I had him this time. "It means 'tobacco' in Cree or Chipewyan."

"But Bright Boy," he replied, "do you also know that it's now part of the English language and also its longest palindromic word?" Try to get ahead of Tall Wall!

The evening held a few bad moments when Bill and Tall Wall, both war veterans, argued bitterly about pacifists who had refused to fight in the war. Bill, although not a prejudiced man, could not understand Wallace's view that perhaps those non-combatants were correct. Fortunately Bill's new fatherhood and Wall's diplomacy changed the atmosphere to one of celebration, and Bill concluded by saying, "At least you're a good medic, and that's for sure."

Stookie said that he hoped that "the little guy smiles when he sleeps 'cause that means he's hearin' the angels sing." He claimed that "the baby shouldn't get scared too bad and too quick 'cause that will make him knock-kneed."

Of course Bill wanted to brag about his new baby boy. Father Bill said "it looks like my son has two cowlicks and that's a pretty good sign he will be clever." He claimed that he knew the infant would have lots of hair because "the wife during her pregnancy had plenty of heartburn." And the fact that she had very little morning sickness proved damn near 100 percent that it would be a boy.

Providing further insight, Bill added "The missus didn't have a pointy stomach so I knew pretty well that she wasn't going to have a girl." The proud father snorted and chuckled, joking that "she must have had a nickel in her mouth when I was plantin' my crop." Apparently he believed that nickels make for boy babies. I shook my head in disbelief, and was about to say something smart when Wallace signalled me to be quiet. Later, he suggested that some of those ideas could be correct because his own mother had taught him some of the same things. That comment from Tall Wall, scholar, teacher, medic and man-of-the-world!

Some of Tall Wall's make-do depression treatments and cures made me smile. He claimed that garlic and camphor kept some communicable diseases at bay; mustard plasters cured chest colds; chewing tobacco stuck next to a tooth removed pain; folded, stiff, brown paper placed under one's top lip stopped a nosebleed; a copper bracelet worn on the wrist prevented arthritis; wearing rubber shoes or rubber boots indoors damaged one's eyesight, and so on. When Wall told me that goose grease mixed with turpentine makes the best chest rub, it was too much for me. "How can you believe that stuff, Wall?"

His obtuse riposte was, "Well, I knew the Bredner baby was going to be a boy, didn't I?" Apparently he knew that boys sit low and girls float high in a mommy's tummy. Damn it, the tallest graduate from the school of hard knocks' was right again.

The conversation, lubricated by moonshine, moved to a new topic: the Cold War and Joseph McCarthy's recent "witch hunts" for communists. For different reasons, Bill and Tall Wall believed that the Rosenbergs, husband and wife, should not have been executed the previous June. Tall Wall argued that history would prove the regime of Joseph Stalin (who had died in March of that year, I believe) caused far more innocents to die than did during the Nazi period. And Mao Tse-tung would one day be found to have exceeded those other two monsters, Wall stated. That really made left-winger Bill angry, and I feared he was going to take a swing at Wall.

Tempers cooled when Stookie said, "You guys don't want to argue 'cause Mrs. Bredner just finished birthin' a new baby and that's why we're havin' this party so we will have a toast to the baby now." Stookie reminded Bill that "Mr. Talleck sure knew how to tend your baby's birth and everything 'cause that snowstorm sure blocked the roads to the hospital."

"We don't want to talk too big," added Stookie. "Them Russians just exploded their H-bomb. I listen to the news on my radio every day ya know." I noticed that Stookie's observations about the threat of war between the U.S. and Russia stopped even Wallace in his tracks. End of argument between ex-soldiers. (Our neighbor, Mrs. Stone, had recently asked if Wallace, myself and she should build an A-Bomb shelter, "just like they are doing in the city.")

Nearly a decade earlier Wallace Talleck's long legs had taken the young medic safely through the waters off the Normandy Beach, June 6, 1944. Wall had a tough time overseas, but he would offer me only vague snippets of information.

During one of our conversations he had told me about one of the dullest soldiers he had ever known who performed an act of bravery beyond belief, resulting in saved lives. Cleverness, according to Tall Wall, would never lead me or anyone else to do anything as significant as was done by that brave soldier.

Once he had shown me nine photos of a Nazi death camp he visited after liberation. "That," he said, pointing to the stack of photos, "gives the world a graduate degree it doesn't need or deserve. The German culture and contributions to mankind have been despoiled by that relatively small group of animals."

On July 16, 1945, the day the first atomic bomb was detonated at Alamogordo, New Mexico, Wallace Talleck returned home from the war. On the way to meet his train, his mother and father were involved in a car crash and were instantly killed. The drunk driver filled with radiator hootch was unhurt.

Welcome home, boy – young man – old man.
Will you smile again?

After the war Wallace worked briefly on his aunt's farm before travelling through East Africa. In Ethiopia a French munitions merchant taught him the Chinese Tai Chi Chuan. Wall next tried university, dropped out, and played piano in various jazz clubs in New Orleans over an 18-month period. He began to teach himself workable Spanish (it is the easiest, he claimed), then Italian, French, German, and Russian. Wallace quoted Goethe, who said, "He who does not know foreign languages does not know anything about his own."

Again assuming I wanted or needed one of his lectures – this time on the word *language* – he told me that the word has its roots in the Latin *lingua*, or *tongue*. He claimed that there are nearly 2 800 different languages and 8 000 language variants or dialects, all of which are divided into about 60 families. The information did impress me, although I didn't admit that.

During the post-war years, Tall Wall gained the suavity of clever conversation, good food, and fine wines – his wine rack was always well stocked. He graduated from Normal School the spring following his return to Canada. Baltic was his second teaching position.

There were times when Tall Wall did or said things which gave rise to my petulant anger. Once he tried to advise me on hitting an inside curve ball, and I loudly demanded to know who he was to advise anybody about something he couldn't do himself. He patted my face with a firmness that was almost an admonitory slap, and said, "Look kid, you're a teacher and you advise, and yet you don't know which way is up. Be quiet and listen."

Wallace never called me "kid" when our students or their parents were around. I admitted to myself that I *was* still a kid, but I didn't like anybody else calling me one. At times I resented my unspoken need for Wall's erudition and wisdom. His inner scars made him seem older, more remote. He was turned in to himself, somehow reluctant to share some of his thoughts. Was that what war did to a man?

I was soon to learn that other Baltic citizens also had their share of scars.

10

Sheba Faye

Canadian girls are so pretty it is a relief to see a plain one now and then. - Mark Twain.

Someone else whose past I often pondered was that of my student, Sheba Faye's. On most occasions her eyes appeared infinitely stupid and gentle – passive and yet not tranquil. Occasionally I saw her angry, and then her crumpled mouth hardened. Most often there was an alternating sadness and a nervous apology in her eyes.

Other district students Sheba Faye's age attended high school in Riga. On school days the Riga school bus picked up and dropped off those students at our school. The bus driver, Mrs. Helen Fowler, who insisted I call her by her first name, said she ran a "tight ship." She was the mother of my brightest student, Marsha, and was one of the few locals who displayed kindness to Sheba Faye. If and when her young passengers yelled insults at my student, Mrs. Fowler's sharp, cold-as-an-icicle look forced the kids into silence. A pretty but insensitive 17-year-old girl in Grade XII (who once called Bill Bredner "Scar Face Capone" and had her face slapped hard by young Casey) yelled from the school bus window, "Hey, Sheep Face, hurry up and get out of that school before my children do." Laughter. The slap hadn't worked. Helen Fowler kicked the girl off the school bus, and almost lost her job over the issue. Helen,

I learned, had been a classmate and chum of Irene, Sheba Faye's late mother. Helen once told me that Irene had been one of the high school's best students.

Why then did Sheba Faye do so poorly in her school work? Mr. Talleck had not taught her, and could offer few concrete answers. The mystery deepened. In early October while in Riga I secured information from the school unit's files.

SHEBA FAYE KLANTY: Baltic P.S.					
Beginning Year	**Beginning Age**	**Grade**	**IQ**	**Academic Average****	**Teacher**
1942	6	1	N/A	90%	Miss Janet Wilson
1943	7	2	N/A	88%	Miss Janet Wilson
1944	8	3	141	94%	Mrs. Janet Kleiner
1945	9	4	104	59%	Mrs. Janet Kleiner
1946	10	5	103	44%	Miss R. Foreman
1947	11	5	99	50% *	Miss Edna Brun
1948	12	6	99	41%	Mrs. Janet Kleiner
1949	13	6	96	50% *	Mrs. V. Debrowski
1950	14	7	97	39%	Mrs. V. Debrowski
1951	15	7	94	50% *	Mrs. V. Debrowski
1952	16	8	89	35%	Mrs. V. Debrowski
1953	17	8			

*Confidential to teacher from Supt. Irwin Clawson, B.A., M.A. (Ed.): It is consistent with our policy of enlightenment that no student spend more than two (2) years in one (1) given grade. If on the second (2nd) attempt (i.e. full academic year) a student fails to attain at least fifty percent (50%) academic such an average will be awarded nonetheless. Teacher should see our handbook for details and/or expansion.
**Rounded to the nearest full number.

The chart raised questions I couldn't answer. How does one give an IQ test to a Grade III student? To put it mildly, was my teachers' college credo, "quantification, quantification and quantification," open to suspicion? Sheba Faye had taught herself to read from a 1914 *Alexandra Reader*. What happened in 1945 to cause the girl's IQ and marks to take such a nose dive? Was it because she was losing her hearing? I decided to consult Mrs. Debrowski, the older, retired teacher I later came to admire. Of course, there was the more personal question earlier asked by Stookie, "Well teechur are you gonna pass her?" Stookie's marriage hung in the balance but school policy would pass her even if I didn't.

I noted that Fred Kleiner's wife Janet took two years off to have and tend her first baby before returning to the battle stations for one more year. I also noticed my name and other current information were missing from the chart, which was understandable.

One of the stories about Sheba Faye originated when she was six years old. Are some people too easy to hurt?

During a Friday afternoon's fun quiz, Janet Wilson asked her pupils, "What is a major export of New Zealand?" The students were silent. One of those famous William Neilson maps hung on the wall, with a picture of a chocolate bar next to New Zealand, and little Sheba Faye piped up, "Crispy Crunch chocolate bars." The other children roared with laughter while the embarrassed girl's long face turned bright red – almost as red as the many British possessions on the map. Then unwittingly the teacher turned to the little girl and said, "If we go to New Zealand we will surely face sheep, Sheba Faye." The kids second wave of laughter set a Baltic record and the girl's nickname was confirmed that Friday afternoon.

During practices for the school's yearly Christmas concerts, a standard joke was that while "shepherds watched their flocks by night," there was always one readily available sheep to play the part. Kids can be damn cruel, and the damage done can't always be measured.

I decided to investigate my poorest student's case further. I hitched a ride into Riga, to check with the Superintendent of Schools, Mr. Clawson, who had hired me. I had signed my contract for $2 150 per year and sent it to him by mail, so we had never met.

At school headquarters I was greeted heartily by a scrubbed, ginger-mustached, heavyset popinjay wearing a fruity cologne, a tablespoon of Brilliantine, and a rich green suit. His neat desk held a small red pot containing seven or eight needle point yellow pencils, Venus No. 3, points upwards.

All business, he intoned pompously, "On behalf of everyone here I welcome you warmly." His studied joviality irritated me, as did his bright, robotic smile and meechy ways. His disturbing kind of servility could not be disguised.

He invited me to his office and proceeded to tell me of the heavy financial responsibilities that he carried in the name of the Riga School Unit. Soon I surmised he loved mirrors. He was a rooster who thought the sun rose each day to hear him crow. For ten minutes or so he tried to impress me with his wisdom and his very hard work, and failed completely. His weak, Cupid's-bow mouth worked hesitantly two or three times before each sentence. His left hand repeatedly opened and clenched when he sat straight in his chair or when he stood, stiff as a board. I finally realized with some embarrassment that he wasn't Mr. Clawson – he was the school unit's Secretary-Treasurer.

In a few moments Mr. Clawson knocked and entered.

"I'm glad you're finished with my colleague," the new arrival said. Two pairs of eyes shot out arrows which crisscrossed in mid-air. It was only then that I began to learn a little bit about the typical power struggle between a School Superintendent and a school unit's Secretary-Treasurer. I hoped that this fellow would come in a very bad second. I was glad to leave that pedantic, plastic smile behind.

After talking with Mr. Clawson for a while, I formed the opinion that the taxpayers didn't pay the man enough. Irwin Clawson was a 38-year-old coffin-faced guy who had worked as an oil rigger, salesman, cabbie, rancher and carpenter. He walked with the fluid grace many fine athletes have.

The Superintendent said that he knew all of his 306 students, formally or informally. And he had studied the chart of one Sheba Faye Klanty.

"What is your response to her situation?" he asked. As I didn't have a good answer, the Superintendent taught me a lesson I hope I'll never forget.

"You purport to be a professional, so you better learn to act like one. Like it or not, fair or unfair, you are responsible for most of the 'nows' your student experiences." He added, "One day schoolteachers will finally recognize the sheer, raw power they hold in their hands and their minds, and they will exert the leadership society has bequeathed them." Perhaps he was dreaming a little, but I believed he was right on target. I wondered what kind of team he and Tall Wall would make.

"By the way," he said, "your student, Marsha Fowler, does not have an IQ of 178 as you reported, because your mathematics was done incorrectly. She is still a very bright girl, however.

Please be correct in your reports to my office." His eyes were bright, hard, unwavering, and filled with curiosity and intelligence.

The Superintendent said that he had noticed the dip in Sheba Faye's performance, but added in his own defence, "How can one administrator personally know over 300 students?" He suggested I contact the school nurse, Mrs. Doby, regarding Sheba Faye. The idea hadn't even entered my mind.

I had to ask. "Is Sheba Faye a health question or an educational question, or both?"

"Young man, let me say it again. Take the initiative. Lead, don't merely follow." His shrewd, appraising eyes stayed locked on mine.

It had been easy to hitch a ride to Riga that Saturday morning because that's where Baltic people did most of their shopping and banking and so on. My short ride home was not scheduled until 5 p.m. so I walked the six blocks to the school nurse's home. Mrs. Doby, a very pleasant, handsome lady with an honest Irish face, introduced me to her husband and three children before inviting me into her small office-study. There she presented me with all her facts on Sheba Faye. The ten-year veteran nurse claimed that Sheba Faye had suffered a rather sharp hearing loss over a one- or two-year period. The suspicious nurse had asked Wayne Klanty point blank if he knew if anyone "had boxed the girl's ears lately." The unruffled Klanty hadn't missed a beat when he admitted he gave "that kid a good thwack now and then, when she needs it – but I haven't boxed her ears. Why, do you think I should?"

Mrs. Doby obviously disliked the man but kept her voice level when talking about the incident. Alert intelligence was evident in her eyes. The nurse told me that she and Janet Kleiner had suggested to Klanty that he have the girl's ears tested by a specialist.

"No damn need for that," Klanty replied, "because anyone can see that she's growing more stupid and lazier all the time, especially around home, the very place I provide for her."

Nurse Doby, gnawing on her lower lip, reported that she had been frustrated but she didn't know what to do about the situation. "Janet, my best friend, and I each had a baby the same year and we took time off from our duties."

It looked to me that Sheba Faye had got lost in the shuffle.

I spent another two hours in the Doby's cheery home, sharing milk and fresh cinnamon buns with the five Dobys. The Doby family exuded contentment and self-satisfaction. The kids took turns on my knee and I gave the three of them the bumps until I got tired. It was fun to treat those children in a way I couldn't treat kids in Baltic. The Doby kids yelled and laughed in my ears and rode on my back as I became their 'horsey.' They pulled my hair, curled in my lap, and listened to a make-believe story. Great fun!

Later on Dalmond Doby, editor and owner of Riga's weekly newspaper, told me about the history of Baltic, his birthplace. His battered good looks and level speech somehow encouraged trust. I'd heard that years ago he had been fired by a big-name newspaper for telling the truth. His booklined study rivalled Tall Wall's collection, I'm sure. Dalmond Doby wasn't one of those guys who focuses on your eyebrows while wanting you to think you are getting an eyeball-to-eyeball connection. He *saw* people and events. His pithy and apposite comments were very enjoyable. While sucking moistly on his pipe he discussed the families of Maggie Jane and Sheba Faye. Even then I had a non-professional reason for learning about Maggie J.

When a person isn't in a real, warm home for some time, one kind of forgets how important it is. When my ride and I returned to Baltic I realized that homesickness was not easily denied.

That evening I walked over to Klanty's to find him "a little deep in my cups," sitting in his throne chair reading Ploetz' *Manual of Universal History*. He said that he found the chronology terrific but the interpretation inferior. He added that he made his own interpretations in any case. Was Klanty really a serious reader?

I believed that Klanty really knew that Sheba Faye simply wasn't "getting stupider and stupider," as he sometimes claimed. He was aware of the girl's hearing problems "long before that big-shot Doby woman told me about it, so there." Klanty wouldn't take Sheba Faye to "that fool Sawbones in Riga so she is stuck the way she is." He added that he wasn't going to buy her one of those "damn fool hearing aids that don't work in any case."

"Besides," he added to cap it off, "that girl isn't going anywhere fast, as any damn fool can see." Then he surprised me by saying, "she'll likely hook up with that young feller,

Wilbur Stook, so what's her problem got to do with me?" Klanty's attitude made me angry so I declined his offer to "have yourself a cool one."

It must have been the do-gooder in me that slowly led to my determination to help Sheba Faye, "the girl on the swing," as I secretly called her. Indeed, there were frequent weekend occasions during that late, warm autumn when I found her swinging slowly and humming softly beside the schoolhouse. Usually I spent Saturday morning and perhaps two hours Sunday afternoon at the school preparing lessons and marking papers. (I wonder if marking papers is what teachers do in hell for all eternity.) Sheba Faye and I had frequent, hesitant conversations, with her on one swing and me on the other. Sometimes she sat on the schoolyard grass, her legs sprawling jointlessly under her. She said that she could better hear some words while she sat directly in front of me. Lip reading, perhaps.

One Sunday afternoon she told me "my only friends are Mrs. Bredner, Mrs. Fowler, Mrs. Stone, Mr. and Mrs. Horvath, and you." I was deeply touched and embarrassed. The only young friend she had acknowledged was also her teacher. It was clear her stepfather cared little about her.

"What about Stookie, Sheba Faye?" Her face's spoiled-yeast complexion, ears and throat burned pink and she didn't answer.

I don't believe that anyone ever saw Sheba Faye and Stookie "go out" together. I supposed that Stookie's work around the town and Sheba Faye's school and babysitting duties must often have kept them apart even if they wanted to be together. And that didn't count the hours the girl spent cooking and cleaning at home. It seemed to me that when she did have free time she spent it alone. That assumption was not totally correct.

11

Conversations

It is the consciousness of a lack . . . that prompt us to preach or to brag. – George Iles: Canadian Stories.

Initially Klanty caused me more confusion than disgust, but after numerous visits to the house on the edge of town, I began to experience pity mixed with my feelings of contempt.

Klanty's brand of sententiousness ran roughshod over my teachers' college work ethic. His viewpoint on material possessions was that "materialistic people and societies become boring as hell after a while." He told me all we get out of life is "a now and a now and a now, and it's just one damn fool thing after another. So why don't you squint a little at life, and see only what you want to see?" As he spoke he scrubbed along his unshaven jaw line with the palms of his large hands, yawned mightily, and bit into two black olives.

I recorded some of Klanty's observations on life in my diary.

Klanty on time: "The man who made time made lots of it, so why get excited about getting something done? I dismiss most people's restless push towards a shaky future." Most people, he suggested, could not stand to admit their own insignificance, but he could. He added that "except in his own, a man is an insignificant character in every other biography – most people are so damned predictable and so pathetically ordinary."

Klanty on old age and death: "When I get really old, the indignities will pile up like snow drifts, so there will be no reason to hang on to life, and I'll be ready to go. It bothers a lot of people that they can't influence their final outcome. People either die too young or else stick around too long, because no one knows how to die at the right time. But I don't give a damn about death."

Klanty on happiness, "one of life's aberrations": he believed that life opens a door for an individual, and then throws wet lime in his face.

Klanty on the birth of the Bredner's baby: "For damn sure, most would-be mothers should abort their fetuses 'cause they'd be doing the babies a huge favor. We all owe one death and we all pay up. You damn well don't forget it."

Klanty on his neighbors: "The only time Baltic people are generous to me is in late summer or early fall when they all harvest too many tomatoes and too much corn, so now you know what people are really like. Life demands more than it gives."

For Klanty, I suppose, a primordial shrug was the only sensible response to life. Some of his arguments seemed distressingly plausible, like his quote from Pascal: "We pursue goals we know to be worthless."

Although his comments would come out increasingly garbled and slurred as he drank, the words almost lost between his ill-fitting dentures and fat tongue, he seemed to believe that his wits were sharpened, not dulled, by the bottle. His questions were like shotgun slugs aimed at changing targets. I can't explain the fact that on some occasions, after drinking heavily, he spoke with increased clarity and pungency. At times he even sounded like an elder statesman. But mostly he was a master of crudity and vapidness, as when he asked, "Did you know that a person's best smile comes just as he lays a really big turd?"

He claimed that he took frequent walks during pleasant evenings, especially along the nearby Riga River. I doubted that very much. Yet in his own way he radiated a strange kind of raucous vitality.

Over the months, I realized Klanty was a strong candidate for the world's "Most Physically Lazy Man" contest. A road crew had desperately needed a flag man the summer before and no one could be found to do the job. With some hesitation, someone mentioned Klanty. After considerable persuasion the big man, along with his chair, beer, and smokes, were moved by truck to the nearby road. From his throne chair Klanty waved red flags and sluggishly sorted out Baltic's rush of traffic. The work lasted seven straight days, which was exactly one week too long for him. Klanty had discovered a new synonym for unpleasantness: work.

"You're right, young feller," he once told me, with a vain insouciance. "I'm free of Mammon's law and work's motivation. Liquid assets aren't the blood of life. So-called idleness isn't bad – it is a bloody, damn fun thing, as far as I'm concerned. They used to say that a hobo will work, a tramp won't, and a bum can't. Well. I'm beyond all three – so there you are."

He believed that it was stupid to work hard in a world full of contradiction and insanity, and that other solid thinkers were only beginning to agree with his viewpoint.

I seldom saw him out of his chair, at least before our terrible trouble began. It looked like you couldn't pry him from it with a long two-by-four. When he did walk, he put his flat feet down ponderously, as if he were planting the dirty, ugly things, creating a field of disturbance as he moved through a room.

There was a certain theatricality about Klanty – he always seemed to be on stage, seated, standing or walking. Klanty once said that we are all actors who wear masks beneath our masks. Can such actors really love someone other than themselves?

During the academic year Wall and I often spent an afternoon or evening with Klanty. When Mrs. Stone warned us our "Klanty visits" would lead to no good, in jest I sang:

We're going to Klanty's in old Shanty Town,
The roof is so slanty it touches the ground.
But that tumbled down shack by the old railroad track,
Like a millionaire's mansion is calling me back.
I'd give up my palace if I were a king;
It's more than a palace it's my everything.
There's a queen waiting there with a silvery crown,
In that Klanty's in Old Shanty Town.

I think Wall tried to smile.

Mrs. Stone said, "I'll ignore your puffery and, furthermore, your parody of that lovely 1932 depression song." More sleepless nights of concern! Perhaps Mrs. Stone's dislike of Klanty added to her displeasure at my version of the song.

When I asked him, Klanty readily agreed that "the bitch lady hates my guts." In a different tone, he added a further view, "Like most women of her kind she uses propriety as a concealment of an earlier shame." I didn't fully understand what he meant, but I often thought about that comment.

Although Wall and I purchased our share of the drinks in Riga, Klanty always provided more than his share of homemade beer and an imported, sickly-sweet apricot brandy he called "bottled poetry."

Once Stookie learned of those visits, our team became a trio. Or it might be more correct to say that slow-drinking Stookie was our largely silent partner. I must admit I attached little significance to him attending, even though he had told me of his interest in Sheba Faye. Not once during our visits did Sheba Faye make another appearance.

Stookie had said he'd come if we'd limit ourselves to two beer each. We promised, but didn't always keep our word. Klanty, Tall Wall and I promised each other that we would come prepared for another person's "presentation." We didn't tell Stookie about that arrangement.

Klanty loved to entertain and, damn it, he *was* entertaining and irreverent and often smuttily ribald during those sessions. There was much alertness and insight in that tub-of-lard. He sat in his mastodonic chair and looked down at us from its height. Tall Wall sat in his usual straight-backed kitchen chair, while Stookie and I shared the couch.

Klanty did most of the talking; Wall asked penetrating and tough questions, and believed little; I, of course, provided the urbanity and wit; and Stookie listened and opened the OP (other people's) beer.

Most of the time, Klanty's raspy voice was punctuated by a heavy smoker's cough, and when drunk, his speech was staccato mixed with whispered vehemence. However, when sober, Klanty's voice was sometimes vibrant, resonant, pleasingly deep and totally listenable. Klanty knew he was a terrific storyteller (and liar, too?) and relished his role. He told me about being a child prodigy on the violin (with short, fat, dill pickle fingers?); a supporter of the One Big Union movement, when he had been physically beaten and knifed (and lost an ear lobe?) during the 1919 Winnipeg general strike; a member of a Chautauqua group in western Canada as ventriloquist and cossack dancer (now there is a combination); a traveller of the Ucavali branch of the Amazon River to Peru; a screwer of eleven women in one week in the same city (he'd give names on request); a boxer in a Kansas City boxing ring (where he had been knocked out by a kangaroo); and a barnstormer with the famed Wiley Post. His parents and only sister had died in the 1918-1920 influenza epidemic which he said claimed 22 million lives world-wide.

I cannot disprove any of his claims. Is not a liar's youth more interesting than the youth of an honest person?

However, on request Klanty chanted the 1919 "Labor Hymn." Upon my insistence, he wrote out, in a clear, legible hand, the hymn made famous during the Winnipeg strike.

> *When wilt thou save the people, Lord? O God of mercy, when?*
> *The people, Lord, the people. Not crowns and thrones, but men.*

It was then that I noticed a faded, fuzzy photograph thumb-tacked to the wall beside his chair. The picture was of a monoplane, a Lockheed-Vega named *Winnie Mae.* On the bottom right corner of the photograph a message had been scrawled: *Warm wishes to W.K. from W.P.*

"That's me standing there with Wiley Post," said Klanty. Damn it; it sure did look like a younger and thinner Klanty!

Klanty handed me an excellent fountain pen and a fancy writing tablet.

"Write these facts down, young feller, and check them out yourself." *Winnie Mae* had been named in honor of the daughter of the airplane's owner, F.C. Hall. Post, affectionately called "the Flying Redskin" because of some Indian blood, was born on November 2, 1899 at Van Zandt, Texas. An errant particle from a drill left him blind in one eye. In spite of that difficulty he was determined to be first to fly around the globe. In 1931, with his Australian-born navigator, Harold Gatty, Post made the remarkable trip. As the humorist cowboy and flyer Will Rogers said, "It was the sustainingest effort that was ever sustained."

Klanty claimed that he was on Edmonton's muddy airstrip when the pair left on their last leg to New York. The *Winnie Mae* is on display in some Eastern big-shot museum, he added. Klanty impressed me by writing out the route taken by the two flyers: New York – Grace – Chester – Berlin – Moscow – Novosibirsk – Irkutsk – Blagoveshchensk – Khabarovsk – Nome – Fairbanks – Edmonton – New York.

My host cracked another beer before telling me about Post's next great adventure. Two years later, in 1933, the flyer spanned the globe in a solo flight. That Lockheed-Vega airplane, said Klanty, was one sweet machine.

"I should know. Three times I rode with Wiley Post, who was a greater flyer than Lindburgh if you really want to know the truth." Klanty's voice actually softened when he told me that Post and Rogers were killed on August 15, 1935, during a short flight with another plane between the Eskimo village of Walakpi and Point Barrow, Alaska.

From his throne chair Klanty reached for a photograph album resting on his messy bookshelves. He showed me a picture featuring Amelia Earhart, Wiley Post, Laura Ingalls and Roscoe Turner.

Klanty shifted his bulk a bit. He leaned forward.

"Amelia Earhart, a brave woman and the best mechanic of the bunch, was shot down by those Japanese just before the war." Again his voice softened. "There's really no mystery about her disappearance in spite of what those damned newspapers print." He moved his polished and filed right thumbnail back and forth across the stubble on his chin and said even more softly, "Yes, Amelia was a great one. The first woman to fly the Atlantic solo."

When I got home I checked Wallace's encyclopedia. Klanty had spoken the truth about Post's career. I had wanted to prove that Klanty was a liar and a braggart! But couldn't he have learned facts and embellished on them? However, the guy standing with Post by the Winnie Mae sure looked like a youthful Klanty.

Although his brain was often marinated with booze, Klanty appeared well read, and could quote poetry to support his arguments. He was especially well acquainted with the romantic poets Wordsworth, Shelley, Keats, and Byron.

"One would expect that," said Tall Wall, who claimed that those romanticists were a quarreling, prickly, wild, and sometimes barbaric group.

Once we discussed the topic, "The most interesting individual in English literature." Tall Wall, who had chosen the topic, gave the first suggestion: Richard III, who, Tall Wall claimed, had been ill-treated by Shakespeare.

My nomination was Lady Godiva, a story first told in 1236 AD by a chronicler named Roger of Wendover. How beautiful was Godiva, the wife of Leofric, Earl of Mercia, one of the great earls of Edward the Confessor. Together they founded a monastery in Coventry. The legend would have us believe that Leofric placed a heavy tax on his Coventry subjects. When his 17-year-old wife objected, he promised tax relief if Godiva would ride naked through the streets at noonday. The long-haired beauty agreed, but only if people stayed inside their homes and shut their windows. A tailor – the original Peeping Tom – brazenly looked out his window at Godiva and was somehow struck blind. A peeping tom, I said, was the worst of the low life. Klanty made a brushing movement with his right hand as though batting away troublesome flying insects.

Klanty's favorite was Defoe's Moll Flanders, who as a whore, "knew how to make a man happy with a little friction, heat and lubrication." Once unwittingly married to her brother, the woman became a successful thief and pickpocket. She was transported to Virginia, where she married a highwayman, and they lived as planters in both penitence and prosperity. He put emphasis on the word "prosperity." "Now that's my kind of woman," Klanty said, chortling.

Stookie simply said that he liked Little John and Robin Hood the best because "they looked after each other and their friends real good and took care of the ladies." Klanty's response? "You can buy Robin Hood by the bag but let him out before he screams." More laughter and spittle.

Behind and around Klanty's chair, which had been clawed by many generations of unruly house cats (Splat's relatives?) there were bookshelves from floor to ceiling, crammed with books, most with broken spines. There were usually five or six resting on his footstool, waiting for more of his red pencil marks. He would look up from a book over the rimless glasses anchored on his empurpled nose and say he "never allowed those damn girls a chance to touch my books." He admitted he had stolen most of them from a Toronto publisher, who was "damn-fool enough to trust pretty near everybody."

During the first part of our sessions, unless he was talking Klanty's eyes were half-closed, eyelids drooping. I could not decide if he was concentrating intensely on the discussion, or if the booze had made his eyelids too heavy, or both. Slowly I came to believe he was concocting his next profane, vulgar comment.

My uncle once told me that self-pitying drunks are the biggest bother. I don't agree. Angry-at-the-world drunks, like Klanty, are worse.

One Saturday afternoon Tall Wall left for the city and Stookie and I were left with Klanty to continue our discussion. The more Klanty drank the more his loose mouth wandered and he made some comments about Tall Wall he surely wouldn't have said to his face.

Stookie defended his friend. "Mr. Talleck's a teacher ya know."

Klanty looked at me. "You're no teacher yet. Even if you do get good at it," he added, "you've got to remember that good teaching is like peeing in dark trousers. You get temporarily warm but no one else knows about it."

What would Wall have said to that? I wasn't able to focus my rebuttal before Klanty went on.

"You teachers teach kids the importance of winning, always winning. You should teach them the importance of losing, because it's a lesson they'll have lots of use for."

I saw something behind his eyes, something that moved and threatened. I left that day feeling angry and impotent.

Our host's foul-mouthed comments eventually became too much for us but it was Stookie who really put a stop to the whole process.

It was during a March seminar, when we were discussing the merits of convent and monastery life. Tall Wall came well prepared, as usual, and spoke eloquently and succinctly about the contributions of many great people who had lived in that manner. Klanty subsequently made his beer hall logic heard.

"Tail is all you young fellers think about, and you can't fool me any more than the sun can get by the rooster."

Something clouded passed across Stookie's face, but he remained quiet for a time. I spoke (predictably) of the biological need to perpetuate the race.

Klanty finished his drink, belched like a gunshot, and responded, "Go to it kid – girls today should be fitted with a baseball catcher's mitt anyway."

Stookie stood, rubbing his reddening face. He slowly stroked the back of his left hand as he stared at the older man.

"You've got two good girls and you talk filthy like that!" He looked at Klanty as if he had a bad smell. In return, Klanty gave him a look of ugly, green hate. Stookie picked up his jacket and turned to Wall and me. "Let's go now, this sure is a bad man."

Klanty turned to Stookie slowly, like a gun on a pivot. There was a tightly stretched silence. A new darkness crossed Klanty's raddled face. Somehow I got the impression that Klanty and Stookie shared a hot and old hate.

In a voice as thick as glue, Klanty said, "Good, get the hell gone, now I can get back to my books." His statement was all the harsher for its soft delivery.

At the teacherage, I expressed my view that inside Klanty was a methodical and strange brutality that fed on itself. Tall Wall disagreed – he thought Klanty's scorn was used to disguise his fear. Klanty was a misogynist, he said; infuriating, intellectually convoluted, but likely capable of brilliance when sober. He added further perspective. Somehow over the years Klanty had changed from the town character into the chief topic of gossip. Such a man might rise each morning to hone old and new grudges, hates and memories. "According to legend," Wallaced added in light defense of Klanty, "even hell-bound Judas Iscariot was allowed to cool himself on an iceberg each Christmas Eve." Stookie thought Klanty was just "a bad onion 'cause he's got lots of rotten layers."

Was it melodramatic to suggest that in Klanty lived an ancient evil, dark and frightening? Or was he all talk? That same Klanty was the (sensitive?) guy who called me one early morning to come and photograph a huge spider's web covered with dew. In any case, Klanty's bogus popularity with us was over and the sessions were no more.

That night my dream featured three identical Klantys, boys of 12 or 13. One held Splat, another a full kerosene can, and the third a match.

Who wouldn't have worried about Klanty's daughters?

12

Anticipation

Hope is a pleasant acquaintance, but an unsafe friend.
- T.C. Haliburton: Sam Slick's Wise Saws.

While my concern over one of Klanty's daughters was mainly academic, I have to admit my interest in the other ran to the more personal. Although the stepdaughter of Klanty I was fascinated with lived in Vyborg, I was determined our paths should cross as often as possible.

Our hamlet, as Stookie had explained to me, used to have a tri-weekly passenger train service. However, the newer, diesel-driven grain trains provided no passenger service. Faint support for my grand crusade! I hoped it was possible for me to travel to MJ's town by bus, but the schedule also made that impossible. She could come by bus to Baltic, on occasion, but had to leave late Sunday morning for Vyborg. It was a bad situation. She had a very heavy teaching schedule, and was also taking two tough university courses by correspondence. Things weren't working out well for us – or should I say for me?

I practically begged tightwad Tall Wall to lend me his new car so that this scholar-in-the-garret could visit Vyborg. But he was one stubborn so-and-so. When I told him that possessions charm most when shared with others, he informed me with the smallest of smiles that the word "car" was originally an Anglo-Saxon word meaning "war chariot," and because war solves nothing, "why should I lend you my potential contribution to more conflict?"

I couldn't even consider the truck Stookie used on his rounds because "she's the town's truck ya know." The upshot was I couldn't travel to Vyborg to see Maggie J.

Tall Wall's tightwad ways with his car did not extend to the Christmas season, when he took me to the city to do Christmas shopping. Even on that winter's day he looked terrific in his canary-yellow sportscoat, silk shirt with French cuffs, cuff links like blue grapes, white-and-blue checkered bow tie, matching blue slacks, and, of course, highly glossed, black leather shoes. His hat and gloves matched his smart winter coat. It was only then that I realized that in many ways Tall Wall did remind me of Oscar Wilde: he dressed flamboyantly, was successful but far too indulgent, and also exceptionally generous with his money. I suppose my Grandpa would have called Wallace a "dandy" or a "fop."

That Saturday morning he dropped me at a cold, crummy, noisy hotel, and then announced he would not be back until Sunday evening. Wall's car purred warmly outside the hotel. Where was he going? What would he do? He didn't say.

In less than an hour my Christmas shopping was finished, and ten minutes later I was bored. I swore at Wall's absence, walked the cold streets of December, and lost (or had stolen) a $20 bill, all the money I had left, somewhere in my perambulations which meant my fun was over for the weekend. Or was it? I sneaked into a fantastic new movie, *From Here to Eternity*. I hadn't known that Sinatra was such a terrific actor. Later that night in one of my most real dreams two other "actors," Maggie J and I, played Kerr's and Lancaster's parts on the warm ocean's beach. (A lot of my dreams seemed to involve water or ice.) I slept late Sunday morning, and spent the rest of the day watching skaters practicing for their forthcoming ice carnival. It gave me ideas for a similar event for Baltic. The teacher in charge, some old guy about forty, skated over to where I stood.

"Look, kid, these girls don't need you staring at them, so leave now!" I *was* watching the older girls pretty closely. I bet their teacher was, too! I left the skating rink, calling the guy "an ugly hypocrite" under my breath.

My hunger did not help my deep funk. By the time Wall and I got home late Sunday night, I was damn near starved. Who ever said carrot sticks and water can't be delicious?

A few nights later, Tall Wall, Stookie, and I had a party to exchange Christmas gifts. Klanty refused our invitation. Wall and I were at school when Stookie stacked his split wood in our back porch, close to that fabulous tin bathtub. That night he tied blue ribbons around two pieces of wood and gave those pieces to us as our presents. We didn't learn until later about the large, fresh wood pile in the porch. Tall Wall gave me very fancy, leather-bound volumes of Thucydides and Herodotus. *Make history your teacher*, he wrote in the card, b*ecause you will then embrace the right combination of hope and fear. History is untidy – just like you*. I feigned a deep hurt and Wall tried to smile. His neat, precise signature adorned both books.

Tall Wall and I combined our giving to Stookie in a wrapped, cardboard box containing a pair of high, heavy boots with long leather laces. I gave Tall Wall thin, softcover copies of Oscar Wilde's *Lady Windermere's Fan* and *The Ballad of Reading Gaol*. When Stookie was out of the room I told Wall that the latter item grew out of Wilde's two-year prison sentence for his homosexual affair with Lord Alfred Douglas, and that the poem should be of interest to him because of Wilde's opposition to capital punishment. Wall pretended that the play and poem were new to him – and that made me feel good.

Then, looking around the front room of our humble teacherage, Tall Wall waved his arms as he repeated the words of Oscar Wilde on his way to prison. "If this is the way Queen Victoria treats her convicts, she doesn't deserve to have any."

Stookie asked us if we thought Sheba Faye would like the snowshoes he had made as her Christmas present. He had soaked and shaped the frames and he had prepared the leather strips and bindings required. They were similar to his own homemade snowshoes which I had noticed in the railroad station's freight shed. How many guys give homemade snowshoes for Christmas presents? We praised his efforts.

I received Christmas cards from all my students' families except the Klantys. Although from their houses one could almost throw a snowball to the teacherage, that afternoon I received cards by mail from Mrs. Stone, Rev. Framm, Reg Woolston, and the Bredner family.

Mrs. Bredner wrote, *Thanks for making my Christmas baby rememberable*. I was touched. Rev. Framm wrote: *I'd like to see you get into one of Mrs. Stone's choir gown*s. I roared until tears came down my face. Chairman of the local school board, Reg Woolston, added a Mark Twain quote to his card: *In the first place God made idiots; this was for practice; then he made school board*s. Under what I had wrongly defined as a vapid manner he had a lovely, self-deprecating humor. Mrs. Stone included a quote from Shakespeare: *Every inordinate cup is unblessed, and the ingredient is the devil.* I'd drink to that!

We three celebrants took two bottles of apricot brandy over to Wayne Klanty's. We didn't stay long, but there I saw Sheba Faye setting up a Christmas tree. It was the decorated tree my students and I had enjoyed for two weeks in my classroom. Sheba Faye had shyly asked if she could "borrow" it over Christmas.

Klanty didn't thank us for his present or even wish us a Merry Christmas. However, while clasping the brandy noggin he acknowledged that "Alice sure as hell didn't find elixir like this down the rabbit hole."

We three returned to the teacherage to enjoy one of Tall Wall's special meals – roast chicken and all the fixings. It wasn't bad, but hardly up to Mrs. Horvath's standards. I asked Wall if this chicken had any extra eggs.

He snorted. "You are an impossible person." However, the corners of his mouth moved in what, in another person, might have been the start of a smile.

Wall played several carols on his piano, and Stookie produced his beaten-up guitar, which he played softly with his big, strong fingers. His singing of Christmas carols was beautiful. I felt warm inside and tears threatened. (Why hadn't the minister ever asked Stookie to sing in the choir?)

Stookie and Wall sang *Silent Night*, and then, with Stookie softly stroking his guitar, I sang one verse of *We Three Kings of Orient Are*. Stookie then proclaimed "you sing better than you sound." (My music instructor at teachers' college said I sounded like an asthmatic rooster.)

Later Stookie, his new boots in hand (he promised that he would "dubbin 'em up real good in the morning"), was about to leave by our front door when he turned to me, and with his version of a smile he said, "oh yeah, I almost forgot this."

I recognized the writing on the envelope which he removed from his heavy shirt pocket. The Christmas greeting was from Maggie J. Stookie had been at the Horvath's post office that afternoon and met the extra mail truck. That loveable innocent, as I called him in his absence, was also a tease. In celebration I played Benny Goodman's classic rendition of "One Sweet Letter From You" on Wall's phonograph. Wallace told me I was revealing my "erubescence." The dictionary search would have to wait!

Accompanying MJ's Christmas card was a breezy two-page letter. She acknowledged receipt of my eight-page letter, and wrote that she understood why I had made plans to hitchhike to my parents' home for the holiday season, as Wall was to spend the two-week holiday in Memphis and New Orleans – apparently two of his old haunts – and there was no suitable train or bus service available. She wrote that she would come home Christmas Eve and again on New Year's Eve to be with Sheba Faye. No mention of Klanty. During the holidays she was going to "knock off" all her university assignments. She concluded with "my hope that you will save at least one dance for me if you can make it to Baltic's New Year's dance."

It was good to see my parents at Christmas, but Hannibal's elephants could not have stopped me from reaching the famed Baltic town hall for the New Year's dance. My eighth ride of the day dropped me at Baltic at 10:45 p.m. I wondered if the night was going to be worth 14 hours of travel, 6 in the dark, and very cold waits.

Under a mad sprawl of stars and lively northern lights, I finally joined over 200 souls, the hastily put-together orchestra from Riga, to say goodbye to 1953 on a cold, clear winter evening. The females sat on long benches, and the men and older boys stood near the front door while examining the predictable talent. Just before twelve midnight – with everyone counting down *10, 9, 8, 7* – Maggie J slipped her arm through mine. Everyone shouted, "Happy New Year." A small, full-bodied and beautiful girl with large eyes and soft lips kissed me long but softly, and then drew her small hands to her chest as if she were a painter who had just finished a masterpiece. Indeed, she had. I thought her kiss had a taste of love in it. It was then that I decided to pursue Margaret Jane Enders with no holds barred.

For some time I heard nothing, saw swimmingly, and drank in the sheer loveliness of that lovely girl. As I held her closely I thought that MJ whispered a name in my ear but it was so damn noisy and there was so much going on that I forgot to ask her about it. A few revellers noticed the two teachers "over there in the corner" by Stookie's stove and whispered to each other.

Young teachers in small towns are supposed to be sexless, bloodless, sterile, and emotionless. While I knew I must act like a teacher (whatever that meant) I simply wouldn't listen to people who told me what that should be. Perhaps dualism is part of teachers' lives because their private and public lives can never be congruent. A teacher is both special and not special.

The boiling hot, post-midnight coffee had been dispensed, along with a choice of ham or egg-salad sandwiches. Granular green floor wax had been freshly applied to the excellent, hardwood dance floor; the dirty cups had been stacked; any babies and small kids had been taken home, or put asleep in (Stookie's) kitchen and behind the benches which circled the rather large dance floor. Before the more rancorous music assaulted dancers' eardrums, the seven-piece orchestra from Riga began a more-than-passable rendition of the wonderful classic "I'm in the Mood for Love." The saxophone was hot and sweet that night, the notes reaching out to the dancers, to Maggie J and me.

"It's our song," I said softly into her neck. She smiled her response.

Why do some people think that the warmest love blossoms only under summer skies?

The truly fine dancers are those people who can do all the fast steps and when waltz time comes, can glide, slide, sweep, bend, move, glissade, with the oneness born from the two. I have seen many big, rural-bred men in hard boots schottische, square dance, polka, jive, and two-step with lightness, smoothness, and a perfect sense of timing. Meanwhile their ladies (in nyloned feet, weather permitting) match and complement the men. The partners obviously have forgotten the tiredness of the long day and the chores which need doing the next morning.

The town bully often enlivens the proceedings with an argosy of power and, of course, the roving police are always at the dance in the next town. The nettlesome, irascible bully usually gets his way while the men of the district silently curse Bully but do little to stop him. The women perhaps better understand the bloodlust in his eyes. (I've been told there is a sexual awakening of sorts here but I don't understand it.) The orchestra members, who have seen it all before, watch from the stage.

You just didn't fight in "Stookie's hall," especially not on the floor which he swept and minded and waxed for the town's dances. Just as men mustn't wear steel clickers on their boots, so must they not spoil the evening. So most of the fights – usually about girls and booze – took place behind the hall or outside the side door where Stookie and I first met. Unwritten rules included: stay above the belt, knuckles not knives, hands not boots, teeth not eyes, one on one, stay down if you're beaten, go home after you fight, and two fights in one night meant "you were lookin' for it, buddy."

The district bully (and our team's best pitcher) was the well-lubricated Jack Klackston, who threatened to spoil the party while dancing with Margaret Enders. When drunk and looking for trouble, Jack had one of those small but somehow vulnerable sneers, phony nonchalance and sullen vacuity worn by younger punks on streetcorners across the country.

I recognized the Riga centre fielder, a loutish guy with a porcupine face, Mortimer Snerd ears, a duck's-ass haircut, mutton chop sideburns, and big boots. I didn't know his name so I called him "Stud."

Mr. Stud tagged Jack's shoulder but Jack, who was not too bright at the best of times, wouldn't give up Maggie J. Jack cursed, and the other man cursed. Anger boiled, and the fight began. The music stopped, and the crowd formed the inevitable circle. Both participants threw a few hard fists. Then Stookie appeared, all five feet of him. With the flat of his hand he hit both men *one-two* high in their chests, fast and hard. The meaty sounds seemed to last a long time.

They fell at his feet. With the click of breaking teeth, Stud's face hit the edge of Stookie's stove. Stookie grabbed one fellow, then the other, by the feet. He dragged them out the side door. He rubbed snow on their faces, and told them to get up.

"It's good to fight out here," he said.

The fighters' zeal had disappeared by then.

Stookie said, "Miss Enders is a teechur ya know," adding, "You're still my friend, Jack, and you're still a good guy for our teams." Stookie told Stud, "We've howdied but never shook so it wasn't so bad hittin' you."

The sheer animal force of the two combatants and Stookie scared the hell out of me. I knew something of Jack's strength and quickness on the ball diamond and the hockey ice, and the power and speed of his fist made me feel puny, indeed. Stud was even bigger than Jack. I had seen him lie belly-down on Woolston's all-purpose counter, and with shoulder and neck muscles straining, eyes bulging, lift a hundred pound bag of flour six inches off the floor with his teeth. He won a ten-dollar bet for his efforts. And my squat fireplug buddy, Stookie, had put both guys out of commission.

Naturally MJ was embarrassed by the fighting. She later told me that she had stayed for the first waltz after the lunch break only because she had promised it to me, she said. She had promised to take her sister home early. Sheba Faye, wearing the new dress Maggie J gave her for Christmas, had sat by herself at the end of the bench the one by the drafty side door during most of the dance. Stookie had one turn on the floor with her, I observed. When I asked why he wasn't dancing with Sheba Faye, Stookie only said, "I got too many things that need tendin' to spend all night dancin' ya know." No one else danced with Klanty's younger daughter. Perhaps I should have danced with my student.

"Stay and have some fun," I said weakly to MJ. The music drowned out my words. The only females left to dance with were married women and high school "jail bait" (most of them "strumpets" by Mrs. Stone's definition) who smelled of spearmint. Please please save me from the sassy, studied languor of high school females who chew gum with their mouths open. On earlier occasions I'd learned that on the dance floor one of the worst dance partners was the rather young and fraudulently vivacious wife of the school board chairman, Reg Woolston. Iris Woolston was a plump, frowsy, raunchy woman with a doughy face, horsey teeth, habitually-parted and overly-full lips, busy hips, the hard, unblinking dark eyes of a predatory bird, and a raspy, slightly breathless voice. She wore big clunking bracelets and brooches, and a dull, pink dress. Rubens would have painted her, but only from the neck down. Duty called on me to dance twice with her, dances which I both liked and disliked. She had a peasant sensuality which didn't remind me of milkmaids and hay barns. Even Tall Wall admitted that "the lady is rather bathukopian and callipygian." It seemed to me that her very red smile had an edge of cruelty to it – she scared the hell out of me. It was rumored that the reckless, full-bodied woman slept far from home far too often.

After my dances, I grabbed my parka in a world-class sulk and headed home to my lonely teacherage. I could hear laughter, shouts, and celebration in the cold, crisp air. Vehicle doors slammed shut. As Stookie had said earlier, there were lots of "wet spots" tonight. All the young people, and older folks too, were having one hell of a good time back in the hall, or somewhere out there in the dark. Guys who attended Riga High School – guys who were my age or only slightly younger than lonesome me – were back at the dance hall with their juices in full flow, no doubt. And I was going home.

Well, Eunuch, I said to myself. *Happy New Year.*

The frozen, wood sidewalks creaked a cold, snappy sound – an angry, alone sound. When I got home I slammed the oven door shut, and it damn well stayed shut for the night. They will never write a great love song called, "All Alone in a Cold Teacherage on a Cold, Cold New Year's Eve." In my dream Iris Woolston evolved into a wet Venus flytrap.

Later that month our hockey team drove to Vyborg for a Saturday afternoon's exhibition game in the town's new arena. I planned to spend the night at the local hotel, and hitch a ride home in the morning. Meanwhile the rest of the team would return home Saturday evening after the game. Maggie J, in response to my letter, made arrangements to borrow a car from her landlady and attend the game with some friends. She and I planned to dine and dance in the next town – all very circumspect. Before the game we exchanged brief greetings. Her friends, including the school principal, seemed friendly enough.

During my first shift on ice, a wild elbow flattened my nose but good. I bled like a stuck pig. I sarcastically asked concerned ex-medic Tall Wall for thick, brown paper to put under my lip to stop the bleeding – and then fainted on our blue line.

The Vyborg doctor repaired my broken beak and temporarily plugged both nostrils to prevent further bleeding. I spent the night in the Vyborg hospital, for observation, they said.

Maggie J came for a sneak visit (while I was sleeping, of course), tiptoeing out on the desk nurse's admonition. MJ left a note saying *Baltic 1, Vyborg 0, Maggie J Enders, 0.* Apparently goalie Stookie got the shutout. We had that in common, for sure.

Next morning the doctor examined me early in his rounds (he'd had too many rounds the night before and had whiskey on his breath). He pronounced my nozzle and me salvageable. Tall Wall and Stookie (who first insisted that "Mr. Talleck" phone Baltic to get the flag down and folded good) had kindly spent the evening in Vyborg on my behalf, and drove me home to Baltic.

It was the first night that Stookie had ever spent away from Baltic. He loved the experience except for one thing –he did not like sleeping in a bed where strangers had slept.

"That could be bad," he said, "because some folks might have died there."

That night at home Tall Wall phoned the doctor and drove me to Riga, where medical wonders were performed, even as I complained about what Wall called in fun "the rosacea of my proboscis."

About a week later MJ sent me a magazine picture of Jimmy Durante, and added her handwritten salutation: *Get well soon, Mr. Schnozzola*. She signed the card *MMMMMMJay*.

During my absence from school, my place was taken by my predecessor, Mrs. Violet Debrowski, a 71-year-old retired, local teacher with a squeaky girdle. One afternoon I watched her work with the youngsters and she was fantastic. I wished I had her gifts – minus the squeaks, of course.

So for a few days, I stayed home from school, read Wallace's books, played his records and his piano, and visited Mrs. Bredner and her new baby and Klanty, and caught him rubbing kerosene on his balding head. I even waved one day to Mrs. Stone.

Things were looking good, and my beak was feeling better. "The rose on my nose," as Stookie said, was fast disappearing, and my girl was coming to town.

Time passed torpidly, but Tall Wall's presents from his Christmas trip to the south helped me to fill the days. I played those 'new' 1953 records daily but failed to discover why Wall thought Rock and Roll (a term recently coined by an American disc jockey) was to become "the music of the future." Among others, the selections included "Crazy Man Crazy" by Bill Haley and the Comets, "Hound Dog" by Willie Mae Thornton, and "Have Mercy, Baby" by Billy Ward and the Dominoes.

"We are going to need all the mercy we can get if your predictions are correct," I told Wall. Wall claimed that this music, if that's what it could be called, had evolved from rhythm and blues, negro spirituals, African drum music, and jazz, or some such combination. Somehow rocking and rolling was tied to the old practice of "bundling" with one's beloved. I didn't understand that connection but I would have been pleased to investigate the phenomenon with Maggie J.

Dancing with MJ called for music, sweet and sentimental, like *I'm in the Mood for Love*. Singing, listening to, or dancing to favorite music connects you to everything else. And it's even better if the right person shares the experience with you. Rock and Roll, a mere craze, couldn't last because guys would remember how good girls felt in their arms.

13

Winter

. . . the frost that stings like fire upon my cheek . . .
– Archibald Lampman: Winter Uplands

Sheba Faye, that lonesome young woman, was the subject of the best photograph I have taken or likely ever will take.

It was an early Sunday afternoon in January when I took my borrowed skis and new camera (a Christmas present from my folks) to the creek. The frozen Riga River had become my open air sanctuary where I could become myself. The hoar frost made the willows white, thick, fuzzy. Winter had sucked the sky empty of all rich color, leaving a hard, low slate ceiling above me. The cold weather sharpened the air. For two miles I skied down the winding river which was covered by eight to ten inches of powder snow. Is there a more coldly beautiful picture than a red-wing blackbird perched on a surviving, perfectly full cat-tail sprouting from a curving snowdrift, with a background of hoar frost and a white-gray sky above?

A small anxious bird faced away from me as I left my skis and crawled toward the cat-tails, camera in hand. It seemed that rabbit berries were everywhere. I could see hundreds of animal tracks, the long slur of back feet and the neat front paw marks. This famed photographer of the avian world got snow up both sleeves and in one boot as he slowly progressed toward the subject. As if one cue, the bird turned its body and black eyes to me, and I clicked the shutter. With a vivid flash from its red and yellow shoulder patch, and a sound like *konk-er-EE* (I was its *conqueror*?) the bird took off – for Tall Wall's beloved Deep South, perhaps.

Wow! Hall of Fame stuff! As it turned out, my best picture was still to come.

I continued down the river, enjoying the cold, the whites, the blacks, the browns and the grays of the perfectly silent Sunday afternoon. The winter sun was softened and diluted as two sun dogs accompanied it across the sky. A few deer and numerous bush rabbits and partridges took turns appearing but they were too skitterish or too far away for a good camera shot. I thought about the feel of Maggie J's recent kiss on New Year's Eve and the afternoon suddenly got much warmer. I could easily have skied another 400 miles as long as I could keep thinking about Maggie J.

It was about then that ahead I saw the mermaid up ahead, sitting on a snowbank with her tail resting on the snow-covered ice. The creature's curving body and tail were only slightly darker than the snow and the winter background, but I could see she was leaning on her elbows while her face looked straight up to the winter sky.

I don't believe in mermaids, but the figure was definitely feminine. I snapped a long-range picture, then skied halfway to Miss Mermaid and clicked the camera again. Just then she slid down the snowbank to the snow-covered ice, and facing away from me, stood up on her tail while stretching her arms, as if she were enjoying a long yawn. A small lower snowbank blocked my view of her from the waist down. My watering eyes (I "cry" in cold weather) didn't help much. She returned to her original spot and my wide-awake dream went "poof." I wiped my wet eyes, took another hard look, and saw that the creature was wearing Stookie-brand snowshoes. The "mermaid" was Sheba Faye Klanty, dressed in her usual off-whites and grays. She must have come directly across the fields while I had followed the river route, which is why I didn't see her tracks. I skied home calling myself an incurable romantic and a damn fool at the same time.

Reality returned splendidly in the form of Mrs. Horvath's Sunday supper. Roast wild ducklings and dumplings garnished with peach halves nearly burst my seams. At 1:30 a.m. Tall Wall returned to our Baltic teacherage from another weekend in the city and poked me awake. How I could sleep in the stuffed chair with my feet in the cookstove's oven, he asked. Easy! Morpheus, the Greek God of Dreams, had been very, very kind to me and that damn Wallace interrupted my desert island visit with a co-operative mermaid.

Over his usual late-night brandy Wall asked if I had read his most recent book selection for me, Katherine Anthony's *Catherine the Great*, over the weekend. I told him I had spent the time with "the mysterious lady of the snows," which was the truth – sort of. Wallace Talleck downed his brandy, and fortunately didn't ask any more questions because of the late hour.

The next day I sent the film to the city for development. On the enclosed note I wrote a special request to handle the work carefully. Results came back in two weeks: the red-winged blackbird was covered by this idiot's thumb, and for some reason the close-up of the mermaid did not turn out. However, my first long-range picture was perfect. I later had that great picture enlarged by the same developers. The distant creature in the picture indeed looked like a fuzzy, gray-white mermaid.

By the way, Sheba Faye didn't hear or see me that day. I told no one about the mermaid story, but I kept the photo. I considered it my best private photo ever.

Later I told Stookie about my experience among the cat-tails. My friend, like so many people in Baltic, chose to lecture me. According to Stookie, cat-tails were a grocery store. Before the pollen developed you could eat the bloom just like corn on the cob, and old pollen made first-rate flour. The stems tasted like asparagus. The roots of the plants could be used "just like spuds," and Stookie had stuffed a pillow with the fluff from many cat-tails' club-like heads. "Cat-tails is good for a guy who knows about 'em," he concluded, "in both summer and winter."

I wondered if Stookie was correct when he claimed that extreme cold could cause a tree "to explode apart real good." Or when he claimed that when muskrats built their houses high, it meant "we are gonna have a tough winter." He also said that beavers left a leathery smell on the piles of mud they used to mark their territory. "It's that castoreum stuff ya know," he added.

The prairie winter often is a uniting thing, not a divisive force. Winter can bring out the best in people who, somehow, know in their bones they need each other. During the winter's roughest anger a lady, a latter-day Queen Victoria, will allow storm-lost strangers into her home and there serve them hot tea in fine china held by hands with callouses and dirty fingernails. Even in the cities, punks you wouldn't want five miles near your daughter rush to your vehicle and with manly chests heaving push your car out of a snowdrift.

Over a long hard winter, cold brings us together. Warmth drives us into ourselves where most of the rottenness and the angers and the hates grow best. So pity the person who doesn't know deep, prolonged cold weather. That cold can kill, but it can also sweep your soul clean with hard, stiff bristles.

Wallace Talleck and I organized an all-day ice carnival for early February. The advertising committee plastered posters on a number of the used and unused buildings of Baltic. *BIGGER AND BETTER THAN EVER*, the posters proclaimed, even though this was the first ever ice carnival to hit the metropolis. Costumes, programs, lunches, music, hot drinks, equipment, adults and kids had to be organized, scheduled, and prepared for the big day and the grand parade to be held at 10 a.m. at the skating rink. The day before the carnival closed clear and cold. Despite tremendous community co-operation, Wallace and I were two tired people.

The next morning, at 8 a.m., I heard my alarm clock and hit the cold deck. The back step and path to the biffy told the story. The good citizens of Baltic had slept through a heavy February snowfall. Dandy. A truth recognized by many great minds is that the gods of open-air skating rinks put large snow magnets under the ice. So, after a quick coffee Tall Wall and I walked to the skating rink, expecting to see a large rectangle of snow. At the far end of the rink we saw Stookie with the elevator's brooms and scoop shovel, finished clearing the rink. Obviously a lot of his work had been done in the pitch dark. He gave "Mr. Talleck" a chance to throw a token bit of snow over the fence and then gave me the shovel to do a similar piece of work.

"Now you can tell people that the three of us swept out the place," said Stookie. He was that kind of guy. I can't say he was grinning, but he looked like someone who had swallowed a large chew of gum.

No snow magnet could beat Stookie; and under a pallid, winter sun and a slate-gray sky the ice carnival was "bigger and better than ever." The crowd enjoyed the program and the mild day. The skit was about to begin, but where was Klanty's daughter? Sheba Faye hadn't shown up. Teachers count kids – I guess it's a good habit. At the last minute I filled in for her by wearing her long black costume (with most of the seams ripped open) and tall black hat, and the 'witch-turned-warlock' skated madly away from the good guys' posse. (I later write in my diary that the costume would have suited Mrs. Stone.)

That evening the parents and our helpers served the school children and themselves at the community hall. The fare was strong coffee, cocoa or milk, baked beans with lots of chunks of rich bacon, assorted vegetables, homemade brown bread, and thick syrup. Terrific! Noisy! There were purposeful people everywhere. The hall smelled of spilled beans, sticky syrup and sticky kids. Wonderful. Stookie acknowledged that "tomorrow I'll have to wash the hall down real good." Even Mrs. Stone made an appearance. I hoped her drippy nose would stay away from the pots of hot beans.

Stookie said it was "a three burp supper."

"Are you ready to open up your 'wet spot'?" I asked facetiously.

He looked around at the crowd, and then shook his head sideways at me. He said the inevitable, "You're supposed to be a teechur ya know."

After supper, some of us burned the used paper plates and cups while Mrs. Stone, the self-appointed matriarch of the hour, supervised the washing of the utensils, pots and pans in water heated on the hall's stove. Most people avoided "Mrs. Lung's" nagging, or at least they attempted to. Could her voice really shatter ear drums and beer bottles? I felt like asking her if she enjoyed being so righteous. "Ugliness etched in Stone," I uttered with questionable humor to no one in particular. Even Wallace Talleck later admitted privately that "the lady-in-question did appear to exemplify a propitiatory air." He further softened his response by suggesting that Mrs. Stone likely had "a humanness" about which even she didn't know. My reply was, "Nuts!"

Wallace and I made the rounds in the hall, thanking everyone for their help including Mrs. Stone, alias Madam Defarge.

Then Wallace Talleck, although usually attuned more to Mozart's lipid strains, leaped to the hall's stage where on the old piano he played "Hail, Hail, the Gang's All Here." Kids and adults loudly joined in the singing. They gave Wall and me a round of applause. As expected, Mrs. Stone had found things to do in the hall's kitchen when all those frivolities took place.

"Don't worry about her because no one is loved or even respected by everyone in Baltic, or anywhere else for that matter," said educator Wallace Talleck. Was he also talking about himself?

At home Wallace, as usual, took his nightly shot of brandy and listened to the radio's late news reports, before heading for bed. I was too happy to sleep. I got out of bed, put on my ball jacket on over my pyjamas, and sat with stockinged feet in our still-hot kitchen stove. Yes, it sure felt good to be a teechur. I spent a long time writing in my diary which had been largely ignored for two or three weeks. During that quiet time "I was learning that being alone isn't the same as being lonely." I reflected on the possible reasons for Sheba Faye Klanty's absence from the ice carnival and the supper. Indeed, she was our only absent student.

I went back to bed and sleep hit me like a huge, woolly pillow. I dreamt about a fat, old warlock whose face was covered by a large hood. For some reason the creature buried huge horseshoe-shaped magnets under the school swings.

During breakfast the next morning, over jaw-cracking yawns, I told Wallace about my dream. His retort was, "You had too much excitement or too much food yesterday." I agreed that the dream was silly, and he added that I had enough things going on in my head without worrying about dreams.

14

Plans

What is more enchanting than the voices of young people, when you can't hear what they say? – Logan Pearsall Smith: All Trivia

Long, quiet winter walks over frozen rivers and lakes allow you to do at least two lovely things: clear your head and heart of their poisons, and focus on a person you need to understand better. I didn't know why, but such a winter's walk at night with a little starlight or moonlight or Northern Lights, can make that clarity and focus come more quicker and sharper. During such times I could even talk to myself and not feel embarrassed. My walks along the Riga River produced many conversations in my head. Perhaps water, flowing or frozen, draws us to it and out of ourselves. Water and my dreams/thoughts often seem to have a connection.

Once Stookie, Sheba Faye and myself went "rat shootin' up the nuisance grounds" on Stookie's suggestion. "It don't stink there when it's froze ya know," he acknowledged. It was the only time I saw Sheba Faye and Stookie together.

It was a mild, snowless, dark Friday night when we cleaned up on 72 rats, thanks to Stookie's strong flashlight, extra batteries, and .22 calibre rifle. We took turns shooting. Sheba Faye and I got about a dozen each, and Stookie nailed the rest. We wounded and lost another dozen or so. He insisted that the dead rats be stacked "like one of them Eye Gyptian paramints so we can see what we got here." Believe me, 72 rats make a good sized "paramint." We walked back to the hamlet single file before midnight. He told me that one of these days he would give me "some shootin' lessons." I left them at Woolston's corner, so Stookie might have walked his girl home.

The *skree-skree* sound of wounded rats echo a long time in one's head.

One night, just for a change, I skied the road past the nuisance grounds and the frozen "paramint" of rats, then past Fred and Janet Kleiner's farmstead. The dark night had an almost brittle cold, and under my skis the snow crunched loudly. Snow lizards wisped their way across the road. The clear cold winter night was uncompromising but magnificent. The silence reminded me of a line from a Robert W. Service poem I had recently assigned my Grade VIII students: "[It is] plum-full of hush to the brim."

Those hard, sharp, stiff bristles of winter went to work and scrubbed my soul until the realization came, *someone* had to do something about Sheba Faye. I realized that Klanty and even the school officials could not, or would not, find a solution for Sheba Faye's problems. Bright Boy decided to find her some solutions for what Superintendent Clawson would call her "now." The crusade, however, called for information.

The next evening I visited Mrs. Bredner. For the sake of my sanity and eardrums I waited until her spoiled kids had been put to bed. She was aware of Sheba Faye's problem, of course, and told me more of the loneliness and hurt her steady baby-sitter had experienced. When Bill arrived home from his curling game he joined our conversation. He asked his wife to tell me about Sheba Faye's "first menstrual (he pronounced it 'men's trial') period." When Sheba Faye had experienced her first female period she was almost petrified with fear. No one had ever told her about the whole process.

"And that old Klanty," said Mrs. Bredner, "sure didn't tell her a thing, so she came to me 'cause she thought she had a serious disease or something."

Why didn't Maggie J explain things to her? I hoped that none of my female students ever asked me about the "men's trial" business because they wouldn't get much help from me. Bill added that Sheba Faye sometimes reminded him of "those poor orphans in Europe I saw there in late 1945." He claimed that Sheba Faye used to be real bright like her mom, Irene, but all she did now was mope around like she was lost. Bill, too, had often seen her alone on the school swings, humming to herself. Mrs. Bredner agreed that Sheba Faye should be taken to a city specialist and not to the Riga doctor.

Surprisingly, Klanty was easy to convince. I told him it would cost him nothing, that Sheba Faye would be of more use to him with her ears fixed, and that he would not have to make any arrangements. I also threw in a bottle of the sickly-sweet apricot brandy he relished.

At my request Wallace Talleck made the arrangements, and very early Saturday morning he drove Mrs. Bredner, Sheba Faye, Stookie and me to the city.

The trip to the city was a first for Stookie and for Sheba Faye as well. After Wall dropped the two women at the ear specialist's, he left Stookie and me for two hours at another doctor's office. There my young friend received a thorough going over from Dr. Alice Krantz, a recent graduate in dermatology. Her confidential advice, treatments, and prescriptions would clear Stookie's skin problems in three weeks. Stookie was so grateful.

When my roomie returned the three of us decided to visit a nearby cocktail lounge. Stookie and I loved the idea; however, as I was underage, I was refused service and kicked out as soon as the drinks arrived.

The theatre across the street was featuring the 3-D movie *Bwana Devil*, and after a little flirting the ticket seller let me watch the movie with those special glasses for five full minutes before the manager booted me out of the place. So I cooled my heels while leaning on Wallace's parked – and locked – war chariot. After a while my two friends emerged. Wall's eyes betrayed his amusement, but Stookie meant well when he said that "you can still come to my wet spots even if you're not old enough to drink if you want to ya know."

Wallace collected Mrs. Bredner and Sheba Faye, and then treated all of us to a fabulous lunch in a fantastic restaurant. Everyone there seemed to know Wallace, and the food and the service were great. Tall Wall paid the huge bill and left a five dollar tip. I couldn't believe the size of that tip. And to think I called him a tightwad!

On the way home Mrs. Bredner discussed the ear specialist's findings. Sheba Faye had a common enough kind of ear problem called Ostosclerosis. During recent years a Tennessee doctor named Shambough further developed a rather simple surgical solution to the problem. As Mrs. Bredner repeated, something is done with the tiny bones, the stapes, which are attached to the ear drum. Hearing improves immediately.

On the drive home (at a sedate 50 mph, of course) Sheba Faye couldn't stop smiling. And for good reason: the doctor had clearly explained the procedure with pictures and diagrams, and said the prognosis was good.

It would be a terrific exaggeration to say that Sheba Faye's smile transformed her into a beauty, but Stookie could hardly take his eyes from her face. He whispered to me, "My lady doctor made me take all my clothes off and everything and it wasn't as bad as I figgered." It was a warm trip home.

Even Klanty's bellyaching about having to prepare his own meals for the day couldn't spoil the evening. Sheba Faye, who couldn't hear well enough to use the phone, asked Mrs. Bredner to contact Margaret Jane with the good news. Mrs. Stone and Mrs. Horvath joined us for Mrs. Bredner's finest English tea, all in celebration. Sheba Faye's unstoppable smile made all of us feel awfully good. Later that night Bill and Stookie came over to the teacherage where, as Bill said, "we destroyed that damn tea taste with some good honest beer and this heavy flagon of porch climber." You'd think that old Klanty would have wanted to come, but no, he turned down the invitation.

Sometime during the evening Wallace chose to quote Wilde again, who after drinking absinthe had said, "After the first glass you see things as you wish they were. After the second, you see them as they are not. Finally, you see things as they really are, and that is the most horrible thing in the world . . ."

"Are things really that bad for you?" I quietly asked Wall, but got no response.

That night Tall Wall repeated that he would look after the finances involved with Sheba Faye's operation. For our benefit he summarized what he had read that day at the University's Medical Library, which is where he had gone after dropping off Stookie and me. You just think you can keep up to Wallace Talleck!

He suggested that one of the most famous people afflicted by deafness was the great composer, Frederic Van Beethoven. While living near Vienna, Beethoven had written, "O my fellow men who consider me, or describe me as unfriendly, peevish, or even misanthropic, how greatly do you wrong me."

Stookie had a partial crying jag when Tall Wall movingly read his handwritten copy of Beethoven's famous statement: "I have been afflicted by an unairable complaint . . . I was soon obliged to seclude myself and to live in solitude . . . . There can be no relaxation in human society, nor refined conversation, no mutual confidences. I must live quite alone and may creep into society only or often as sheer necessity demands. I must live like an outcast." The words applied so vividly to Sheba Faye.

Tall Wall's research allowed him to mention several nineteenth century medical pioneers who had worked in alleviating the problems of conductive deafness: Miot, Black, Kessel, Corti, and Jack. I pretended to be fascinated with his long descriptions as Wall explained that people like Sheba Faye usually experienced a gradual hearing loss, with some days better than others. Eventually such patients heard only nonsense words and bits and pieces. They could not hear and understand a conversation unless lip reading were involved. For them, music was something to be felt more than heard.

Then Wallace said things about bones and inner ears and canals but I was too tired or lazy to listen attentively. How the hell could Wall absorb so much information in such a short time? When my colleague discussed the works of the mid-nineteenth century Irish ontologist and oculist, Sir William Wilde, I perked up. As soon as Stookie and Bill were out of the room in typical fashion I almost destroyed the good mood by saying, "I suppose you're going to tell me that your Dr. Wilde was related to your 'secret homosexual hero', Oscar Wilde."

"Yes, you arrogant Smart Ass," whispered Wall, "Oscar was the good doctor's son."

"It's too bad that Daddy didn't give Sonny an operation of a different kind," was my retort. Wall didn't answer but his eyes had a hard glint.

After awhile Stookie said "some of my back teeth here is hurtin' somethin' terrible," so the celebration came to a slow conclusion. As Stookie left by the front door I said to him, "Save your teeth, Stookie, and next time use a beer opener."

He stopped, turned around, and walked the few paces towards me. "Them teeth of mine isn't the question 'cause the real good thing is that Sheba Faye's ears is going to get fixed so that's why she was smiling all the way home to Baltic from that city doctor you and Mr. Talleck here arranged for and everything so you two is the best friends I guess any fella can have and you will sure come to our wedding if she gets her Eight but that's up to you 'cause she'll be able to hear everything a teechur says ya know."

Now there's a speech! The weepy Stookie squeezed Wall's upper arms and then squeezed mine even harder, and added, "Somebody else too must have been prayin' for Sheba Faye and thanks for what ya done for her." I wiped my eyes and Tall Wall honked two times in his crisply-ironed handkerchief.

After our friends left, Wall said, "You know, Bright Boy, that station clock will sound happy to Stookie tonight. You did well. And thanks to you, Stookie and Bill are now my friends, too. You all accept me – with certain reservations," he said, looking in my direction, "so I must consider you fellows as my friends."

Despite the veiled reference to my attitude towards his homosexuality, that was the finest thing Wall had ever said to me. I responded, "Lucky Sheba Faye will soon be able to hear clearly the dulcet tones of England's wartime songstress, Mrs. Bredner." Wall's hard glance told me to keep quiet and leave a good thing alone.

I wondered if Stookie had proposed to Sheba Faye.

Later that night, over his brandy, Tall Wall chose to lecture me about the father of the famous poet, fiction writer, dramatist and critic, Oscar Wilde. The father, the good doctor from Dublin, Sir William Wilde, was a very successful ear and eye surgeon in the Irish capital. There he founded a hospital and wrote what was to become the standard textbook on aural surgery. Sir William also held the honorary appointment of *Surgeon Oculist to Queen Victoria*.

"You'd like him," said Wallace with a trace of a smile, "He was accused of using a little chloroform on one Mary Travers in order to seduce that young lady."

He dryly added: "William used chloroform in the 1860s and you use my liquor in the 1950s with the same stupid goal in mind. You would be smart to remember G.K. Chesterton's famous statement about sex: 'The pleasure is momentary, the position is ridiculous, and the cost is excessive.'"

Obviously Tall Wall had given me too much credit in that department – at least so far.

15

Rendezvous

When a man is in love for the first time he thinks he invented it.
- Robert C. (Bob) Edwards: Calgary Eye Opener.

To think that Maggie J was my girl was either optimism or sheer arrogance. Like many youths, I was a mixture of dogmatism and uncertainty. However, she had more than brushed my lips with hers at that happy-unhappy New Year's dance. I took the incident as a sign of something even more wonderful to come. MJ and I had known each other since September but had only infrequent conversations during her visits. I was becoming more intrigued by "my little schoolmarm" with whom I hoped I had an understanding. I decided to settle some issues during her next visit to Baltic.

We planned a ski trip and winter picnic down by the creek, but the flu and cold that very weekend soldered my nostrils shut. Damn! Mrs. Stone's admonition, "Feed your cold and starve your fever," did me no good.

We had another weekend date, to attend a Saturday night whist drive in the town hall, but I had to leave right after the game – before coffee and sandwiches, and my walk home with MJ. For no reason my nose started bleeding and the fool thing wouldn't stop. Eventually I tried Wall's idea involving cardboard under my top lip and ice on the back of my neck. It worked, but by then Maggie J had retired for the night. Three times my beak had separated MJ and me. I guess you could say I didn't have a good nose for romance.

I asked Tall Wall if a man can rightly be accused of being overly possessive if he is the one who is captivated.

With one of those mini-smiles of his he replied, "A dopey boy in puppy love would have to grow up to be a man first."

I threw my shoe at him. The tall first baseman handled it cleanly.

"Too bad you can't throw that well from third base," he commented.

"Just wait and watch and be amazed, Streak," I replied, picking up my other shoe. I was beginning to enjoy Tall Wall's company very much.

MJ was often in my dreams. I once dreamed that I couldn't remember her face, and woke with a start. Damn it, her face still would not come into focus on my usually dependable eye screen. So I added wood to the still warm kitchen stove, sat in my chair with my slippered feet in the oven, and willed her face to appear. It (she) would not. I refused to cheat by looking at her snapshot taped to my bedroom mirror.

Around 4 a.m. Tall Wall found me cold and asleep in the kitchen, and pointed me back to bed. In the morning I told him about my dream. I saw a cynical comment building on his face, so I said, "Forget it, Mr. Fag."

"Okay, Mr. Glands, but just remember that you have no more right to trust your heart than does anyone else." That sure didn't sound consistent with what his mother taught him.

One Blakean nightmare featured Maggie J and me in summer clothes skating for miles and miles under a lemon sun, down the nearby Riga River. As Tall Wall once said, a dream of a journey is itself a strange kind of journey. The land was scoured clean and pure, just for us. The new ice was near perfect, and I saw countless lucky pennies frozen just under the surface. Summer birds sang, all the trees wore their greenest green and in the slight breeze trembled their private greetings at us. Along the creek's edges, millions of flowers of all colors grew from the ice surface. At first the sun in cerulean sky was hot on our bare arms and legs, then cumulonimbus clouds, ebony and heavy with water, appeared, showing their smooth, flat underbellies to our world.

The Dream Master had just one rule: if either skater slipped or stumbled, Maggie J somehow would fall through the ice and forever disappear in the dark, deep, cold water. Wouldn't you know it? I tripped on a fallen, leather-like flower petal. Luckily I awoke before the Dream Master could do his evil work. I never told Tall Wall about that nightmare.

Of course, there were long and fluid dreams about Maggie J and me, more than mildly involved in Tall Wall's new car (dream the impossible dream!), in Bill Bredner's hay stack under fulgent sun, on the school's new tumbling mats, and so on. One of my favorites had to do with the big bathtub in the teacherage's back porch.

My dreams and realities demanded that certain preparations be made for Maggie J's next visit – nose permitting of course! If I had not been a teacher, would I have made such secret and devious plans? But hadn't my teachers' college instructors told me to be both innovative and thorough in my professional planning?

It appeared that a little honest larceny should be the third ingredient. I "borrowed" Stookie's yellow key with the red head, and one bottle of Tall Wall's best wine. (I had thrown aside some of my usual, brittle caution.) Both properties would be returned or replaced on completion of my assignment. The Horvaths had been informed that "certain" duties would make me absent from supper.

After the school children left that Friday afternoon, I sat at my school desk, shoved the globe and my students' assignments aside, and listed on paper the equipment and things to do for my late winter's Odyssean adventure and my most important night class.

chilled wine	*two wine glass*es
matches	*candle*
key	*cushion*
dice	*shave*
bath	*new tie*
polish shoes	*brush teeth, mints*

I reread the list and stroked out *cushion*. After all, Maggie J was a lady (even though I was no gentleman). I added my old Boy Scout jackknife to the list. One can't be too prepared.

With the equipment in my trouser and parka pockets, I secretly made my crusade through the winter's early night, past the Bredner house and down empty Third Street, across the little traffic bridge and frozen creek, across the graveyard road (I didn't whistle) and toward the south end of the trestle. The long route was the safe route and my plans demanded I not be seen travelling to and from the scene of my anticipated conquest. And to be sure, my own self-consciousness and my need to protect M.J.'s reputation were good reasons for making my plans in secret.

The night was clear and brisk and there was that sharp smell of coming snow. Under a penembrous, fishhook-shaped moon I crossed the high trestle, chin out, determined to follow the railway tracks behind Klanty's place leading to the railway station – the only place in Baltic I could take her. My candle was broken during my safari. A bad omen?

Inside the station I struck a match to the pre-laid paper kindling and the wood stove cheerily came to life. The station would be warm in an hour or so. My "props" were in place. As when Stookie and I were there earlier, the vase on the windowsill contained the usual (frozen) flowers. This ever-careful knight-of-the-night returned to the teacherage by the same secretive route. The gut-tingle of excitement felt great. I hummed the hit song, "Once I Had a Secret Love."

After my sponge bath and shave I dressed, then found Tall Wall in the "parlor" (his old-fashioned term for the living room) by the oil heater, reading Simone de Beauvoir's best seller, *The Second Sex*, while listening to one of his favorite records featuring Sibelius' *First Symphony*. (He claimed that the Finn's music best described the moods and character of a harsh climate like ours.)

He invited me to sit down and relax so we could discuss the music, but the world's smallest grin told me that he had surmised the nature of my plans for the evening, which just happened to coincide with my birthday. Well, I sure as hell wasn't going to tell him anything. I muttered something about needing to eat and left Tall Wall whistling reedily to the music.

I made a thick salmon-and-pickle sandwich and left the teacherage eating my culinary masterpiece. I could feel my heart beating behind my eyeballs.

I stopped sharply in front of Klanty's yard and blew into my cupped hands – even in the cold air my breath smelled like seventeen salmon gone bad. Damn. I quickly chewed so many hard mints so fast that my teeth hurt.

"Gargle, gargle, in the night, only idiots could have this plight," I said to the spirits of the evening. I popped one more mint and knocked on Klanty's door. Houses look bigger in the dark.

Maggie J opened the door and slipped out immediately. She tossed her parka hood over her head, did up the top button, took my arm, and turned to me. In a voice somewhere between hot maple syrup and ripe apples she said, "You smell like a candy factory. Any for me?"

I nearly tripped over my tongue but managed to get out, "Certainly, fair snow maiden," and kissed her. I felt obliged to kiss her again. More maple syrup. More ripe apples. She felt bigger in my arms than she was.

She drew back, chuckled in her throaty way, and then cuddled back in my arms. The fur on her parka hood tickled my cheek. The stars were so low I asked Maggie J if I could pluck a few for her.

I suggested that we "go see the train come into the station."

"Yes, I can hear it coming," she hesitatingly replied, playing along with my game. So we walked from the Klanty property through two snowdrifts to reach the railway tracks, and followed them to the station.

"Walking these tracks is becoming a habit for us, isn't it?" she said with a small laugh. Little did she know how that evening I had practically worn out the railroad track! I almost wished the Cyclops eye of one of our grain trains would appear to complete the picture.

The lovely old stove had performed beautifully and the station greeted we two travellers with warmth. I refilled the stove's belly with more wood. We dragged one of the tall-backed benches closer to the stove, removed our overshoes, and placed four slightly cold and wet stockinged feet against the metal ring circling the hot stove. I lit the broken candle and placed it away from the windows even though the glass faced the tracks and not the hamlet of Baltic.

Fussily gallant, I hung our parkas on the tall, old-fashioned coatrack which stood near the door. Feeling a bit smug about my plans, I opened the door to the ticket office, and glided in faint light to the far side of the wicket.

"Over here, please, ma'am," I said, "and get your ticket." Maggie J, almost uxorial, walked to the customer's side of the small wicket.

"But Mr. Station Man," she plaintively asked, "where can you take a poor girl like me?"

I rolled the two dice and, pointing to them, announced, "I can take you *there* right now." Double entendre at its best, or so I thought.

Margaret Jane Enders gave a swift intake of air before a montage of amusement crossed her face. Then she laughed so hard the tears came. Maggie J sat on our bench holding her stomach as if in great pain while I worried she could be heard in the hamlet.

"Yes," she said, "a trip to pair-a-dice would be wonderful." She added that it was the worst pun she had heard in a long time.

It was no joke. It was part of my careful plan. And here the very object of my romantic cogitations was nearly on the floor, her sides splitting from laughter. And it was my birthday! My ego, or something, went down considerably.

What did the aspiring young teacher and scholar do next? I tried to shake off my hurt, mixed feelings by adding unnecessary wood to the fire, moving the candle closer to our bench, restacking some wood that didn't need restacking, and commenting on the increasing threnody of the wind (sometimes it had the voice of a living creature).

As if making a decision, Maggie J drew her feet to herself, hugged her legs and placed her chin on her knees, and exhaled long but softly. Then she rose, took my hand and led me to our bench by the hot stove. She brought our parkas over. Placing my parka on the bench, she sat on it, and then sort of squirmed her waist and shoulders into my arms which seemed to know what to do.

Maggie J pulled her own parka over her legs, stretched out on the bench, and said with a tiny whisper, "A soft kiss says sorry best." It did.

With fractured grammar I asked Maggie J, "Is there more best yet to come?" History immediately repeated itself. Again. And again. The fire crackled happily but all the fire wasn't in the stove. My dice and bruised ego were forgotten. A kind of a sweet comfort rested deeply in me. After a long, silent time my arms ached with tiredness, but I would have eaten the burning candle before admitting it to this small, warm, soft lady.

By the candlelight I studied her closed eyes, high cheekbones, the clean and sweet line of her jaw, and that tracery of veins in her left hand. I wondered if I'd ever be mature enough to put a ring on it. Her femininity and very life seemed visibly warm in a lucent, blue vein at her temple. The small tendrils of her hair tickled. She looked like a sleepy, amiable, contended, and kissable 16-year-old girl.

I waited for her to stir. Was she asleep? I felt the gentle guilt of one who watches a loved one asleep. However, the big railroad clock ticked its approval. Its tick was very, very soft and I knew that Stookie was correct about the sound of the clock.

I could teach kids the elements of sentence structure and grammar, but I didn't know how to say, "I love you, Maggie J." But then to be truthful, I wasn't sure.

Maggie J stirred, stretched and yawned, pushed parkas aside, and announced that she was hot and thirsty. The waiting room was getting very warm. I had just the thing. I rubbed my left arm from its deep and prickly sleep and placed Tall Wall's bottled best on the bench with a fine flourish.

Damn: no corkscrew. With implicit permission from Lord Baden-Powell, I butchered the cork with my ever-handy scout knife. The wine was terrific but the tiny pieces of cork failed the taste test. I made a grateful and silent toast to Stookie, Tall Wall, the scouting movement, railroads, grape growers, wine glass manufacturers, and the world in general.

"Let's dance," Maggie J said in a husky timbre. So we put on our shoes and waltzed to her soft humming. She remembered our favorite song from the New Year's dance and sang that sweetly and softly.

I'm in the Mood for Love simply because you're near me;
Funny, but when you're near me I'm in the Mood for Love.
Heaven is in your eyes bright as the stars we're under;
Oh! Is it any wonder I'm in the Mood for Love?
Why stop to think of whether this little dream might fade?
We've put our hearts together. Now we are one, I'm not afraid!
If there's a cloud above, if it shall rain we'll let it,
But for tonight, forget it! I'm in the Mood for Love.

We each held a rather full wine goblet in one hand as we danced.

"Let's put the wine down," I said, "so we can do some serious dancing."

My Miss Enders replied, "No, we might get thirsty again."

"Then let's drink up to prevent that possibility."

We did. The wine had a smoky, flinty taste and was wonderful. I placed the two goblets beside the dice on the wicket counter. The line that I had prepared and memorized came into my head but I couldn't deliver it. *Let us, Maggie J, allow our feelings to be guileless, and believe that there is only a warm now for us.*

As if answering my unspoken thought, my dancing partner suggested we dance to the inside kind of music, the kind that is *here* and *here*, she said, pointing to my chest and then to hers. I was having trouble breathing under the gentle, suffocating impact of love. Our combined orchestras were very loud and every note was right.

Outside our music and dancing, quiet clung to the night. MJ's softness and vulnerability and fluid grace joined me completely as we danced by the rosy glow from the eyes of the stove. My right hand felt the muscles of her back, pliant and moving. I liked her hair even better when she removed two blue barrettes. Lots of clean, soft hair. Sometimes concurrently, hours shrink to minutes and minutes stretch to hours. We didn't need music from Stookie's old radio – we danced to the music only we could hear.

We returned to the bench and rearranged our parkas and ourselves. She collapsed in my arms with a warm and trusting somnolence. For some reason I remembered a poem from my teachers' college English class which discussed love's sweet oblivion. With the night's black arms wrapped conspiratorially around us, we held each other for a long, long time, and I kissed MJ far too often. Baltic didn't exist. The world had a population of exactly two people.

MJ made the smallest movement, received my long kiss, and said softly, "Oh, Con."

Ever been sucker-punched just below the heart? I experienced an actual physical constriction in my chest. My right leg was asleep but in one second flat I stood up.

"My name isn't Con!" I damn near fell on top of her as I tried to stamp the sleep from my leg.

"Who in the blue hell is Con?" I asked with cold avidity. My face felt hot as I relit the shrunken candle.

The bruised capital *O* of her mouth gave a stretched look to her face. Silence grew to fill the room. MJ stood up slowly and returned to the bench. A sob built in her throat and she turned wet eyes toward me. Her tongue arrowed out to catch a tear droplet. She reached up to touch my chest but I walked away from her, over to the tall clock, as if its large, pale face knew something I didn't. The *tick-tock* sounded loud.

With a flourish of anger I knocked the vase of frozen flowers across the station floor. Without comment Miss Enders rose and gathered the scattered flowers in the near dark, placing them in the unbroken vase which had somehow survived my temper. Something estranging and wounding had come between us. I finally realized that Con was the name she had uttered at our New Year's dance.

Silence, slow as treacle. I felt the silence like a draft.

Looking down at the darkened base of the station's stove she began speaking slowly, stutteringly, and so softly that at first it was difficult to understand her. Then she said, "There's a lot I'll tell you about Con, my stepfather, and others," she said "but first let's go away from here."

16

Conrad James

Lay him low, lay him low,
In the clover on the snow!
– G.H. Boker: Dirge for a Soldier

We checked the stove, replaced the benches, gathered my tools of seduction, and locked the station. Walking behind MJ, I held the wine bottle behind my back and let the remnants pour out. A strange thing to do, perhaps. The wind was stronger and the snow drifting. Just past midnight we returned to the Klanty house – my first visit there since the "seminars" with Klanty had concluded.

Klanty was in bed, probably passed out, and Sheba Faye was babysitting at the Bredner's. MJ brought several photograph albums from the bedroom she sometimes shared with Sheba Faye. While drinking hot chocolate, we sat without touching at the heavy, fat-legged, oak kitchen table where in a low voice she told me about her hurt.

Maggie J knew her mother, Jane, for just ten years, and her father, Benson Enders, for only four. Benson Enders had been gassed in World War I, and had spent years convalescing in a London hospital. In 1927, he married Jane, "my happy-go-lucky English nurse and part-time flapper," as the printing under a photograph announced. They moved to Toronto, where they borrowed heavily to purchase a then-prosperous bookstore. Jane loved the bookstore and fast became a devotee of the printed word, but the war veteran's lungs and poor health demanded he rest often. The Enders had a few happy months together before the economic crash of 1929 led to bankruptcy and the loss of their business. Their baby, Margaret Jane, arrived a year later. Jane could not find work as a nurse, and her husband's health deteriorated. Ben Enders' lungs lost the fight they could not win, and his widow somehow raised her little girl while working at depression-level wages in someone else's bookstore.

In 1938, Jane met Wayne Klanty, a publisher's salesman and frequent caller to the bookstore. The photo showed a well-dressed, heavily-built, broad-shouldered man standing beside a Model A Ford. They used to take little Margaret to one of the city's parks where they discussed good books and exciting ideas. Jane was lonely. Wayne Klanty seemed to like her daughter. So the young widow agreed to marriage – a practical if not a loving partnership. Wayne promised to cut down on his heavy drinking.

Wayne Klanty eventually lost his job and attempted to find solace in any brand of liquor, as long as it was wet. He apprenticed with a barber for a while but that didn't last. In order to meet expenses, Jane took in typing at night. One January morning in 1940, Margaret Jane, age 10, got up for breakfast and found her mother dead from a heart attack, sprawled over the cheap typewriter. The landlord tried to contact Klanty but he remained missing for three weeks.

Little Margaret Jane, her teacher, the preacher, the mortician, the bookstore owners, and the landlord (who kindly arranged for six volunteer pallbearers), buried Jane Enders at the height of one of Toronto's famed snowstorms. She could not remember specifics about the graveside ceremony, other than one pallbearer saying to another, "It's cold as hell." The little girl stayed with her mother's employers until Klanty returned.

Other than sleeping and crying, Maggie J remembered little of the storm-delayed, seven-day train journey west with her stepfather. They travelled by coach because sleepers were too expensive. But when they got there, they found Klanty had been wrong when he told his stepdaughter that business was better out west.

Sheba Faye's father, Henry, was killed by Japanese bullets in Hong Kong, on Christmas Eve, 1941, less than three weeks after Pearl Harbor. The young soldier was one of those largely forgotten Canadians (Winnipeg Grenadiers and the Royal Rifles of Canada) who, after a stiff fight, fell or surrendered on that far field.

For a while Henry had enjoyed Hong Kong. He hired a private servant for 60 cents per week. A rickshaw ride or a cold beer cost him or his pals a ten cent piece. The day of infamy ended all that.

The ill-prepared Canadian, Indian and British defenders were told all sorts of lies by some of their superiors: the Japanese were poorly equipped, badly-trained and few in number; the invaders couldn't see well at night because of their eyefold; their tendency to get sea sick would favor the island's defenders. In fact, the 50 000 experienced Japanese were skilled, tough and successful soldiers.

Perhaps Henry was one of the 'lucky ones,' at least he was spared the horrible ordeal subsequently suffered by other Canadian soldiers in Japanese prison camps.

Before the war, Henry, an ex-coal miner, had married Irene Spansky, a top graduate of Baltic's high school, who gave birth to their daughter ten months after they married. Little Sheba Faye knew her father for five years. Maggie J showed me a photo of Henry and Irene riding horseback at the edge of some thick, tall trees. Henry was supporting his three-year-old daughter, whose little legs could hardly straddle the horse's back.

A second, earlier photo of Irene featured an unattractive, small, curly-haired young woman standing in front of the Baltic high school. On the back of the photo was written: *The girl I'd most like to take to a coal mine*. Another photo showed Irene and Henry in front of a well-tended and attractive house. Four-year- old Sheba Faye sat on her tricycle next to her father. Obviously the house in the picture was the Klanty house, the one in whose kitchen I was visiting at 1 a.m. I suspected that the tricycle was the old one with that missing back wheel.

Maggie J saw my look of puzzlement so she continued her story. Even in the poor light I could see the silvery tears on her cheeks.

"Here, the going gets a little tough," Maggie J said with a break in her voice. She asked if I really wanted to hear the rest.

In a brotherly fashion I awkwardly kissed her on the left temple, and asked her to continue. Even then she smelled of violets. Outside the wind stopped as if to hear her story.

It was in late 1940 that Klanty made his first payments on the Baltic pool hall. He was a gregarious man full of the dirty jokes and rough language many of his male-only customers enjoyed. He believed that he could get along with most people because he didn't bother to develop deep feelings for them.

The improved war-time economy helped his business and he soon added a barber's chair to the pool hall, where he plied his trade. Behind the chair, next to a large cracked mirror, he added a small sign printed in red: *Klanty's Tonsorial Emporium.* A moth-eaten, taxidermic nightmare of a moose head hung above the inside door. (I hadn't noticed these when Stookie and I first visited the deserted pool room.) Klanty succeeded financially, but he chose to live by himself in a small, booklined room at the back of the long pool hall. He owned a four-year-old blue Packard (now rusting in his backyard). Some said he had won the car plus a lot of money in poker games. (I wondered if Klanty could beat my teachers' college janitor.) Margaret, his stepdaughter, lived full-time with Mrs. Stone (that surprised me somehow) who also had a little girl, Jenny, the same age.

Klanty again stopped drinking. Even Mrs. Stone, who hardly approved of "pool hall riffraff" once begrudgingly admitted that Klanty might not be all bad. She even shook his hand once – at church in the spring of 1942 – the day he accompanied Irene and little Sheba Faye to the Sunday service at which Margaret sang her first solo in public. Three weeks later Irene and Wayne Klanty were married.

Irene sewed her own wedding dress, and Klanty wore the uniform of his generation, a blue serge suit. They had no honeymoon. Klanty, naturally, planned to move into the house built by Irene's first husband, Henry. The house soon became known as "the Klanty place." After Klanty married Irene, he made plans to move his "stuff" from the pool hall residence to "my new home overlooking the trestle and stream." Twelve-year old Margaret Jane and Mrs. Stone's daughter, Jenny, were big enough to help.

So on a warm Saturday morning Jenny Stone and Margaret Enders, coins in their hands, went to the Shanghai Cafe for ice cream cones. For some reason Margaret dawdled with other youngsters while Jenny went behind the cluster of business buildings and knocked on Klanty's back door. She heard nothing so she walked into the room to begin packing books into cardboard boxes.

In a few moments Klanty entered the room using the inside door. He saw Jenny, smiled, and left briefly, only to return with a large candy bar. He sat on his bed and smiled broadly at his little visitor. Klanty told Jenny if she was going to lift all his big books, she should first sit up here and eat this treat. He patted the grayish-white pillow while he spoke. Jenny wasn't sure what to do. Then Klanty asked if she had any little treats for him? At that moment Margaret entered the back door of the pool room residence.

The widow Stone learned of the conversation as described by her daughter. She believed Jenny. She was suspicious of the man's insistence it was all very innocent because she learned that while Jenny was inside Klanty's, the front business door to the pool hall was locked from the inside.

Klanty said "of course the door was locked, I was away from the cash register for a bit of time." The few doubters noted that during business hours no Baltic business locked their door. It was suggested that Klanty would never close his doors as long as a dime were to be made in the pool hall.

Mrs. Stone was not a popular lady. Most people believed Klanty, who was a newly-married man. And Margaret Jane told Mrs. Stone and others that she thought everything was fine when she walked in. But the incident plant a seed in Margaret Jane's mind.

So that was how, on about 2:00 a.m. on that winter's night, I learned why Mrs. Stone hated and distrusted "that Klanty," and why she didn't approve of the not infrequent visits to "that Klanty place" that Tall Wall, Stookie and I had made.

Maggie J agreed that no court of law would have convicted the man back in 1942. However, in small communities, rumors and doubts can grow like weeds on a vacant lot. Mrs. Stone suggested that Klanty should have been put on the "Indian list" years earlier. Even I knew she was referring to the liquor interdict list.

According to Maggie J, Klanty seemed to care for his new wife, Irene, and her little daughter, Sheba Faye, who was given the Klanty name. Margaret moved home from Mrs. Stone's house and the Klanty home and yard became more beautiful, thanks to Irene's hard work. Maggie J told me that her stepmother, Irene, was a warm Christian woman who had accepted Margaret Jane as her own. She certainly made her new husband behave – except for his drinking. Maggie J said, "Sheba Faye and I grew to love each other very much."

At Christmas, Easter, and Mothers' Day, Klanty accompanied Irene and the two girls to church. Secretly Mrs. Stone sniffed. "He can't fool me – not even for a minute. He's like a cockroach on a wedding cake." It bothered that proud woman that she had been wrong about Klanty before – the time she actually shook his hand in church.

During the war years and for a few years after Klanty's business prospered. His illegal, late-night poker games were very kind to him. But things were changing. School centralization meant that Baltic's high school students were bused to Riga. Bigger farms meant fewer farmers, fewer young people, and fewer dollars. Even before passenger and freight train service ended, several of the town's businesses had folded. The hardware, grocery store, pool room, drugstore, and café, among other businesses, were all victims of the move to urbanization and centralization. (I recalled the lost businesses Stookie had identified from the grain elevator's roof.) In 1949, the last weekly movie was shown in the Baltic town hall. A year later, two of the three grain elevators were dismantled. The once prosperous town had become a nearly deserted hamlet. As if to emphasize that finality, the 1951 polio outbreak touched five families in the Baltic district and Irene Klanty succumbed to the terrible disease. (Dr. Salk's famous vaccine appeared two years too late for Sheba Faye's mother.)

"I just buried my second wife, you know," Klanty frequently told the citizens of Baltic. Apparently he loved to recite and discuss the lengthy elegies of his great pains. Only Margaret Jane, the 21-year-old university student home for the funeral, knew how hollow his words were. She believed that Klanty's life was wrapped with many layers of lies, short-cuts and deceits. She told no one that Klanty had not attended her own mother's funeral 11 years earlier. Margaret was convinced that Klanty had married Irene to receive a free house from his second marriage.

It was while she was staring at Irene's sealed casket (apparently the bodies of polio victims are not for the eyes of the living, hence, the sealed casket) that Margaret Jane made two somewhat contradictory decisions: one, she would watch over Sheba Faye, and two, she would move permanently away from Baltic. Conrad James, who had accompanied her to the funeral, fully supported her decisions.

About a month after Irene's funeral, Klanty approached Margaret Jane as she hurriedly hung wet clothes on the outside clothesline, which stretched from the house to the stone fence built years earlier by Sheba Faye's late father, Henry.

"Here, I'll help you," Klanty said to Margaret. Things went well enough until it came to her dainties, near the bottom of the basket. The drunken Klanty made "certain bad comments" as he handed the items to Margaret. She turned crimson. Klanty put a heavy paw on her left shoulder and muttered something about "you're the woman in my house now, and you must know what that means, especially now that your big soldier boy is leaving." Margaret Jane's mind flashed back to the pool hall incident involving Jenny Stone.

She lowered the basket and went into the house, where she calmly phoned Con. Then she walked stiffly to Mrs. Stone's house to wait. She stumbled up Mrs. Stone's canted, cracked walkway and the sway-backed steps, only to find the inside door locked. So Margaret had to weep in anger and disbelief while sitting alone in the glass-enclosed front veranda. Con arrived at the backyard of the house to find Margaret Jane on her knees in front of the outdoor toilet, convulsed with dry heaves. Sergeant Conrad James carried his "Margie" to the screen door at the back of the house and forced it open. He poured warm water from the stove's reservoir into the bathtub and wordlessly pushed Margie inside the small bathroom. "Hurry," he said, "the train will be here in less than an hour."

When the young woman was finished her warm bath, she walked out to her "Sarge," the man she loved without hesitation. He listened to her story about Klanty, making no comment and asking no question. He quickly took Margie to his car and sped the short distance to the Klanty pathway. He found Klanty and gave him this gentle warning: *I will gently remove your guts and use them for garters if you ever touch her again.* Sergeant James then "roughed him up a bit."

After Con released Klanty's shirt the older man rubbed his hurt neck and chest, and sat, flummoxed and temporarily defeated, in his throne chair.

"I tried to show Margaret a little warmth and this is what I get," he squawked.

With both hands Con again lifted Klanty to his feet and said in a steady, steely voice, "Fish might enjoy you if they're not too particular. Don't forget that." He pushed the fat man backwards into his huge chair. Klanty looked like the guy who had stepped on a rake, and got nailed, but good. Both Klanty and his stepdaughter knew that Con meant what he said.

The train was late, so Con and his Margie had a little private time sitting on a hard, worn bench. The station agent left his wicket and locked the door to the station in their honor before the train arrived to take the soldier away from Margaret Jane Enders and to the Korean Conflict.

At approximately 9:30 a.m., June 10, 1952, Conrad James, decorated for bravery, had just straightened up from tying his muddy boots when a partially spent sniper's shell caught him flush above his left eye. Sergeant James, age 24, was killed in the Korean Conflict. Though he had been Margie's fiancé, they had never made love.

Maggie J closed the photo album, sipped a little tepid liquid from her cup, and said in a clear and unwavering voice, Somewhere in my story is the reason why I twice called you Con."

She told me that since Con's death I was the only man who had embraced and kissed her. She added that together we had briefly rediscovered a magic. I was about to tell her that it sounded rather Hollywood to me when I saw the truth in her eyes.

Was my immaturity allowing me to be jealous of Con, a dead man? I was more than slightly piqued that Maggie J insisted on using Con's death as the watershed in her life. Con's type of two-fisted masculinity intimidated me.

Inside I didn't know whether to laugh or scream when Maggie J said awkwardly, "Bill Statiuk has asked me to marry him. He is such a fine and decent human being. I wonder if I should, even though he knows I can never love him."

For a moment I didn't know who this Bill was. Then I remembered him from the hockey game we had played in Vyborg, the town where Maggie J taught school. That wonderful-terrible screen behind my eyes allowed me to picture a round-faced man, bald as a peeled egg, with a red bow tie and a substantial overbite. "Bill" was the school principal who had accompanied Maggie J and her other friends to the Vyborg-Baltic hockey game!

The words jumped from my mouth, "Mr. Bow Tie is an old guy and I think you're out of your mind."

"You talk and react just like Con would," Maggie said, adding that Bill Statiuk was not that old – only 44. She concluded that she missed Con so very much, but her real loneliness came because she had no one with which to share her little events and momentary thoughts. Bill Statiuk liked to listen to her because he was so patient.

"Don't I listen to you?" I asked angrily.

I was really steamed. First I had been asked to compete with a dead soldier, and then with a man 25 years older than myself, a guy who should be in an old folks' home. So I told her so.

A little bit of fire appeared in her eyes when she reminded me that if I was 25 years younger than Bill, that would make me 19 – not 24, as I had told her. I could only blush. MJ patted my hand, and I felt very young, like I should be asking her for a late slip to present to my homeroom teacher.

"If Statiuk asked you to marry him, how could you lie to me by saying no man since Conrad James has ever held you and kissed you except me?"

"Because it's true," she replied. She and the school principal occasionally met other teachers for lunch, at school meetings, in the hallways, and in downtown Vyborg. They would 'group date' at movies, sporting events and the like with other friends. Not once, however, had he made any advances toward her. Bill Statiuk's mother was elderly, and he was lonely.

I loudly told Maggie J to run, not walk, from 'Uncle Statiuk's' marriage proposal. I guess I sounded like Stookie when I said "you're a teacher, you're supposed to know what life is all about – you're supposed to have solid judgment and common sense, and you talk that way about a nice, lonely guy who is supposed to keep you warm at night?"

Still experiencing too many emotions at one time, I asked, "What would you say to one of your high school students who announced that he or she planned to marry someone 21 years older?" Maggie J muttered something about the age of consent. However, a flicker of doubt showed in her eyes.

There was little more for me to say other than, "Thanks for a lovely evening, the hot chocolate was delicious." Two tiny brackets of discontent appeared at the sides of MJ's mouth.

The snowfall was arriving. Large, heavy individual flakes joined the waiting, white blanket below. The hamlet's street lights were haloed with wavering nimbuses. I slipped and fell hard at the end of Klanty's path and hurt my behind, right elbow and dignity. The night was full of winter and there was a chiselled quality to the late evening. In ten minutes I was at home with my slippered feet in the stove's oven, unable to sort out the night's happenings. It was clear that I wasn't mature enough to understand and evaluate – all those things educators supposedly can do – the most memorable night of my life to that point. I washed the two wine goblets instead.

My whole head felt like cold air on a bad tooth. Meanwhile, my heart seemed to hang heavy and sick in my chest and my tongue was a dry stone. A sort of ugly weariness crept over me. I spoke the words of our song softly and angrily, and realized how real they seemed, especially the fifth line.

Why stop to think of whether this little dream might fade?

In the morning Wallace Talleck, with fingers steepled like a Zen master, asked me if I had enjoyed his wine. (How had he noticed the absence of one bottle?) I told him was that I'd had a very, very tough night and he did not press me for details, thank goodness. I felt drained of all vigor and inspiration.

"Either your denouement wasn't what you wanted it to be or else you really did not experience your novitiate," Wall said.

All I knew was that frustration left a bad taste in my mouth – like the awful cough syrup mothers force-feed their kids – and it stays there a long time.

I made plans to return Stookie's key to its key chain. The replaced wine, a Chambolle-Musigny, was to cost me exactly half my next teacher's cheque. I returned the Boy Scout knife to my desk drawer at school. There were tiny pieces of cork stuck in the slots of its handle.

It seemed a long time since I had held MJ, since we danced our silent dance before the hot-eyed stove, the stove where a young woman had held her Conrad James for the last time. Was I a replacement of sorts?

I didn't understand the weird emotional geometry inside me. The trouble with illusions such as mine is that you can never know if and when and how they will release their power. The night with Maggie J seemed somewhere between a dream and a memory. Should a person pick at memory's scab? Or does one dare ignore it? Of course, I put the whole damn thing in my diary.

Through the teacherage's big, front window I saw Sheba Faye Klanty close the Bredner's front gate on her way home. Her overnight babysitting chores were complete. How could I know then that this second Klanty daughter would have an even more profound impact on me?

17

Interlude

A pretty girl who is naked is worth a million statues.
– ee cummings: Collected Poems

Waiting for Sheba Faye's surgery was tough on all of us. During that time she might well have been on Mars, instead of in my classroom. Doing Grade VIII arithmetic can't match the probable reacquisition of one's hearing, and she looked forward to her operation because she obviously could well remember the years when her hearing was excellent. During those days of anticipation I noticed some subtle and not-so-subtle changes in Sheba Faye. For example, her knees got to know each other – before they had been rather distant strangers when she sat at her desk or on the school swing. I guess you could say she had instantly learned to "sit like a lady," as my grandmother would define the term.

Before Sheba Faye's eyes had been shyly averted whenever I looked at her. Now she looked directly at me with a trust and openness that was almost scary. Confidence straightened her spine. What would she be like after the operation? She had once told me that "silences are not all bad because I can't hear all the people's insults." Soon for Sheba Faye conversation was no longer to be a jigsaw puzzle with important pieces missing.

As expected, MJ was delighted with the good news. On the second Saturday in April she drove to Baltic in her landlady's car, as a surprise for Sheba Faye. The younger sister was not to be found at home, the Horvath's, the Bredner's, or Mrs. Stone's place, so MJ walked over to the teacherage to ask me if I knew Sheba Faye's whereabouts.

This was the first time I had seen MJ since our rather recent train station evening – and immediately I started to wonder if the train station were available again. She wore blue jeans and a loose plaid shirt and looked sensational even in a ponytail. Because I'd just left the school I knew exactly where Sheba Faye could be found. So Maggie J and I walked up the wood sidewalk to the school swings.

As we rounded the southwest corner of my portable blue, Sheba Faye saw us, rose from her swing seat, and ran into the arms of her sister. They embraced long and hard and weepingly. Pure, shared joy. That was no time and place for me.

About an hour later MJ knocked on the teacherage door, and without hesitation said, "I've just spent a wonderful time with the most important person in my life, Sheba Faye." (Was I now fourth fiddle after her sister, Conrad James and Bow Tie?) She thanked me for my "leadership," and left a thank-you note for "Mr. Talleck" who again was spending a weekend in the city.

MJ told me of the great happiness Sheba Faye was experiencing. The two sisters had enjoyed a long visit on the swings. She gave me a kiss on the cheek which I hoped would slide into something several thousand percent better. I responded to the kiss with my best gee-whiz grin.

MJ suggested that I come by her place late that evening so we could go for another walk on the trestle. I accepted her invitation but added I thought we should "check out her landlady's car for any potential mechanical problems."

"Do you think you can use the brakes?" she said lightly. I didn't ask about Bow-Tie.

After her departure I wrote in my diary that MJ's visit with me seemed to have held more potential passion than caring. Not that at nineteen I was opposed to the former!

After sampling Mrs. Horvath's best I enjoyed a long, cool tub before hauling my carcass to Klanty's shanty. For old time's sake I took the famous Third Street route past the Bredners, across the Riga River bridge, and over the high trestle to the spot on the railroad track closest to the Klanty place. My fear of heights was disappearing.

The April night was surprisingly warm. In total darkness I walked along the south end of Klanty's property, as defined by the partially completed stone fence. The house's lights bounced off the dead Packard supposedly won by Klanty in a long-forgotten poker game. I glanced at a lighted window and saw through the well-lighted rectangle nature's most wonderful creature – naked woman. She was humming and dancing to the New Year's Eve song which belonged only to MJ and me. The dancer had opened the tired storm window from its top hinges, and raised the inside window so as to enjoy the warm spring air. Through that window with its partially lowered blind I watched that golden woman dance to *I'm in the Mood for Love*.

It was about 9:30 p.m. I had arrived perhaps thirty minutes early. (I wanted to prove to MJ that I didn't know how "to use the brakes.") Sheba Faye was babysitting at the Bredners' and Klanty was likely getting drunk in his big chair. And here was Maggie J, that lovely, tiny, full woman, in grand display through the window. It delighted me that while preparing herself for our big date she was playing "our song."

The sound from the record player allowed me to hear only slight swatches of her voice. The partially pulled dark blind and the inverted V of the dark curtains provided an imperfect triangle of glass through which I could gaze at her moving, womanly perfection. For a moment the crossbars on the raised inner window were like a rifle's crosshairs on her navel. That damn window blind cut off the dancer's head so I hunkered down and crunched my chin into the stone fence so as to see her face. It didn't work. If I lowered my face and eyes behind the fence, a rock on the uneven surface blocked the lovely view.

Parts of me showed definite signs of excitation. Ashamed of myself, I walked 15 or 20 feet towards the corner of the property, stopped, dismissed my temporary attack of decency, and returned to my post. I hated myself for being the Peeping Tom I had so roundly scorned during that earlier "seminar" in Klanty's home.

The ceiling light directly above the dancer formed a nimbus about her shoulders, allowing me to see that she was glowingly matured with a surprisingly wide and fertile spread of hips. I realized that one of my old pal's crude observations was correct: a woman's behind is always bigger when it's bare. Her buttocks were like large, hard, ripe pears. I studied the knuckles of her spine and the xylophone of her ribs playing against shadows and lights. Her nakedness held shadows, voluptuous curves, firm haunches, secret places and small, thrusting rose-tipped perfections (I focused the crosshairs on each one) as she placed her hands on the flexuous incurves of her waist. She danced in one spot, hugging herself lightly.

I willed the blind to raise a few inches and the dancer to bend her knees. I desperately wanted to see MJ's hair, her face, her eyes, her hair, her mouth, to complete the most fantastic picture I'd ever witnessed. My chin again ground down on the stone wall and my eyes looked up at the sharpest possible angle. Still no luck. Neck down only. Some guys would have been satisfied. Not me. The essence of womanhood meant completeness. I vaguely believed that by seeing all of "my girl," my Peeping Tomism would somehow be more decent, defensible, and justifiable. I could have walked closer to the window but something held me back.

I should have walked to the ice-cold creek for a long, cold swim. Wallace Talleck is correct to say that most men are goats who think with their nuts.

The nubile dancer stepped slightly to one side, and, as I could clearly see, picked up another record and placed it on the turntable. A new sound travelled out to me, Johnnie Ray's bestseller the year before, "Cry." That song and the flipside of the record, "The Little White Cloud that Cried," were favorites of MJ.

The young composer-singer had suffered a sharp hearing loss, so I decided right then I would purchase the record in the city as a celebration present for Sheba Faye.

That Dallas-born singer combined gospel music and black blues, loud and clear, and the music encouraged the dancer to perform more energetically. I was glad my little schoolmarm had brought home a record player, even while I despised myself as a voyeur.

Fifteen seconds into "Cry" the naked girl lifted the phonograph needle and the music was no more. The bedroom lights stayed on, but my dream moved sideways into the room. Out of sight but not out of mind.

I still had time to waste so, unseen, I walked the Klanty path east to the skating rink. The faint beam of a streetlight picked out hockey nets left to sulk in the spring mud. No doubt Stookie would soon collect them and place them in the freight shed at the train station.

I willed myself to think of the February ice carnival when I had skated madly while wearing that stupid witch's costume. Then I tried to remember the circumstances around the "sure" goal I had missed in our 6-5 home loss to the Riga hockey team. But no matter how hard I tried, nothing would erase the image I had no right to see and enjoy beyond words. For some reason I recalled a twelfth century quote by Peter Abelard: "The sin, then, consists not in desiring a woman, but in consent to the desire."

It soon became time to head back to Klanty's place, and a few minutes later I knocked on the front door. No mints this time. After three more hard raps the door opened, and Sheba Faye, barefoot and dressed in her usual off-whites and grays, greeted me. She immediately explained that Klanty was in bed dead drunk, and "my sister asked me to give this message to you."

The note said that Bill Statiuk had suffered a severe heart attack and MJ was driving immediately to Vyborg. I noticed the time written under MJ's signature: 7:45 p.m.

I damn near fainted. As I sprawled in Klanty's tall throne chair, the realization came quickly: the dancer I had slavered over at 9:30 p.m. was the girl who had just opened the door to me. Apparently MJ must have left her record player and her records with her sister to enjoy once her hearing was restored. And I'd been too taken with myself to notice that MJ's usual borrowed car hadn't been parked at the Klanty house. It was my 17-year-old, Grade VIII student, who had danced and crooned and gyrated to the Gardners and Rays of the music world.

I felt feverish, sick and dizzy. All my joints felt as if they were unscrewed. After mumbling good night to Sheba Faye, I walked back to the muddy skating rink where I was physically sick. It didn't help one bit to remember that I hadn't known the window-framed dancer was Sheba Faye. She was still my student, and I was her teacher. Sometimes shame sneaks up on me. On other occasions it lands like a huge, muddied boulder.

What would Stookie do if he knew about my night's adventures? Wasn't he the crack shot of the Riga River valley? And what would be the reactions of MJ, Tall Wall, the Horvaths, the Bredners, and especially Mrs. Stone? What would my parents think? I didn't even want to think about the Superintendent of Schools.

What evil comments would come from Klanty's lips? More importantly, what would happen if Sheba Faye ever found out my secret?

Another question remained unanswered. What the blue hell did I think of myself? I was no scholar, certainly no gentleman, and surely no professional. Self-hate weighs a great deal. I told no one the story and that made my shame even heavier. And my next sensations didn't lessen the weight. My eyescreen featured the slow transformation of a sheep to a mermaid to the most beautiful female figure in the world. I loved and hated it at the same time.

At home with my feet in the oven, I got thoroughly smashed on my absent colleague's best brandy – and wine. After all, satyrs are supposed to keep company with Bacchus.

My eyescreen wouldn't stop showing its sensual movie. With eyes closed I stood by the stove, wobbly, snifter glass in hand, and pretended that I was again dancing with MJ in that warm train station. Then I "measured" out with my hands the dimensions of the girl in the triangle of the light. Were not the stepsisters almost physically identical from the neck down?

Around dawn I made it to halfway to the two-holer out back before my stomach erupted again. I hoped Mrs. Stone couldn't hear me. I ended the night with a drunken crying jag, and don't remember making it back to the teacherage.

When I woke up around noon I hadn't any idea where I was. After a long stuporous moment I realized that, drunk as a skunk, I had crawled into that huge, empty tin tub in that totally dark and windowless shed, the scene of so many swimmingly good hours of tub hedonism – and had lain there like a soaked mattress for seven hours.

I had removed my shirt but my loosened tie was still around my neck. One foot was sockless and shoeless. Yawning and gritty-eyed, I took four aspirin, stripped naked, and washed off the smell of the evening. After dressing slowly, I left the teacherage.

I didn't try Stookie's for a "sure cure for them hangovers – chopped onion and a raw egg mixed in warm milk." My neck was still stiff and my 100-pound head pounded often and hard. Something or somebody was trying to push a skinny icicle shaped like a corkscrew through a vein in my forehead. Meanwhile my stomach fluttered with more nausea, like a freshly caught perch on a wobbly dock.

After apologizing to Mrs. Horvath for missing lunch, I walked in lead boots to Reg Woolston's emporium for some of his tepid coffee. Rex, the king of mange and bad breath, was sleeping by the antifreeze. Irene Woolston, wearing a low sweater of venomous green, and tight, red slacks, approached me from behind and slapped me on the shoulder – causing my skull to explode.

"Gettin' much, kid?"

"You and Klanty sort of complement each other, don't you think?" I replied sourly.

She sucked her teeth in the Klanty style and said she didn't know what I was talking about. Sitting fatly on her heels, hammocked abundance swaying, she stacked day-old bread on the shelves. Without socks, Iris' sandals clearly displayed her dirty ankles. I walked away leaving my unfinished coffee and doughnut. Standing up hip-shot she said too loudly, "Hey, guy, come back and pay for this 'cause you don't get anything here unless you pay for it."

Just then Chairman Reg (as I called him behind his back) came in and the incident passed. The three of us sat on the café stools and talked about everything and nothing while insincerity saturated Iris' voice.

I spent the rest of the afternoon coming back to life while bringing my Baltic diary up-to-date and rereading it from the beginning. Diaries like mine call for either a great ego or a consuming diligence, or both.

The reading took place on "Sheba Faye's" swing for no good reason other than that it was a soft, early Spring day and I wanted to be unseen and alone. My thoughts were fuzzy at the edges and writing helped clarify them. Although Tall Wall agreed with a comment made by Voltaire: "To hold a pen is to be at war," I felt writing helped me find peace and satisfaction. And catharsis.

Sheba Faye's operation took place a few weeks later, and was a complete success. It seemed she and Stookie got rid of their health problems at the same time. Tall Wall paid all the bills, as promised, and provided the transportation. I was thoroughly delighted and perhaps a little bit smug about it all. I had provided leadership of the kind my school superintendent had advised me to.

I still hated myself for being Baltic's Peeping Tom – thinking more of my reputation and private shame than about the unseen insult I had imposed on an innocent individual. But the next few events were to give me even more perspective. The chopped tempo of this time invaded, sliced, brutalized, pounded and further altered my definition of early manhood.

18

Shootin'

Hast thou named all the birds without a gun?
– Ralph Waldo Emerson: Forbearance

As thick, dark clouds slowly scudded southward on a Sunday afternoon in April, Stookie, Sheba Faye and I took a .22 rifle and a 30-30 rifle to wage war on "them crows that need shootin' down the crick." Why did Stookie carry a large, folded piece of cardboard? Why did he include the 30-30 in our arsenal? I sometimes wondered if there was some dark, deep atavism in Stookie's love of guns.

We were headed to a place not too far from where I had seen the mermaid in late winter, so I hadn't wanted to "go down the crick," but Stookie insisted. Sheba Faye's nakedness was far too fresh in my memory, and during school hours I kept my eyes averted from her.

Of course, Stookie broke trail. Sheba Faye, behind me, tripped going down the riverbank, so instinctively I opened my arms to catch her, and she plowed me down flat on the shore's gravel and mud. Parts of her landed on parts of me parts of me that obviously had a tactile memory. It felt wonderful: she weighed just right. Everywhere.

How could Mother Nature put a sheep's face on top of her beautiful body? Why was I so rotten to think the things I was thinking? She was my student!

Stookie, thirty yards ahead, didn't see Sheba Faye stumble and fall. Awkwardly she rolled off me, brushed herself, and bent to wash her muddied hands in the cold, shallow water. Just below the bottom of Stookie's heavy jacket, Sheba Faye's beautiful behind stretched the bright-blue slacks she wore for the day. Since her operation Sheba Faye's clothes had brightened considerably. I suppose there is some kind of cause-effect relationship there.

While bending like a baseball catcher she shook water from her hands, turned on the balls of her feet and looked directly into my eyes. "Gee, that's good," she said, "'cause this is the first time since my ear operation that you have even looked at me. Have I made you angry or something?" She had no idea about the excellence of my eye screen.

Stookie decided it was time to stop for lunch. The wind died down just as Stookie's fire came to life. I still couldn't light a kitchen match like he could with his thumbnail. Against the fire's early smoke Sheba Faye's face had the hues of a newly exhumed corpse.

We had brought tube steaks, buns, mustard and Mrs. Horvath's dill pickles. (Their snap could scare deer for miles around.) Stookie insisted on "havin' no beer 'cause Sheba Faye shouldn't be drinkin' with her teechur ya know." He advised that "you always want to build small fires like Indians used to and then you sit between 'em and keep warm. Too many guys make their fire too big." A small handful of coffee thrown in a coffee can along with crick water can make the best brew in the western world.

Sheba Faye told me that Margaret Jane would soon be home, but nothing was said about Mr. Bow Tie and his heart attack. The two sisters now had frequent conversations on the telephone and Sheba Faye had been thrilled to hear her sister clearly. (I wondered how Klanty sounded to her.) I was planning a river picnic with MJ, or if the weather turned bad, another evening in the train station. There would be cushions this time. It was a happy afternoon "down the crick."

While Sheba Faye looked for "the ladies' room" somewhere behind us, Stookie, as he had promised, proceeded to teach me shootin', using the 30-30 as his teaching tool.

He reminded me he had promised to teach me how to hit something for a change. "If ya want to hit your target ya got to know where your bullet is goin! A fella with a good eye and a good hand also gotta know two things – wind drift and the up hill and down hill ways your bullet needs to go unless you're shootin' straight across like on a prairie."

"Let's say you got a 10 mph crosswind," he said, "and you're tryin' to use this 30-30 rifle carryin' a 150 grain round-nose bullet like this one. Well I used lots of big cardboard targets I cut and painted in the station shed, and took them down the crick with my 30-30 and brought the taped yardstick the school threw away. Then I figured out pretty close what the gun will do for me and even for you if you got the eye and the hand."

He extended his arm straight out and drew an imaginary trajectory in the air. "In that crosswind at 10 mph your shell will go sideways pretty near three inches if you're 100 yards away. But if you're 200 yards away she'll go 12 inches sideways. Ya don't want to shoot no deer at 300 yards but if ya do the bullet will go pretty near 30 inches sideways. Ya gotta know about wind drift. My huntin' magazines at the station say all ya got to do is multiply by two if ya got say a 20 mph wind, and so on. I figure you must know all this stuff 'cause you went to college. Those fellas writin' in those magazines are mostly right ya know."

That surely was Stookie's longest speech!

Then Stookie withdrew a flat tin object from his breast pocket. I took a deep breath and then whistled long and soft through my teeth. It was a protractor.

My friend reported, "You're Sheba Faye's teechur so ya know all 'bout angles and things like that. But if you're shootin' up or down more than say 10 degrees your gun needs to get aimed lower. Let's say your 30-30 is zeroed in for 150 yards. But s'pose ya gotta end up shootin' 250 yards instead. She'll drop pretty near 15 inches. But if your target is say 15 degrees up or down she'll drop 'bout half an inch less. At 30 degrees it will be two inches less."

Using the protractor, Stookie showed me what would happen if the angle to the target changed to 45 degrees either up or down.

"She'll drop five inches less. The stiffer angle ya got up or down, the less your slug will drop. But like I said, ya probably learnt all them things at college but if ya want we can try 'em out."

After Sheba Faye returned Stookie stepped off the proper distance, stuck the piece of cardboard, which he unfolded, in a late snow drift, and supported it with dead branches. The centre of the target was a solid red circle two inches in diameter. The outside circles, six inches apart, reminded me of my science teacher's attempt to teach us about "electrons and their friendly nucleus."

The cold crosswind seemed to be about 10 mph. I followed Stookie's instructions as closely as I could and the results were impressive. Stookie brought me back to reality, however.

"She's different for sure when it's alive and when it's movin' fast. Anybody can shoot cardboard. But those book fellas sure know their stuff 'cause they found out the same things I did." (How many educators have that kind of innocent self assurance?)

By raising and lowering the target Stookie proved that shooting uphill or downhill, if distances remain unchanged, "ya got to aim low on both targets." That was news to me, and maybe to many hunters.

We got only nine crows that day, and no magpies. (Is there a smarter, more fidgety bird than a mature magpie?) We didn't make a crow "paramint."

On the way back, on that chilly and windy day, I noticed a small, lovely incident. Stookie slipped his heavy jacket over Sheba Faye's shoulders and did up the front buttons with his big fingers, then raised the big collar around her neck. Something soft passed between them and I thought he was going to kiss her. My squat, and by now better-complexioned, friend and his girl looked right for each other.

The most wonderful thing, of course, was the obvious fact that Sheba Faye could hear. She rejoiced in the gurgle of the river's rushing waters, the crunch of feet on stones and on last autumn's stubble, and the sound of human voices.

19

Race

Tomorrow we will run faster, stretch out our arms further.
– F. Scott Fitzgerald: The Great Gatsby

Our first baseball practice of the season was the first week in May, in the early evening. Our team looked good, according to our captain, coach and manager. It appeared that Stookie was trying to get us ready for the baseball season in a few successive nights, however. Riga's May 24 Victoria Day ball tournament would be the season's first big test. Wallace would be present for that tournament, but would have to drive in from the city for the games in July and August. That was alright with our coach. Stookie let it be known that "Mr. Talleck is a teechur and should be allowed to miss some practices."

Stookie asked Tall Wall to bring "one of them city library books with lots of pictures which tells about how the big league coaches 'specially Casey Stengel do their spring training." Tall Wall and I learned that Stookie could read far better than his grade IV schooling would warrant.

After a short practice, some team members assembled at the teacherage for cold beer and hot conversation. Tall Wall's radio had picked up the astounding news from Oxford, England. Bannister (who was a year or so older than Maggie J) had set the sporting world talking by running the mile in 3:59:4. Our left fielder and our short stop, our team's two fastest runners, agreed that the four-minute mile was now just a question of "your head over your legs." In fun, each bet the other a dozen cold ones that he could run the mile in 4:40. Soon numerous side bets were placed, and the conversation and laughter got louder. I saw Stookie whisper something in Wall's ear, and our tall friend waved his hand for silence. He dangled his car keys as if to mesmerize the ball players. Wall said, "Stookie has a great idea."

Under Stookie's direction all of us, some with beer in hand, walked down to Woolston's Corner. The runners, still in baseball uniforms, changed their cleats to running shoes while Stookie and I synchronized our watches. The race was to begin at exactly 10:00 p.m. on that beautiful, still May night. Of course, Reg Woolston and his wife heard all the commotion, as did much of the hamlet, and Reg agreed to help me in the all-important job of time-keeping.

Both runners sneaked over the barbed wire fence to empty their bladders behind a rusting, ancient Case tractor. By 9:30 p.m. there were at least 40 people, kids included, by the locker plant, and another 35 or so out at the finishing line past the nuisance grounds.

It was so damn much fun. The fine citizens of our hamlet had never seen anything like it. Everyone was laughing, talking too loudly and making friendly bets. By the streetlight I noticed the Bredners, with babe in arms, the Horvaths, the Framms, Sheba Faye, and even Klanty (likely on one of his infrequent evening strolls) in attendance. Sheba Faye stood by the self-appointed organizer, Stookie.

Stookie asked the two runners to shake hands just before starting time, which they gladly did. Stookie then announced "there's no more bets gonna be made now." Wall, Jack Klackston, Reg Woolston and I drove straight north on the nuisance ground road and placed a rope across the road, exactly one mile north. No one doubted the odometer in Wall's car. As it was getting dark, we arranged that after returning to the starting line, Tall Wall would follow the runners with his car's high beams to light the way. At 10:00 p.m. sharp we heard Stookie fire his 12-gauge straight to the stars above and the race began.

Those of us a mile away had our watches set and Stookie had supplied us with a few flashlights. Three sets of car lights further illuminated the area just south of Fred Kleiner's farmstead. He and Janet arrived just in time to learn of the race.

The road was so flat and level we could see Tall Wall's car lights a mile away. About three minutes into the run I could see the runners. I glanced at my watch and shivered. It appeared that the two runners might come close to matching Bannister's record. However, the last five to six hundred yards were the toughest. The two gasping runners eventually crossed the line in a tie.

Chairman Reg and I consulted our watches. The time was 4:55. Too much winter, beer and fun! The runners hugged each other, laughed, rolled together on the dirt road, and demanded cool beer. Then most of the crowd got in Fred Kleiner's truck-box, or in one of the three available cars, and headed for Fred's half-empty, cavernous hayloft. In single file we passed the barn's deep, dark stalls and the chop bin, and crawled up the dirty, strong ladder to the "dance floor."

Sweet and harsh smells filled our nostrils. The gang back at Woolston's Corner heard about the plans so most of those people came, too. The people with small children went home.

In short order kerosene lanterns, a violin, a banjo and an accordion appeared, and the impromptu celebration began. Fred played the violin, and Tall Wall and Mr. Horvath shared the accordion and banjo.

Stookie and Sheba Faye danced every step together. She could hear, and as Stookie said, "I don't have to sweep and mind this loft and everything ya know." For the first time I saw Sheba Faye wearing a ribbon in her hair and earrings, and she wore a green blouse and bright yellow slacks. Gifts from Maggie J?

It was the kind of night when everything went right, the kind this romantic assumes helped our pioneers through tough times. After one hour or so, Stookie announced "she's all over now 'cause we all sure had a good time with the big run and the dancin' and everything but tomorrow will be here too quick ya' know." He thanked Fred and Janet, and then called on "the two Roger Bannisters to stand up and be clapped." He added, "Ya know I was feelin' all the time I was runnin' with them runners." I knew how Stookie felt.

At the teacherage I played the piano for an hour and then tried to listen to more of that damn fool rock and roll, including some from Elvis Somebody. Wall told me that only a few copies of the records had been produced.

"That's a blessing," I replied.

I soaked in the big tub, wrote home, and then tried to put Maggie J and Lochinvar in perspective. In fifty years she would be 73 and I would be 69. Big deal. Men marry younger women so why shouldn't women marry younger men?

But with whom could we discuss the whole business of sex, given that both of us had never had it? Should we discuss the issue with Reverend Framm? When? Should I propose marriage and buy an engagement ring with the money I'd made during the summer at my construction job? (I had signed on with the oily, green-suited Secretary-Treasurer to work on the school unit's repair crew.) Would MJ and I when married have sex every night except during her "men's trial?" How could we afford to have kids if I were to attend university? How in hell could young teachers get married when their salary was less than what a casual laborer earned? Could MJ love me as she had loved Conrad James? I asked myself both silly and sensible questions

All those musings, plans, dreams and hopes darkened the next day, Thursday, May 7, 1954, the very day General Castries surrendered Dienbienphu and French Indo-China to the communists after a 55-day siege.

20

Rails

Ah, sorrow, how close you tred on the heels of enjoyment.
– T.C. Haliburton: Sam Slick

The morning after the big run saw me still in bed at 8:40 a.m. and classes started at 9:00 a.m. Roosters have the wrong attitude about mornings.

Wallace Talleck, as usual, had been in his classroom since 6:30 a.m. "Those two hours in the morning," he often said, "are the ones that make my work most productive." Believe me, I never tested his theory. I splashed cold water on my face and wherever, drank a large glass of warm pineapple juice, and headed for the salt mines. For reasons teachers will never understand, the kids were terrific that morning. Co-operation everywhere. Meanwhile, my head was in great pain, and I have only muddy memories of recess.

After two more aspirin I began to look forward to Mrs. Horvath's lunch. During the barn dance the night before she had asked Stookie and me to bring "that young Mr. Talleck to lunch tomorrow." So after the kids left for lunch, Tall Wall and I walked to Baltic's remaining grain elevator, where Stookie was helping elevator agent Jack Klackston fill a grain car. Wall and I were to collect Stookie and proceed to one of Mrs. Horvath's culinary masterpieces.

The diesel engineer and two brakemen were shunting grain cars as Wallace and I searched for Stookie. As we walked into the long shadow of the grain elevator Wallace couldn't resist the chance to give me another one of his damn history lessons.

"In 1930 #1 Northern Wheat fell from $1.40 to $.60 per bushel. During one three-day stretch my parents couldn't see the sun for dust. Four years later the grasshoppers were so bad that when people walked down village sidewalks, it was like crunching thousands of peanut shells under your feet. People actually had to clean their shoes of grasshopper juice."

I believed the grasshopper story, at least, because back home we used to catch the 'hoppers and make 'em spit "tobacco juice." His response was, "You'll never really know or remember the real horror story of the depression." Was I supposed to apologize for being that young? Or for not having his memories? Doesn't each generation discover its own realities?

Just then the diesel gently and slowly shoved another full grain car past the side of the elevator. Even above the mighty engine's roar we heard the sharp scream. Another shout followed immediately. We saw Jack Klackston dash to the tracks behind the stopped grain car. We joined him in two seconds flat around the end of the grain car.

The first things I saw between the rails were what I thought to be a pair of high leather boots lying about three feet apart, not far from where Stookie had tossed our two beer from the elevator roof last August. Then I realized the boots weren't empty.

Stookie had fallen, and the unforgiving train wheels had caught him just above his knees. The rest of his legs and trousers were left in those fine boots Wall and I had given him for Christmas. Stookie was screaming, then mewing, writhing on the cinders and small stones next to the railroad track. His face was contorted in a rictus of agony. Blood spurted from both stumps.

Immediately Wallace Talleck took charge. He fired his key chain to me and yelled "car!" To the brakemen, "Come here, now!" As I turned on my heel to go, Wall yelled to Jack, "Church bell!" Even as he shouted ex-medic Wall was ripping off his silk tie and removing his thin leather belt.

All my actions and thoughts seemed to be in slow motion. The world was a grainy, black and white movie as I ran through hot honey to the teacherage to get the car. Each second expanded thirty fold. Yet in another sense I felt peculiarly detached, as if I were watching a runner (where was Bannister when you needed him?) from high above the hamlet. My run seemed more steep and difficult than Hillary's climb to Mt. Everest. I think I left a little second-hand pineapple juice somewhere between the tracks and home.

Before I reached the car Jack had begun pulling the *EMERGENCY ONLY* rope attached to the church bell. Not until I reached the automobile did terror rise like bile in my throat. In my haste I couldn't unlock the car door. I fumbled. There were at least a dozen keys on the key chain. Which key was the ignition key? Number five or six worked. Sweat blinded me and my face was greasy with perspiration.

Mrs. Stone, who must have seen me running by her house and heard the church bell, pounded on the passenger door, demanding that I let her in. "What's the commotion all about, and didn't you young fellows have enough of it last night?" she demanded.

I answered her in one terse sentence as I tried to start the car. I stalled the motor, and couldn't get it going again. "You damn fool," Mrs. Stone yelled. "Push the gas pedal to the floor." Her magisterial manner and habitual severity of mien were gone. Not until later did I think to be shocked about Mrs. Stone's language.

We tore down to Woolston's Corner, turned east up main street, and made a new trail through early weeds north to the grain elevator. Mrs. Stone kept saying, "Go faster, go faster." My face, body and hands were covered with an oily sweat and I could feel the drum-like thud of my heart.

We pulled up next to the elevator and rushed to Stookie's side. Some of the local people, including a few students, were already there. In the distance we could hear Jack still ringing the church bell. Mrs. Stone gave a wretched bleat of terror when she saw the front of Wallace's white shirt, soaked with Stookie's blood. The engineer was vomiting heavily beside the now-stilled diesel engine.

Wall pointed a bloody finger at the car. "Head for the city."

He ordered Reg Woolston to phone ahead to the hospital as he picked up what was left of Stookie, and ran to the car where he placed himself and Stookie in the back seat. Just as I was about to gun the motor, Sheba Faye Klanty jumped in the front seat. Klanty appeared, shouting at her to get the hell out. The girl snapped the door locked. She began to weep copiously but silently as I gunned the motor.

For a long time I had wanted to drive Wall's powerful car, his "war chariot" as he called it. *But please God, not this way,* I said to myself. As we sped by Riga, 15 miles away, I remember that the sawbones there had retired and moved to the west coast in early March.

The bloody interior of the powerful automobile smelled like wet copper pennies and worse. Trees, posts, buildings and herds of cows flung backward past us as we drove the sixty miles along the gravel highway. I was so alive I could almost feel our planet turn beneath the powerful car's tires.

In the back seat Wallace worked on Stookie, remaining totally silent and concentrated. Sheba Faye, with knees on the front seat, had turned around to watch her Stookie and the ex-medic. She prayed and cried all the way. I passed vehicles on curves and on blind hills, and because of traffic had to pass a tractor on the wrong side. A large jackrabbit was nailed solid and left the red evidence on the bumper and grill.

Forty minutes, a century later, I braked hard at the hospital's emergency entrance. Thanks to Woolston's phone call the medical team was waiting for us. As they lifted Stookie from the car I saw that circle of white around his mouth. A doctor had once told me that was a sign of impending death. I felt furious, frightened and helpless.

In a few moments Wallace, Sheba Faye and I met in the hospital's small lounge. I looked up in surprise as Dr. Krantz, the dermatologist who had treated Stookie, entered the lounge. Wallace thanked her for coming in response to his phone call, and she kissed him on the cheek, hugged Sheba Faye, and heavily shook my hand.

The doctor turned to Wallace Talleck. "Well, old friend, Dr. Abramovitz will brief you on Stookie's condition. Miss Klanty, however, will now come with me." And she put her arm around Sheba Faye's shoulders and led her away. As the squawk-squawk of her rubber-soled shoes receded down the corridor, I knew she was the right person to talk with Sheba Faye.

Some time later, it may have been minutes or it may have been hours, a tired-looking surgeon solemnly introduced himself as Dr. Abramovitz. He got right to the point with Wallace and me. "Your friend's condition is critical. We've done all we can for him at this time."

He couldn't (or wouldn't?) provide us with the odds on our friend's probable fate. In deference to Wallace's friendship with his colleague, Dr. Krantz, Dr. Abramovitz agreed to give us the facts about the accident. Somehow I felt that knowing the specifics would help calm the unwanted pictures playing continually on my eyescreen.

"An injury of such magnitude," Dr. Abramovitz began, "is an immediate life-threatening assault. The patient would lose about one pint of blood a minute, post-injury. Clearly, unless some intervention took place, he would not survive more than a few minutes." The doctor paused as if collecting his thoughts.

"Two things might be important here. Firstly, cleanly cut arteries have the ability to contract and to retract surprisingly, on occasion, to such an extent that the blood loss is reduced considerably, if not controlled completely. This appears to have happened to the patient you brought to my hospital. Secondly, an astute bystander with some medical knowledge," here he nodded toward ex-medic Wallace Talleck, "would perhaps be able to fashion some sort of tourniquet."

I remembered how Wallace had used his silk tie and narrow leather belt to once again "make-do."

"By using the pressure of the thumbs over the femoral arteries, at the mid-point of the upper and inner thigh, blood loss could be controlled while tourniquets were being applied." The doctor raised his eyebrow at Tall Wall, who nodded quietly. Wallace had ordered the brakemen to place their thumbs where the doctor had indicated.

"Assuming that all this must have been accomplished in, let us say, three minutes, the victim was saved from immediate death, although his hold on life would still be precarious. Despite tourniquets applied above the wound, he would have still lost blood from oozing of the damaged muscle, and I would estimate by this stage he had lost 50 percent of his total blood volume."

"By now the patient was probably in the process of transportation to this hospital, hopefully being carried in the head-down position to maximize cerebral blood flow."

Again Wallace nodded. As I thought about it, I remembered Wallace holding Stookie in what I thought was an awkward way.

"During transportation the victim likely showed signs of continued vasoconstriction. Did Mr. Stook's fingers, skin, nose, or ear lobes become cold and white?" Dr. Abramovitz asked, and received a "yes" from both Wallace and me at the same time.

The doctor nodded. "That would be due to blood loss."

The doctor's voice softened a little and he indicated we should sit down. "Nature provides a protective mechanism in these cases – endorphin release. This might be evident in a gradual subsidence in pain levels, and the patient might even become quite comfortable."

I remembered with some feeling of relief that at one point Stookie told Sheba Faye "I'm feelin' pretty good," and how he had asked me to make sure the May 24th ball tournament in Riga went well for our team.

"Our procedure when your friend was brought in," Dr. Abramovitz continued, "was an aggressive intravenous fluid replacement, with IVs set up in both arms and subclavian veins, pouring in lactate, albumen, plasma and unmatched group *O* negative blood. We also applied oxygen and endotracheal intubation to control respiration."

The doctor seemed to have no more to say, so Wall and I thanked him for the information and shook his hand. We asked him to take extra care with "Mr. Stook" and to let us know as soon as there was a development of any kind.

The police arrived, asked the appropriate questions, examined and photographed the interior of Wall's car, and thanked Wallace and me for our co-operation. Both of us signed written statements. Then the police headed for the scene of the accident.

"Take Sheba Faye home in the car," said Wallace Talleck. His blood-soaked shirt contrasted sharply with his gray-as-dirty-chalk face. For once he seemed unconcerned about his appearance. He told me he would take a taxi to his apartment to clean up. From there he would contact the proper authorities, and then drive back to Baltic in his sports car. I hadn't known he had a sports car, let alone an apartment. That explained why he had all those keys on his key chain.

A hospital worker quickly gave the back seat an inadequate wash and we used a hospital blanket to cover the seat. Dr. Krantz had given Sheba Faye a needle to make her "comfortable." Without it, she likely would have insisted on staying at the hospital.

Three or four times during our drive to Baltic, Sheba Faye reached to wipe my eyes with a handkerchief Wallace had supplied. Her left arm circled my right arm tightly while her head fell on my right shoulder. Tragedy wiped out the student-teacher relationship. She cried and wiped her eyes. Tears joined tears. Did the trip home take one hour or one decade? I didn't know. Near Riga I spotted the large jackrabbit I had hit on the way to the hospital.

Though worried sick, I realized that Sheba Faye was wobbly beyond devastation. She and I recalled that it was only the previous night that Stookie had told the crowd in Jack's hayloft "tomorrow will be here too quick ya know." Stookie was more correct than anyone could know. As Sheba Faye and I entered Baltic she asked that I drive her to the train station. I was totally, unabashedly perplexed by her request.

Sheba Faye extracted a key from a red plastic change purse with a broken zipper, and opened the train station. The tall clock ticked loudly as the girl grabbed the green vase and flowers resting on the windowsill. She told me that it was a gift to her from Stookie. Quickly she grasped the stems and carefully put them in the beautiful black stove. She added old newspaper, lit it with two paper matches, and then replaced the empty vase on the windowsill. Sheba Faye turned to me.

"Nobody knows but now I have to explain it to somebody."

21

Mrs. Stone

A woman is more influenced by what she suspects than by what she is told. *– Robert C. (Bob) Edwards: Calgary Eye Opener*

As we sat on the bench I once shared with her sister, earlier by Conrad James and his Margie, my student, her dark eyes deepening, told me how "no one except Mrs. Stone has ever known about Stookie and me."

For almost two years Stookie and Sheba Faye had been visiting occasionally, on those very benches, winter and summer.

"It's not far from our homes you know, and after dark no one could see us coming to our secret place. Once my stepfather passed out at night it was safe for me to come here."

Now I understood why Stookie had kept the train station cleaned, polished and painted. When Sheba Faye told me that Mrs. Stone, the supplier of all those beautiful flowers, helped to arrange all their "together times," I damn near fainted. Ma Stone had a side to her I hadn't seen. Sheba Faye scared me a little by saying, "I don't think I can take any more pain from kids or adults."

Knowing that Sheba Faye was in bad shape, I took her to Mrs. Stone's place. I sped to Klanty's pathway and stopped. On my eye screen I saw Klanty's ugly face and mouth, pressed to the car window, shouting to Sheba Faye, "Get the hell out of there!" I knocked and without waiting for a response, entered Klanty's place. He was drinking his fifth or sixth beer while resting his 300 pounds on his throne chair.

"Well," commented Klanty, "that young Stook got his cut off today, eh?" His eyes were as shiny and dark as wet coal.

There was no way I could trust myself with a response, so I announced that Sheba Faye would spend the night at Mrs. Stones' place.

"Good riddance to the little bitch. Don't worry, I know where she's been going some nights. I followed the stupid, deaf whore a couple of times when she thought I was asleep. I know what she and that Stook have been doing in the station."

For two years plus the "girl on the swing" and Stookie had been doing just fine, thank you, at ye olde railway station with its clock ticking happily and softy. I left Klanty without a word.

I washed up at the teacherage. My eyes were sandy, and for some reason most of my bones ached. Splat had again decorated the back porch. After some hesitation I headed for Mrs. Stone's place.

My neighbor lady had prepared a warm bath for Sheba Faye and given her a strong sedative. The girl was soundly asleep. My hostess, pouches of weariness under her eyes, prepared hot tea and sandwiches. Only then did I remember that my pineapple juice breakfast was a long time ago.

I told Mrs. Stone that Sheba Faye had told me about Stookie and herself and the train station. Haltingly, at first, Mrs. Stone explained why she had tried to make things happen beautifully for "those two young people for whom few people have ever really given the time of day."

Because they were 'different,' Mrs. Stone explained, the townspeople had taken advantage of Stookie and scorned and teased "that sweet, young girl."

"Small towns," she said, "can be the unfriendliest and cruelest places in the world in which to live. I ought to know. Nearly everyone in Baltic, including you, treat me as if I were an old witch or something dank and evil."

I remembered my diary and felt the blush and heat rise from my neck to my forehead. Mrs. Stone didn't seem to notice.

"I know what I am and people will have to like it or lump it. Then she vacantly asked, "Who is going to hold my hand when I die?"

She started rambling, saying she realized she had done a terrible thing to her daughter, now 23 and a student in London. She had taught her daughter to hate and distrust all men.

"You see," Mrs. Stone said, and her voice broke into pieces, "my late husband, a remittance man, started to drink heavily after he lost everything except an insurance policy in the 1929 stock market crash. He started to beat and abuse me terribly. This community knew nothing about my problems."

"Booze killed him," she said bitterly, "and it wrecked our lives together." She took a sip of tea, and continued.

"When that horrid Klanty tried to entice my little girl in that awful pool room of his, well that was the last straw. Actually it was Margaret Enders who likely saved my daughter."

What, if anything did Mrs. Stone know or suspect about MJ and me? I pretended that the information was news to me. Mrs. Stone reported that she had drilled her daughter about the evil ways of men.

"I told her that all men were as bad as her father and Klanty. I know that was wrong but that's what I did. My daughter, who will never give me a grandchild, will have nothing to do with men now."

It seemed to me that Klanty had been correct when he talked about Mrs. Stone's propriety being a concealment of an earlier shame. We sat in silence for three or four minutes, and then my neighbor made her final point.

"You see, young man, there is a reason as to why I've helped little Sheba Faye, who's like another daughter, and why I supported Stookie in his search to find at least some worth and love in this horrible town."

She added, "Every small community has cankers, and Baltic has more than most. This place is merely another affirmation of the very bad and the limited good to be found in people." Her body seemed to pull in on itself. Across her hard, high cheekbones her pale skin clung tightly to her face.

I was a bit embarrassed when she said, "I know it was you who arranged for that poor lonesome girl to get her hearing back."

Mrs. Stone poured me another cup of tea, went to check on Sheba Faye, and then stopped at the top of the basement stairs.

"It has been twenty years since I've used swear words like the ones I used on you today in Mr. Talleck's car. Please accept my apology. It seems like I'm running out of sap."

Almost as an afterthought she added, "Bring the car around to the back lane, please." In a few moments she appeared behind our outhouses, with pails, water, soap, towels and rags. We worked until nearly dark cleaning Stookie's blood from the interior of Wall's car. The blood looked black on my wet blue rags. Perhaps the back seat would have to be recovered or replaced.

I don't think we said two sentences during the whole process. We rinsed the pails, returned the materials to her basement, and placed the wet rags in the garbage. An unasked question presented itself. *Who will collect the garbage now?*

As I left by the veranda door, on impulse I lightly kissed her low on her cheek.

"Please accept my apologies, Mrs. Stone, for a lot of things."

Her eyes watered and she uttered a soft "thank you." Her long horse-face sagged even more. But before I had taken six steps she called me back. Standing on the top of the veranda steps, the tall thin woman looked down at me at ground level.

"I've one request, young man. After people left I gathered Stookie's legs and wrapped them in oilcloth and put them in Woolston's locker plant. I burned the bit of trousers covering the boots. Of course Big Shot Reg didn't like the idea but no one else knows about it. So it is done."

Then she gave me an order. "You will look after Stookie's legs in the right way and at the right time." With her usual jerky abruptness she ended her comments with a curt "Good night, young man."

I felt numb everywhere. I hadn't even remembered about Stookie's legs, stuck in the very boots Tall Wall and I gave him. What do you do with legs? Give them to the police? Mrs. Stone had more humanity to her than I'd ever have. I realized how wrong I had been about her.

22

Farewell

He whom the gods love, dies young. – Menander

Just as I parked the car in front of the teacherage, Tall Wall, wearing clean clothes and an unreadable face, drove up in a yellow sports car. Feeling self-righteous, I reported what Mrs. Stone and I had done with his "luxurious, 1953 DeSoto FireDome V-8, with its Tip-Toe Shift, Power Steering and Power Brakes, Air-Conditioning, Fluid Torque-Drive, White Walls and all."

"Shut up, Bright Boy," said Wallace Talleck flatly, "Stookie died just two hours ago."

I stared at my colleague and friend, ashamed and afraid.

"I drove here to deliver the news personally rather than phoning. The doctor didn't know how Stookie lasted as long as he did. His heart stopped three times. The third was the last."

I felt a sharp needle enter my heart.

Wall's face displayed bruised weariness and deep sorrow as he softly gave me his second-ever compliment. "You're one hell of a driver. I don't know anyone who could have done better." His well-meaning words meant nothing under the circumstances.

The coroner's report would have called it an accidental death. No one learned how and why Stookie fell under the train's wheels. Luck wears millions of masks, including tragedy and disaster. The Stookies of the world are supposed to be always *here*, aren't they? Echo: *I don't fall where I don't want to.*

We told Reverend Framm the bad news, and he agreed that he should accompany us as we made our rounds to some of Baltic's homes. If there were any coolness between the minister and Wallace it didn't show.

After hearing the news the Horvaths collapsed in each other's arms. Mrs. Bredner bawled loudly while Bill sniffled his way to the cupboard under their kitchen sink where he kept his bottle of home brew. We declined his invitation for a drink.

Reg and Iris Woolston were also shocked to hear the news. Iris shook our hands and kissed my cheek, saying, "I'm really sorry 'cause I know he was like a brother to you." Her warmth surprised me, and it was then that my tears first threatened.

Chairman Reg exercised his father-figure role, and took me into the restaurant part of his service station. He sat me down on the rickety wicker chair and told me to stay there quietly for 15 or 20 minutes, and then join the others when I was ready.

"Every man," he said, knawing on a knuckle, "needs to be alone when he is hurting badly – and you're hurt bad – and I know what it's like to lose someone – I love Iris and she loves men – I'm in her dog house most of the time – I've lost my wife you must know unless you're totally blind – so you just sit here alone and drain your pain."

It sounded to me like he was talking about an oil change. Nonetheless, I cried wetly and hard. King Rex, asleep on the other half of the seat, kept his mange and bad breath to himself. I reach over and scratched the ugly dog's ears. As usual he was sleeping on his back with all four paws bent in the air. Apparently the world was created to admire Rex's maleness.

As we left the Woolston's I thought about how Reg was an unhappy husband and Iris an unfulfilled wife. What I had vaguely defined as Reg's back-woodsiness and Iris' horniness, I could now identify as their humanness in both cases. As a result, I felt a little more human myself.

Wall and I visited a few more homes and then returned to the teacherage. I was learning just how loved was Stookie. Obviously Mrs. Stone's comments about Stookie's popularity were wrong. We had agreed not to disturb Sheba Faye and Mrs. Stone until the morning. To hell with telling Klanty, given his earlier comment to me about Stookie.

"Just think," I said to Tall Wall, "only last night Stookie was so alive, so much fun, so in control of 'his' Baltic. He ran the baseball practice, organized the 'Bannister mile,' danced every dance at Fred Kleiner's barn dance, saw his girl home and now he's dead, gone, kicked the bucket, bought the farm, gone west, wiped out, deceased, passed away, likely 'resting' in some S.O.B's funeral parlor." Meanwhile his legs and boots were freezing stiff in Reg Woolston's locker plant. Even brilliant Wallace Talleck was shocked to hear that information.

Back at the teacherage I made tea as strong as turpentine, and the two of us sat silently, four feet in the cold oven door – Wall on his kitchen chair and yours truly in the stuffed chair – while we went through hours of "remember-the-time-that-Stookie-said-or did . . . ." Wall made two trips to his bedroom for handkerchiefs into which he blew loudly and without apology. I wasn't doing too well myself.

About 2:00 a.m. there was a light knock. We opened the front door to reveal Mrs. Stone. Without greeting us she said, "Stookie didn't make it, did he?"

After I gave her my slow response, the local WCTU president turned to Tall Wall and said, "I'll have a double brandy, a stiff one, please."

As she reached for her drink I noted for the first time that she wasn't wearing a wedding ring. The skin on her hand looked like tightly stretched parchment and her face was as gray as cold ashes. It had been 35 years since she had drunk any liquor, but she rather quickly tossed back three of Wall's best while he and I finished my latest pot of tea.

"I saw your lights on, boys, so I thought I should come over." Deep bone-weariness shadowed her eyes. The sharpness of her face now looked rounded, blunted.

"I don't sleep well at night in any case," she added. "Don't worry, in the morning I'll tell Sheba Faye about Stookie. There are many instances when only women must tell women about their men."

Wall and I were relieved. I whispered to Wallace, "Let's drink to the WCTU." His pointed shoe got me lightly but squarely on the shinbone. I got the message.

Mrs. Stone needed to talk so we moved into the parlor, as Wall called it. She repeated what she had said about the sins of her late husband and her loneliness and also retold the reason that Klanty was her private nemesis and *casus belli*. She expanded on her Cupid's role with Stookie and Sheba Faye, and reported that she had four stillborn babies before she gave birth at age 46 to her daughter.

Perhaps the booze allowed her to say too much.

"You know, these terrible deaths always happen in threes. I wonder who will be next." She sat silently for a few minutes.

"I lost another young man who was like a son I never had. I guess you fellows wouldn't know about Conrad James who was killed in Korea, would you? He was engaged to that lovely Margaret Enders who used to live with my daughter and me many years ago – but you wouldn't know about that either." Her voice was marked with as much anger as grief. I didn't correct Mrs. Stone on my knowledge of Margie and her Sarge.

The weekend was terrible, full of funeral arrangements, long and short conversations, and a deep sense of loss. The guys on the baseball team dug the grave and left it tidy and ready.

I couldn't stand the unctuous, smarmy solemnity and mannered subservience of the funeral parlor operators. The night before the funeral, at the church, Tall Wall and I heard one of the Riga morticians say nasally to his colleague, "I'll sure be glad when these next few days are over. We've got seven funerals to do in five days. We'll have to try to get back to Riga tomorrow as soon as possible."

Do butchers, professional killers and undertakers develop a certain indifference toward death? The mortician knawed nervously on a large thumbnail and spit the pieces on a small rug on the church floor. Wallace told him to pick them up and put them in his pocket. He did.

Outside the church, the man felt a little better when Wallace paid him cash for the services he and his funeral home provided. His lips and chin were glossy and pink, as if he had badly applied funeral home cosmetics to himself, and his hands fluttered as he accepted the money.

The lowery gun-metal sky foretold of a coming downpour. Thunder pounded with hard fists but nothing much resulted, and lightning transfixed our world only intermittently.

On the day of the funeral, Tuesday, I awoke with my body drenched in sweat, on the edge of a bitter, sour scream. Rain had hammered most of the night. Now it was a blowy, blustery bitchy morning. The wind increased in strength, causing one of our shingles to beat violently and arrhythmically against the roof.

You never feel so alive as when you are a pallbearer. The Horvaths had asked Wallace Talleck, Bill Bredner, Fred Kleiner, Jack Klackston, Reg Woolston and me to serve in that capacity. With Reg Wolston's co-operation, at dawn Tall Wall and I delivered by automobile Stookie's frozen legs and boots to the church. Apparently the police and the morticians thought the hospital had the legs for disposal.

Stookie's coffin had been placed in front of the pulpit during the previous night so that people could pay their respects. I don't know how to describe the strange experience of carrying a friend's body parts, opening the coffin, unwrapping the oilcloth, and adding the stiff, frozen legs and boots to Stookie's quiescent body.

Acting on Mrs. Horvath's advice, the undertaker had dressed Stookie in his usual corduroy trousers, wide belt, tightly buttoned white shirt, and baseball jacket. As noted, Wall and I had only one important thing to do, stuff the frozen boot-covered legs inside the pant legs. In the tenebrous light of the church Wall didn't notice that I quickly placed a baseball in Stookie's jacket pocket and his soft leather gloves by his side. Maybe it was childish or sacrilegious – I wasn't sure.

We took one last look at our friend's still face. At least they had removed the terrible fixed expression of pain which had been there for most of his last hours. I supposed that an undertaker was a type of beautician who tried to obscure and disguise death. There was almost a beatific contentedness about Stookie's expression. I thought about death's intractability, its imperviousness to argument. I glanced up at Wallace's face which was pale as a marble mask. He looked as dead as Stookie.

We lowered the coffin lid. No, you never feel so alive as when you are with a dead person, especially a person for whom you had great respect and affection. In the church our voices seemed to ricochet like stones in a large wood box.

In anticipation of a large attendance, some of us had arranged loudspeakers and other equipment to be placed in the nearby town hall. The hamlet's nervous air of respectability had arrived in time for the funeral. By 8:30 a.m. the church was filled. Stookie's place at the back pew was taken up by the green vase from the station, brimming with Mrs. Stone's house flowers. By 9:00 a.m., when Reverend Framm started the service, the hall was filled as well.

It was the largest funeral ever held in Baltic. League hockey and baseball teams were well represented. The engineer and the brakemen were there (it was a terrible time for them). Most Baltic students, including the ones who were bused to Riga, were also in attendance. Wallace and I arranged for Mrs. Violet Debrowski and Mrs. Janet Kleiner to take our classes on that Tuesday, but we later learned classes were hardly a qualified success. It was only to be expected.

Jack Klackston sat on one side of me and Fred Kleiner on the other and both wept through the service. Wallace, who sat next to Fred, frequently used his handkerchief. In fact, all six pallbearers were in bad shape. Mortimer Snerd, the New Year's Eve brawler, the stud with the missing front tooth, sat behind me. I didn't remember much about the details of the service, but I remembered most of Reverend Framm's comments, which I duly recorded in my diary.

> *"Let's celebrate our love for our Lord, and indeed, for our friend, Stookie. Yes, we will refer to our friend as Stookie rather than by his formal name. The memory of him will be our monument to him. A tragedy such as this slits open the false skins and coverings we wrap around ourselves in some kind of defense.*
>
> *Stookie had fibre, and we will miss his tenderness, strength, wisdom and his undiluted passion for busyness and happiness. Somehow he knew that the glue that holds us together is the need and the desire to be of service.*
>
> *Stookie's death and dying invite our repudiation and hostility. However, we must mourn and mourn now, or else you will mourn later more discordantly and for far too long. Express as much grief as you actually feel because grief has its own slow wisdom.*
>
> *There is much good to be found in an Irish wake or a Jewish shiva. Our ancestors wore sackcloth, tore their garments, fasted and publicly wept. Abraham, Jacob and David were open and unashamed in their grief. Please remember that people in mourning see life from a different vantage point. Take time now to assess your relationship with God and with other people. You should confront Stookie's death because it puts you in touch with your own mortality and limitations.*
>
> *Please remember Jesus's words as recorded in Matthew 5:4. 'Blessed are those who mourn, they shall be com-*

forted.' We have come to think of death as natural for very old people, but not for the likes of Stookie. That is not true, life is a gift, not one's private possession. No one, even a clergyman, can remove your pain. However, we can walk together and support each other with God's help."

I surely had underestimated Reverend Framm. The impact of his words on the congregation was immense and helpful. Catholics, Protestants and Jews joined in common sorrow.

The three mourners, Sheba Faye and the Horvaths, rose with the congregation to read the Twenty-third Psalm.

After the congregation sat down Reverend Framm softly cleared his throat and announced that one of Stookie's learned friends, Mr. Wallace Justinian Talleck, would deliver a short eulogy.

Believe me, I had never before experienced or heard or felt five minutes more real than those which followed. Without pause Wallace spoke to the congregation, and as he talked he looked old and shrivelled. His collar seemed too large for his neck.

Wallace compared the modern English poet, A.E. Housman, and his attitudes toward life to the young man whose body rested just below the pulpit. Both Housman and Stookie, he said, liked structure and disliked carelessness and controversies. For them life was a duty and a pleasure. Wallace then quoted from Stookie, suggesting that Housman could not have said it better: "I guess a good person is kind of noble-like when they keep doin' things for people even though it's kind of frustratin' sometimes."

Those words brought a few more snuffles and sniffles from the congregation. Our friend, claimed Wallace, believed that, in Housman's words, "Luck's a chance, trouble's sure." Stookie would have further agreed with Housman, said Wallace, who quoted: "The troubles of our proud and angry dust are from eternity, and shall not fail."

That shared fatalism allowed them, "to eat, drink, and be merry for tomorrow we die." Both men of words used charming sophistications, deceptive simplicities, catchy and quick turns or phrases, subdued melancholy and easy recklessness – one with clever written words and the other with his unschooled but beautiful, spoken words.

Housman and Stookie would agree, suggested Wall, that their different but quiet countrysides taught them fortitude in the face of haphazard cruelty. They instinctively knew that in life there is beauty and happiness to be grasped, but there is endless injustice to be endured as well. Both the poet's and our townsman's works were tinctured by quiet humor and a certain bravado. Housman was known for his verbal ferocity and formidable aloofness, but Stookie would remain loved for his kind words and openness.

Then Wallace lowered his voice and said that in spite of "the noted similarities of spirit and thought" there were major differences – many young men in Housman's poetry found suicide to be a solution, but it was a cold, cruel accident that took Stookie's life.

It seemed to me that Wallace was looking directly at Stookie's girl, Sheba Faye, when he said that.

"Yet," added Wallace, "I believe that Stookie would agree that it was just his time to go."

I was reminded of Stookie's comment which he made to me on the elevator's roof so long ago, "Everybody has a time to die ya know."

"I believe," Wallace continued, "that Housman thought the world was evil, and that people are untrue. However, Stookie knew better than all of us that that idea is false." Wallace said that "the way Stookie lived his life tells us that he knew the opposite is true, and that the world can be a decent place, and that people can be true to those they love. Stookie wouldn't say it in so many words but he actually believed that those ideas are needed for the sake of our sanity."

Wallace paused, removed his glasses briefly, and then reminded the congregation of the recent "Bannister race" which Stookie organized, of his role in baseball and hockey, of his prowess as an athlete and of his importance to the community he loved.

"Stookie," said Wallace, "was one of the most learned men I've ever known." It was then that Wall quoted from memory A.E. Housman's famous poem, "An Athlete Dying Young."

The time you won your town the race
We chaired you through the market-place;
Man and boy stood cheering by,
And home we brought you shoulder-high.

To-day, the road all runners come,
Shoulder-high we bring you home,
And set you at your threshold down,
Townsman of a stiller town.

Smart lad, to slip betimes away
From fields where glory does not stay,
And early though the laurel grows
It withers quicker than the rose.

Eyes the shady night has shut
Cannot see the record cut,
And silence sounds no worse than cheers
After earth has stopped the ears,

Now you will not swell the rout
Of lads that wore their honours out,
Runners whom renown outran
And the name died before the man.

So set, before its echoes fade,
The fleet foot on the sill of shade,
And hold to the low lintel up
The still-defended challenge-cup.

And round that early-laurelled head
Will flock to gaze the strengthless dead,
And find unwithered on its curls
The garland briefer than a girl's.

Wallace looked slowly down at Stookie's coffin. "Goodbye, townsman of our stiller town."

As Wallace walked jerkily to our pew, I dismissed Housman's platitudes. To me Stookie's death simply and cruelly meant that a good life had unnecessarily been taken – stolen – from Baltic's midst and from me.

Maggie J, accompanied by Mrs. Stone, rose to sing "Nearer My God to Thee." Later someone from the congregation in the town hall told me her voice sounded splendid, even through the loudspeakers. As she sang the last line I saw her lower lip wobble, and from my distance I could see shimmering, tearful evidence of grief brimming in her eyes. She sat down quickly.

Reverend Framm got up and gave a brief biography, fulsome in content and warmth. The choir sang its second hymn, and the service concluded with a prayer from the pulpit. The congregation from both buildings went outside the church and waited as the preacher, undertaker, and pallbearers made their way down the church stairs with the coffin and through the crowd of people to the hearse.

Because of the parking problem and the small bridge, Reverend Framm had wisely suggested that most people should walk to the cemetery. I wondered how long ago, if ever, Baltic had had a parking problem. Those of us who travelled by car waited for nearly 20 minutes for everyone to arrive at the grave-site.

Overhead the saturated dark clouds hung in the bruised and swollen sky. As we lowered Stookie to his final resting place at the foot of Elma Bea Stook's grave, a few viscid drops of rain fell and beaded the top of his casket, spangling the one wreath of flowers provided by Sheba Faye and the Horvaths. The minister said a short prayer, and then a few people dropped handfuls of soil on the coffin before they left the cemetery, on their way back to the hamlet.

Sheba Faye motioned to me, needlessly reminding me to stay. When we were alone she said in a scratchy, tight whisper, "Break it now, please." So I drew a small ball-peen hammer from the inside pocket of my jacket, and from my side pocket produced the pale green vase which had been Sheba Faye's gift to Stookie – the vase from the railway station.

She had said the vase represented all the love she had for Stookie, and "now it must be broken just like my heart." I didn't know that people, especially young people, thought and spoke that way in our day and age. She added dully, "I wish I could be dead like Stookie." I had promised myself to talk later with her about such a statement.

Sheba Faye placed the vase in a kerchief on the nearby grass. My hammer's aim was true and the young woman emptied the shards of glass on the casket below. I had to grab the full of her dress back because she almost fell into the grave.

Sheba Faye took my arm and we walked silently to Klanty's. There, with vacant eyes, Maggie J greeted us at the front door and kissed us both on the cheek. She took her sister by the hand and said goodbye to me. The three of us had decided that we would not attend the post-funeral lunch at the town hall.

Sodden with weariness, I took the long way home, the route I had used during that special night with Maggie J. This time I stopped in the middle of the high trestle, sat on the edge, and dangled my feet. I felt grainy and spent. My fear of heights was gone. So was my friend.

From my height I could see four of my baseball teammates with shovels at work, covering the grave. I decided to stay on the trestle until they finished their duty. Tomorrow we would have to add the final touches because the rain, which had been threatening since dawn, finally came like Billy-be-damned just as the four fellows left the cemetery gate. Driven by a rather sudden, hacking wind, the storm had began with gusts and spits. The northwest wind increased in strength, and the rain was hard and cold. As everyone knows, sideways-blown rain is the wettest kind. It stopped quietly, just as I reached home.

Later that night I told Tall Wall about Sheba Faye's near-fall at the cemetery. He said something about me having quick reflexes, and, of course, had a comparable story to tell me. It seems that an eighteenth century British poet, Thomas Chatterton, was walking with a friend through a London churchyard. The young poet, who was gloomy and melancholy, was reading the various tombstones when he fell into a freshly dug grave. His friend helped him out, only to have Chatterton say, "I have been at war with the grave for some time, and I find it not so easy to vanquish as I imagined." Three days later the poet killed himself.

At dusk I walked over to the town hall and brought down the flag which was flying at half-mast. I still had Stookie's keys. The slate sky promised that the rain would return.

23

Attack

He's like a walking phallic symbol.
– Malcolm Bradbury: Eating People is Wrong

Small towns aren't always the caring and warm places they are purported to be. Under Baltic's facade, I had discovered, were hates, hurts, angers, distrusts, jealousies and dark secrets. There were secrets I couldn't have anticipated when I first arrived in the hamlet called Baltic. *Was the community just a microcosm of this whole crazy world*? I angrily asked myself. However, at the same time what I had learned in my own small hometown was reinforced: people in small communities can come together with intensity and in surprising numbers if the motivation and/or leadership are right. Stookie's death brought people together in body, mind and emotion. Perhaps loyalty and sorrow can combine to become a greater power than love.

The day after Stookie's funeral, Tall Wall and I returned to our duties at the portable blues. We had been told that we were not to fly the school flag at half-mast even though Stookie had once been a student there. We did it anyway.

The morning dragged by somehow. At lunch Stookie's chair was terribly empty, but Mrs. Horvath set a place in honor of him. Mr. Horvath, delayed briefly at the post office, was a few minutes late for lunch. That mild, sweet man's dark eyes watered when he saw Stookie's ready plate, glass, cup, saucer and utensils. He looked warmly at his wife, slowly shook his head, gathered Stookie's things and took them to the cupboard. He patted his wife's shoulder and said, "No more. We have his picture and our memories, and now he's in the good earth."

My noon-hour appetite disappeared so I excused myself from the table. I sat on the garden well wondering if drowning Ophelia-like in deep well water could match the horror of Stookie's death. Ten minutes later Mr. Horvath found me. He asked that I invite any of the team ballplayers to lunch or to supper, because his God-fearing wife needed to serve others with the thing she did best.

"She needs you and those boys to replace our son lost to the Nazis." Mr. Horvath stroked his face with his large brown hands. "Stookie was like our lost son because he was so close to all the things that count in life."

For fifteen minutes or so the postmaster gave me a brief history of himself, his wife, and his people.

"We are Magyars," he said, "We are a special people. Do you know what Magyar means?"

He looked at me and for the first time I noticed he had the fierce penetrating gaze of a mystic.

"We are related to the Estonian, Samoyed and Finnish peoples. We invaded Europe from Asia around AD 900. 'Magyar' means an individual of the Mongoloid race who now deeply loves the country called Hungary. We understand why some people think power is important. They are wrong, of course."

For reasons I didn't understand, Mr. Horvath made me promise to tell no one of his family's history. He and his wife were born in Budapest, Austria-Hungary, in 1884 to Magyar and English-speaking parents. Before the Great War they met and married, then purchased land east of Budapest where they had a very profitable vegetable garden business.

Before long, five trucks and wagons filled with their vegetables regularly left their farm for the markets of Budapest. Young Horvath was in good financial shape.

In 1915, wearing his corporal's uniform, he had actually saluted "Kaiser Bill." In late 1942, because of some Jewish blood, the Horvaths and their beloved son were taken to Auschwitz. The parents somehow survived that death camp which consumed so many other Hungarian Jews, but the son did not. Three years later the still grieving parents made their way to France, and then sailed for Canada. I remembered the nine death camp photos Wallace had showed me. Mr. Horvath, the swarthy ex-corporal, had lost his son to another ex-corporal, Adolph Hitler. It became clear to me that Stookie had replaced the son they lost to the gas ovens.

Leaning on his spade, Mr. Horvath told me of the rights and wrongs of Baltic and the rest of the world. He told me nothing more of his family background. I didn't know why and how the Horvaths had come to Baltic. It seemed many of the hamlet's citizens had come from someplace else. Was that the nature of our country? With that thought in mind I returned to school for the afternoon's classes. Not surprisingly, Sheba Faye was still absent.

With rakes and hoes over our shoulders, Wallace and I left for the cemetery immediately after supper. A new, low wind honed the edge of the damp, May cold. Thunder had cracked and rumbled all afternoon across a sky of tarnished pewter. As we walked through the cemetery gates, we saw Sheba Faye on her knees beside Stookie's grave. She had already finished the smoothing-out job we had planned to do, and was now transplanting a few geraniums in the freshly turned and rain-soaked soil. Without disturbing the girl we returned home. I decided to make a cross to match the one on Mrs. Stook's grave. I wondered if humanity was the only animal that buried its dead with dignity. I asked myself, *Why can't one person come back and tell us about it? Why didn't Lazarus write his memoirs?*

Mrs. Stone called to us from her verandah, her face taut with unshed tears. She asked, "How is Stookie's grave now, boys?" Her glacial manner had disappeared, and she looked old, shrunken and weak. Since Stookie's funeral she said she had suffered a migraine which turned whispers into shouts. She told us that on the following day she, Mrs. Bredner and Mrs. Horvath planned to check on Sheba Faye, who had returned home. None of them would go to "that Klanty's place" alone.

Tall Wall and I glanced at each other, and knew what we had to do. We replaced our tools in the school's shed, washed up, and headed for Klanty's. Maybe there was something we could do for Sheba Faye during her long hours of sorrow. After all, I was now the only young friend left for the "girl on a swing." Was I wise enough to counsel her?

Wall agreed to collect Reverend Framm and meet me at Klanty's. Maggie J, with whom I'd not been able to visit during those terrible days, had left for Vyborg on the night of Stookie's funeral. My dithery-dreamy thoughts of her now seemed silly somehow.

I was at least forty yards from Klanty's house when a short scream reached my ears. The sound seemed to come from the rear of the house. In near-Bannister time I reached the front door and entered the house to see that the throne chair was empty. I heard a muffled cry from behind the girls' closed bedroom door. It was locked. Another scream, louder and longer this time. It was not a difficult thing to shoulder the door and burst the light lock. In fact, my momentum ended me on the bedroom floor, Hollywood style.

Sheba Faye, her mouth working softly, stood before me stripped naked except for one sagging, gray ankle sock. Her hands, which hung loosely by her side, opened and closed, and she made no attempt to cover herself. I sensed the red, sexual appetite in the room.

Klanty, also naked, rose from the far side of the first single bed. He stood very quickly and made two drunken stilt-like lurches towards me, then stopped. He was quaking and quivering like an excited bull. His hard pecker was the mere length of three thimbles my grandma used to use. Sweat glistened on his heavy chest pelt. He examined me with the controlled purposefulness of a cougar about to get his bush rabbit.

Anger replaced my gelid fear. I yelled at Klanty and charged. His right fist hit the centre of my chest like a flat rock. A short left a split second later caught me in the solar plexus.

My belly became a sac of liquid pain. My knees loosened. Soft putty replaced the marrow in my bones. Even the panicky strength a drowning person knows couldn't raise my arms in self-defense – like tentacles they had no bones.

With the flat of his two fat, wide hands he slapped my face *one-two* and I fell at his feet.

"Want some more, kid, to teach you to mind your own damn business?" Klanty grabbed a handful of my hair and clothes, flipped me over on my stomach, and pushed my face hard to the floor. I heard him grunt with the effort. Then I heard my nose breaking like cornflakes under a slow, heavy rolling pin.

Klanty ground my face to the floor, slowly and heavily. My blood felt slippery on my forehead and chin. Would he slam me hard and get it over with? Briefly, I thought he might puncture me with that knife he kept on his throne chair. Then with two hands he twisted my left arm behind my back and jerked harply. A hot wire stretched from my wrist to my shoulder. A ty, swirling, purple montage floated out there somewhere. uick red pain, silence and blackness.

24

Rope

I have been half in love with easeful Death.
– John Keats

What happened next I learned later. Wallace Talleck and Reverend Framm had arrived a few minutes later. Sheba Faye sank to the bed, screaming and clutching a small, round pillow to her body.

As Wall and the Reverend rushed through the bedroom door the big man was ready. His ham-sized fist met the glass shelf of Wall's jaw with such force that the tall man's feet left the floor as if he were jumping backwards. Wallace was out cold on the floor. Then in sheer desperation the short, tubby preacher drove two stiff fingers directly into Wayne Klanty's eyes. Klanty, temporarily blinded, roared like the animal he was. Feeling his streaming eyes with the flat of his hands, he waved his huge arms and fists, trying to reach Framm. The preacher buried the tip of his small right shoe deeply in Klanty's manhood. Klanty howled and puked beside the bed. Rising, he shook his head, rubbed his clearing eyes, and turned to the preacher. "Framm," he said, "you are about to make your wife a widow."

Those were Klanty's last words for some time. Sheba Faye picked up Maggie J's portable record player and with a sideways swing caught her stooping stepfather flush on his left temple. (Stookie would have been proud of her baseball swing.) Klanty slumped down on the floor.

Framm, as they say, rose to the occasion. First he covered Sheba Faye with one of her own rough blankets. Then he dragged the unconscious Klanty across two linoleum floors to the front room and used his own tie to secure Klanty's neck to the heavy leg of the oak table. The good minister tore strips from tea towels and tied Klanty's ankles tightly together, securing the man's wrists behind the table leg. Another strip of cloth provided a gag. The minister found Klanty's shirt and used it to cover him as he lay naked in a fetal position. The rapist was going nowhere.

Reverend Framm phoned the Riga police, then Reg Woolston, who ran the town. It didn't take long for Chairman Reg to bring half the Baltic-area citizens to the Klanty place, although this time no one rang the church bell.

Reverend Framm poured a pitcher of cold water slowly over Tall Wall. No one had to awaken me – pain did. My guts ached and my arm and scrambled-egg nose hurt like hell. Jack Klackston said he would guard the naked and trussed Klanty until the police arrived, and then he ordered everyone else out of the crowded house.

"We'll attend to you soon," said Tall Wall to me, lightly touching his sore chin. "But our first priority is Sheba Faye."

Apparently sometime during the chaos Sheba Faye had quietly slipped out, telling the good Reverend she was going to Mrs. Stone's. When we arrived at our neighbor's house, we found Mrs. Stone had placed her charge in a hot tub. We could hear a scraping sound coming from the bathroom.

"I gave her a dipper and the poor girl keeps pouring water over her head and shoulders." Through the bathroom door we heard the words, over and over: "I'm dirty, I'm dirty, I'm dirty."

I was in considerable pain, so Wallace drove Sheba Faye, Mrs. Stone and me to the city, where doctors confirmed that the girl had not been raped. Apparently my arrival at Klanty's place had been just in time.

Both Sheba Faye and I spent five days in the hospital. In less than one hour the cartilaginous tissues of my nose were fixed – a bit crookedly, I think – and a large, heavy cast, supported by a frayed sling, stretched from my elbow to my wrist.

Sheba Faye received counselling and advice from a psychiatrist, and from another young woman who had been raped four years earlier. Sheba Faye came to my room during visiting hours and reported the sessions to me, and so gradually the story of her attack came to light. When I asked, she assured me that never before had Klanty beaten or molested her.

She told the psychiatrist how, the day of Klanty's attack, he had read and drank most of the afternoon, and begun to drink even more heavily after supper. Sheba Faye had just finished her sponge bath in the bedroom before her babysitting job at the Bredner's when Klanty burst into her room. She was wearing only her underwear. The large man told her "with your Stook out of the way you're the woman around my house now. You know what that means." In mere seconds he had torn her panties and bra from her. He slapped her hard and threw her on the bed. Apparently it was at that moment that I had arrived.

The psychiatrist explained that Klanty's attempted rape was not a sexual act but an act of violence and aggression. The other young victim claimed that the crime against her had affected her in spirit, body, memory, and in her ability to sleep.

During one visit with me Sheba Faye brought the other rape victim with her, and that young woman insisted that Sheba Faye was not to be left alone when she returned home. The woman suggested that Sheba Faye should have friends watch her carefully because she might do the very thing she herself had once tried – suicide.

Daily Reverend Framm drove to the city to visit Sheba Faye. On one occasion he brought Mrs. Bredner and Mrs. Horvath with him. They came by my room for a short visit, and I began to realize how important these people were to me.

During this time, two detectives interviewed me on three separate occasions about the attack. I phoned my folks to report that my nose had been broken and my arm hurt.

"It's baseball season," I lied, not wanting to worry them. I planned to tell them the truth once the smoke cleared. Much to my parents' pleasure, I announced that, after thinking things over, I had decided to leave Baltic at the end of the school term and attend university. Obviously unhappy events had influenced my plans.

Klanty awaited trial in a small jail not a mile from the hospital. The *show cause* process was quickly concluded, and Klanty was not allowed bail. For some reason he insisted I pay him a visit. I agreed to, partly from curiosity, as soon as I was out of the hospital.

From behind heavy protective screen and glass, Klanty told me how he had been out on one of his evening walks, and had seen me watching his stepdaughter, dancing and moving to music. In that moment I felt like I should be on the other side of that protective glass along with Klanty.

"You know the night I mean," he said, looking me straight in the eye. "Boy, you're the person who started those visits to my house. I was alone before you came to Baltic. For that reason I won't squeal on you."

I was beginning to feel almost grateful toward the big man when he added, "But you know, young feller, she looked pretty damn good through the window, didn't she?" He laughed, spraying the glass between us. "Her dancing like that gave me ideas, that's for sure." His eyes were as merciless and warm as drill bits. I couldn't leave him fast enough.

On a beautiful late May evening Wallace arrived at the hospital in his sports car for Sheba Faye and me. The psychiatrist had a few parting words for us, saying that Sheba Faye was "a tough young customer and would be fine in time." Her words quieted the anxiety the other young rape victim had aroused in my mind, but didn't completely erase it. I still worried about my young student.

Sheba Faye quickly got in the back seat of the little car and locked both back doors. I sat in front with Wallace as he drove at his usual sedate 50 mph. It was a long, quiet ride to Baltic. At dusk we dropped Sheba Faye at Mrs. Stone's.

During the next few days I rested, recuperated, and did a lot of thinking. The purple loops under my eyes were gradually disappearing, my nose had once again survived, and my imprisoned arm was progressing as well as one might expect, with a little help from painkillers. Memories of the success of Sheba Faye's ear operation, the fun we had on the hockey ice and baseball diamond, new friendships, and especially a sense of belonging, were working at changing my mind about leaving. Why not stay in Baltic, preferably with MJ at my side? Bow Tie couldn't match my prowess, appeal and youth, could he? And with Tall Wall as my colleague, everything would be fine.

I was beginning to accept more readily the faults of others, and of myself. The latter was becoming a full-time job. But after placing my faults alongside the animal wickedness of Klanty, they looked more modest and forgivable. Too often Klanty's suety face sort of swam across my eyescreen, his stubby hard fingers and freshly cleaned nails acting as quotation marks to either side of his large, fat ears. A crazy description, but a true one.

Baltic rightly considered Reverend Framm to be a genuine hero. Even Jack Klackston, pitcher, brawler, and elevator man, went to church the next Sunday. Jack, not exactly a biblical scholar, nonetheless informed me that "Jesus had done the same thing as the Reverend with the temple's money changers. Framm has got balls, for sure," he concluded.

A week of rest did me some good, and the next Saturday I was at my school desk, preparing for my return to work the following week. A hot, dog-day somnolence had descended that afternoon when Sheba Faye walked noiselessly into my classroom. I don't know how long she had stood there before I noticed her. I was startled by a movement and her soft, unexpected voice.

"It's a rotten world, isn't it?" she said. She spun the globe at my elbow. "I'd just as soon leave it for good."

I got a kink in my neck as I quickly raised my head to look at her. It was the first time I'd seen her since her return to Baltic. She looked terrible – drained, disillusioned, abysmally weary, haggard. Old at seventeen. She was wearing her grays and off-whites again.

Slowly, Sheba Faye said that she would never again return to the Klanty place. She had taken Mrs. Stone with her and retrieved a few things she wanted. She handed me a record. It was *I'm in the Mood for Love*.

"I think you and my sister love this phonograph record so I'm giving it back to you before some policeman seizes everything for evidence or something."

I realized then that her cadence and use of words resembled those of Stookie. Brokenly she said, "I lost my everything when they buried Stookie and . . . when I was . . . hurt." Sheba Faye spoke almost as if she was in a trance, seeing bad shadows from her past. The psychiatrist had told Wallace, Reverend Framm and me that she had tried, unsuccessfully, to get Sheba Faye to use the words "death" and "rape." It was important that Sheba Faye confront their reality.

Trying to reassure her and instead sounding perhaps a bit patronizing, I reminded her that both of us would be ready to return to classes on Monday. No response. Of course: how was she to face her classmates and the citizens of Baltic, given her recent humiliation and the countless earlier ones, for that matter? Everyone in town knew that she had been stripped naked by Klanty, whose rape attempt was the talk at most supper tables.

Sheba Faye left my classroom as quietly as she had entered. I continued to work at my desk, my mind more on Sheba Faye than on my work. Someone would have to talk to her – could Wallace help, or Reverend Framm? I certainly didn't feel up to it. Maybe Sheba Faye should return to the city for more counselling? Through the window I saw the swing ropes move, and knew that Sheba Faye was on her swing, but I didn't hear her humming this time.

The girl's visit, my aching arm, and the pain killers ruined my concentration, and in a few minutes I raised my eyes to survey my academic kingdom. I gave the globe a fast spin. Where was my place and what was my role? Did it really matter? Was life a cosmic joke? *You're supposed to be a teechur, ya know*. Maybe Klanty's shrug was the only sensible response to the world. An old Sunday school song returned to me and I wondered, if God saw the little sparrow fall, did He see the fall of Stookie? I felt a bit childish for thinking about my Sunday School days. From my desk I looked through the windows to my right to the brilliantly blue sky. The answers were up there, weren't they? I said a silent prayer, halfway between a cry of help and desperation.

My eyes fell back on the papers before me, then I glanced for the hundredth time at the names of my students written on my cast. It took several seconds for what I had seen through the windows a moment ago to register in my dulled brain. A second glance through the window confirmed the message: there was only one strand of rope hanging from the swing where there should have been two. The remaining rope was tied in the middle of the swing's crossbar. Seated, I couldn't see what was below the end of the rope.

Rising quickly I shouted, *Sheeeeba Faaaaye*! Because of my forward momentum my right knee caught on the desk's open drawer, and I went down hard, hitting my head on clever little Marsha Fowler's desk. My damaged left arm slammed to the floor and a scream of pain escaped my throat. Down the rows of desks, down the three front steps, I lurched rather than ran.

As I rounded the corner her back was to me. Sheba Faye Klanty's feet were three feet from the ground and her head was slanted away from the school building. The swing seat was lying on the ground. She must have cut the rope to use as a noose, but I couldn't spot her knife.

I hobbled to her and took her weight below her hips with my good arm. She was warm enough to be alive, and I prayed that she was. She smelled terrible.

My useless left arm was of no assistance. I yelled, shouted, screamed for help, but no one heard me. As I held Sheba Faye close to my face I looked upwards to see signs of life, but her bunched-up bloused prevented me from seeing her face.

No choice. My arm couldn't hold her up any longer. I lowered her gently and ran-stumbled to the portable blue. My Boy Scout knife was still in place. I returned to Sheba Faye and, opening the knife with my teeth, stood on my tip toes. Even jumping I couldn't reach the rope with the blade. I threw my arm sling to the ground and tried to use my damaged left arm to hold Sheba Faye to my body while attempting to use my right hand to cut the rope. For only three seconds I held her as the excruciating pain under my cast coruscated from shoulder to finger tips. I screamed and took her weight again with my good arm. No good.

Back to the school for a chair. Keep your knife open. Forget your banged, wobbly knee and redamaged left arm. Go back. Stand on chair. Cut rope. Catch the girl with bad arm as gravity claims her. Drop the knife and take her with your good arm. Lower her to the ground, loosen the rope around her neck, yell for help. Feel her pulse, pinch her nose and open her mouth. Blow. Pump her back. Smell her smells. Weep. Wipe your bleeding nose on your sleeve. Keep blowing and pumping, blood and tears of impotence on her face and neck. Was her neck broken? Was she dead?

It was Bill Bredner who a thousand years later pulled me from Sheba Faye. "Let her be," he said with gravel in his voice. "She's gone."

Bill gently closed Sheba Faye's staring eyes, placed his light jacket over the dead girl's cyanosed face, and seated me on the grass. I leaned against the building's outside wall where I tried to vomit myself inside out. Bill contacted Wallace Talleck who in turn communicated with the Riga Police, Mr. Framm and Mrs. Stone. No one else in the hamlet could see or hear what was happening.

In fifteen minutes the Riga police arrived, their turbulent sirens going full bore. Dalmond Doby, newsman, arrived a few minutes later.

The officer who had arrested Klanty just a few weeks earlier turned to me to ask why I hadn't seen Sheba Faye climb the swing's uprights – they were clearly in my line of sight. The questions went on and on. Didn't you hear or see anything? Didn't she even hint that she was contemplating suicide? Or did you even bother to listen to the kid? I could only answer each question with a dull, inadequate "no." Is there any emotion heavier than guilt?

The authorities confirmed that my 17 year-old grade eight student had climbed the swing's uprights and cut the ropes, then secured the noose from where she sat high on the crossbar before she jumped. As her last involuntary act her sphincter muscle opened and she defecated even as death arrived. Later the police found Klanty's large knife where she had thrown it into some nearby weeds.

The ill-formed noose had allowed her to live briefly after she jumped. My school had provided the gallows. And some of the motivation? If I had been half bright wouldn't I have noticed her actions and saved her? Echo: *I just as soon leave it for good.*

It was a late night. The coroner stayed for ninety minutes, then declared that no autopsy would be required. After the police finished their questioning, investigating and photographing, they concluded that Stookie's death, Klanty's attack, and Sheba Faye's suicide were connected. I noticed they took the noose with them when they left the schoolyard.

Later Nurse Doby arrived and gave me a powerhouse pain killer that almost put me to sleep. Finally, at 1:30 a.m. Wallace was allowed to take the body away. Moving like an over-the-hill athlete, he carried the dead girl down to Mrs. Stone's. Here was the same man who ran while carrying an injured Stookie, who once picked me up and held me, frozen with fear and feet dangling before slamming me to the floor – but now Sheba Faye's limp, cooling body was almost too much for him.

Wallace was again the one who contacted the Riga funeral home, but there was no answer, so he phoned a city funeral home. The manager there assured him his people would be at his service first thing in the morning.

It was very clear that I wouldn't be returning to work on Monday. My left arm was in bad shape, and my ineluctable guilt didn't make me feel any better.

Reverend Framm, the Horvaths, the Woolstons, the Kleiners, the Bredners, Helen Fowler, Mrs. Stone, Wallace and I, the unlikely and unlucky thirteen, gathered in the teacherage parlor where Mrs. Horvath served scalding tea and scones. Next door Sheba Faye Klanty grew cold and stiff. Mrs. Stone and Mrs. Horvath had bathed and dressed her. It seemed right that she be given peace and quiet and aloneness amid Mrs. Stone's heavy, Victorian furniture.

We all knew that other Baltic lights were burning. Other late night conversations were stretching into early morning. It was as if a slow miasma hung over the hamlet like marsh gas. A dozen or so people came by, mouthed words to us, and yes, special words to me – the clumsy, slow, unobserving, ineffectual, worthless, man-boy with the Boy Scout knife. Everyone seemed to agree that the coroner, the police and Mr. Framm had made the right decision about keeping the body in Baltic until Maggie J arrived from Vyborg. It was strange. A few hours earlier we had referred to her as Sheba Faye, but now we spoke of "the body" and "the deceased."

I have to say that there were a few phony hugs and handshakes that night. As Mrs. Horvath reached to give me a genuine hug, her sleeves rolled part way to her elbow and I saw the pale blue Auschwitz numbers engraved on her arm.

The police had not allowed me to phone Maggie J until well after midnight, but she was due to arrive soon. While we waited for her, I became aware of certain animosities and distrusts developing between the people assembled there. Did the day's horrible event allow those angers to escape?

Soon the room was sour with vehemence. Iris Woolston, in a snarly way, suggested that it would be better to get a singer she knew from Riga for Sheba Faye's funeral or else a certain war-time songstress would want to sing a solo during the service. Mrs. Bredner replied by telling Iris not to worry, *she'd* be sitting beside *her* man, but by which man would Iris sit? Iris turned to Reg, who made a brief study of the floor, shook himself, and told Mrs. Bredner instead of blathering so much she should be home doing what she did best, breeding more ugly, noisy kids. Now that didn't sound like the Chairman Reg I knew. Bill Bredner scratched under the elastic of his eyepatch, stood up, and told "Big Cheese Woolston" he only thought he cut a wide swath around the town, so he'd better tell that frump of his to shut up.

Quietly I asked Reverend Framm to stop the two-bit bickering. It was such small stuff compared to the gravity of the day. He whispered to me, "Let them get the poison out. Healing will result."

Then Mrs. Stone appointed herself as peacemaker by telling Mrs. Bredner she didn't sing all that badly, and suggested to

Iris that the Lord, if asked, would forgive her transgressions. My tall, bony neighbor-lady hardly helped the situation. Iris told Mrs. Stone it was no wonder that no one gave a tinker's damn about her and Mrs. Bredner nodded in agreement. "Now, now friends," said Chairman Reg, "there's no need for profanity." Fred Kleiner told the three women to shut up because they sounded like heifers in heat. With her head turning like a gun turret, Mrs. Stone fired back, saying "it's no wonder you stubble jumpers live near the nuisance grounds."

When Mrs. Horvath suggested quietly to no one in particular that they were acting like children, Mrs. Bredner responded with "you're a few pickles short of a jar – you have no children, so how do you know how children act?" Was I the only one there who knew of the Horvath's difficulty in Nazi Germany? Helen Fowler, dispenser of iron will to ill-behaved teenagers and usually a strong talker, said nothing. She really disappointed me. Her lips were tight, and her face looked desiccated. Again I looked to Reverend Framm, and then to Wallace to stop this insane infighting. Both men put their fingers to their lips as if asking for silence from me. The whole thing was a Chaplinesque blend of sick humor and pathos.

Mr. Horvath then spoke his first words of the evening. He leaned over to his wife, gently pushed up the left sleeve of her sweater, and said, "Our martyred son had one of these."

Everyone but me gasped when they saw the blue tattooed numbers. Mr. Horvath said, "Now our world has lost another child, Sheba Faye, and you people fight with all the hate you can find. Be ashamed. May God forgive you." He fixed his eyes on his wife's face and haltingly asked her to forgive him for breaking his promise.

He turned to us and said that before he came to Baltic he had been a lot of things in his life – a student, failed poet, sanitation worker, soldier, vegetable farmer, prisoner, displaced person and grieving father. "This whole world is bigger than your hearts," he concluded. "Be ashamed."

I was ashamed in the same way the prisoner felt guilty in Kafka's *Trial*. That individual didn't seem to be able to find out the nature of his guilt, either.

There was a silence and we all heard the car approaching. A car door chunked shut and there was the sound of high heels running up the wood sidewalk. As Maggie J entered our teacherage only Mrs. Stone, with a nervous twitch to one side of her mouth, rose to greet her. They stood at arm's length, motionless as cataleptics, and then embraced, silently and long.

Then the young beautiful woman did a remarkable thing. She shook hands firmly with the dozen people present, walking in a somnambulistic, jerky way from person to person, saying "thank you for coming" to each. There was no extra pause as she greeted me. I could see those dark lashes over dark blue eyes holding back tears. Something tiny but strong reached inside me and pinched my heart. Without another word she and Mrs. Stone left to visit the body of her beloved Sheba Faye.

After they returned it seemed important to everyone there that all the duties and funeral details be discussed. Maggie J uttered a soft "thank you" after each suggestion. Obviously Reverend Framm believed that it was good therapy for MJ to have this experience because it detracted from the horror of her sister's death. The planning and discussion acted as catharsis to me as well.

Reverend Framm quietly took charge, his eyes smoothing into blank neutrality. His first words of the evening were, "If one cannot love, one cannot mourn – all of us here mourn." He said that Margaret Jane Enders, the dead girl's only surviving relative, was our first priority. MJ kept her reddening eyes level. It was agreed that Mrs. Stone and the minister would organize Sheba Faye's funeral service. I was to make what they call a short presentation from the pulpit. Wallace, a model of diplomacy, asked if he might have permission to take care of any financial considerations. Bill Bredner, with the help of others, would prepare her grave – next to Stookie's.

At one point Wallace, Reverend Framm, and I were gathered in the kitchen, discussing plans, when Reverend Framm said, "Mr. Talleck, I strongly disagree with what you do, but your acts of generosity are those of a Christian gentleman. Your offer tonight and your payment for Mr. Stook's funeral are acknowledged. Your generous ways must please God. I shall pray even harder that you will change your 'secret' ways."

The shocked Wallace Talleck slowly collapsed to the floor like a Daddy Long Legs Spider, crossed his long legs, put his elbows on his knees, and his hands on his long face.

"Yes, Sir, please do," mumbled my remarkable friend, "if that's what you think you must do." In a moment he rose, his eyes wet behind his thick glasses. Then the short, fat, preacher and the tall, skinny teacher embraced warmly.

How in hell had Reverend Framm known about Wallace's homosexuality? As far as I knew, Wallace had told no one in Baltic except me. Now I understood something about the aloofness Mr. Framm had always displayed towards Tall Wall. The preacher had special radar.

The three of us returned to the parlor with two more pots of hot tea. Reverend Framm served the tea and then asked for everyone's attention. He began to speak, and every word appeared to be like lifting a heavy rock.

"Let me speak without clerical banalities. It is important for Margaret Jane that we talk about the death of Sheba Faye. We must encourage and allow Margaret Jane to dwell upon her sorrow."

Everyone there looked as though they were in agreement and Reverend Framm continued.

"As people who cared for Sheba Faye we have to try to understand her motivation. Suicide is as old as Cain. Depressed people are often unable to express their real emotions. They say and do things the rest of us ignore or misunderstand."

"All of us are part of her death, even though we deny it, even though we deny our own guilt. Indifference led to this disaster. It is typical that Sheba Faye retreated from her community and her so-called friends, because, often, they appeared to be her enemies. We share a common sin of omission. Yes, I include you, Margaret Jane, you teachers, you neighbors and myself. We missed the signals."

No one had missed more signals than her own teacher.

"Youngsters in school," Reverend Framm continued, "must share the guilt. Who among us had not heard people call her 'Sheep Face' and the like, and who among us did something about it?"

Helen Fowler had, but as I watched her face her expression did not change.

"We must not forget that a sheep or a lamb – timid and gentle creatures – are often pictured with the Good Shepherd, our Lord. For our own sweet lamb, Sheba Faye, the prospect of death held fewer terrors than did life. So in two days I must conduct a funeral service for that poor child of God."

Her voice quavering, Maggie J interrupted. "But surely," she said, "life should not end like my sister's. My stepfather cannot be correct." MJ's mouth was twisted like that of a crying child. "Please tell me otherwise." MJ paused for the longest time before turning directly to me and asking in a broken, husky voice, "Where were you when my sister was suffering? Were you both blind and deaf? I only pray I can forgive you for your negligence." Her words cut deeply, but no one there disagreed with her.

Was she wrong? Apparently it didn't matter that Klanty took me apart during my defense of Sheba Faye. But, damn it, I *had* failed Sheba Faye over the months, and certainly on the days and moments preceding her suicide. My earlier small victory in getting her hearing restored looked so insignificant now. I recalled my smugness.

Then Mr. Horvath put his hand on my shoulder, turned to the grieving young woman, and said, "Margaret, there will be another time. We all hurt. Yes, we all do."

By unspoken consent everyone rose to leave. Mrs. Stone had Maggie J lie down on our couch, then informed us she would sit with the body of Sheba Faye for a while.

The pearly luminosity of dawn couldn't keep us awake. Exhaustion and intensity had left Tall Wall silent. He looked bleached out, a spectre, and went to bed without a word. Anomie engulfed me. I felt a chill no rising sun could dispel. Life had lost its sharp edges.

Maggie J fell asleep on the sofa. I removed her shoes and tucked a warm blanket around her, and placed my pillow under her head. She suddenly moved, pulling my head and shoulders down to her with such compulsive insistence that I had to sink to my knees beside her. Her strength hurt the back of my neck. Hers was an act of tremendous sorrow, not of love. Great tearing sobs tried to rip her apart. My heart squeezed for her. After what seemed a long, long time her sobs tapered off to irregular hitchings of her chest and exhaustion claimed her. She was away for as long as the gods willed. I knew that our "romance" was finished. I was the guy who allowed her sister to commit suicide, wasn't I?

25

Reflection

Reflection, you may come to-morrow.
– Percy Bysshe Shelley: To Jane: the Invitation

After taking two more painkillers I lay in my bed, kicked my shoes to the floor, and tried to understand, to use Stookie's words, "people, thinkin' and things." I added a fourth: events. Those four – people, thinking, things and events – had surely crisscrossed the lives of Klanty's daughters. I wondered if there really were cause and result. Was there a plan to it all? Was Reverend Framm correct when he said our lives could be painful mysteries acceptable only by minute revelation of His divine design? Or did God say to Stookie and to Sheba Faye, "That's enough for both of you?" Most of us carried on our lives as if we lived permanently on the earth, and as if everything began and ended there.

My thoughts returned to Sheba Faye and her suicide. People had teased and scorned her most of her life. And, damn it, a dead soldier and the sweetheart he 'most wanted to take down a coal mine' had birthed Sheba Faye, nourished her, loved her, hugged and kissed her, changed her, presented her with a tricycle. They must be weeping in their graves, even as I was weeping on my pillowless bed.

Perhaps it was anger that dried my tears. I couldn't forget that "Sheep Face" (there, I said it!) took her life not fifteen feet from me. Why did I have to be the guilty one? Her dead weight, her bulging dead eyes, her terrible body waste smells – all sorts of scenes were replayed on my eye screen. One of those scenes even featured Sheba Faye dancing naked to the music of *I'm in the Mood for Love.*

I was glad to be alone so that I could marinate in my own juices of despair, anger, frustration and guilt. I heard an echo in my head: *I wish I could be dead like Stookie.* For awhile Stookie and Sheba Faye came together on my eye screen, and I realized there had been such a waste of warmth, secrets, firm flesh, young juices and a long future. I knew that it would take a long, long time for my knots to untie. Finally sleep poured all over me and, fully clothed, I lay like a dead thing for six hours. I dreamed once more about that fat, old warlock who placed magnets under the school swings.

When I awoke just before noon, I found a note from MJ telling me she was at the Bredners. Tall Wall was at school. A thorough sponge bath, a change of clothes, and Mrs. Horvath's lunch made the world look a little better.

When I returned to the teacherage after lunch, I found Delmond Doby out front, note pad in hand. He said he had decided to write a series of articles on teenage suicide and wanted to interview me. He maintained that teen suicide should be of concern to journalists, as well as the clergy, educators, parents and the public. The medical profession and the clergy, he said, were still pretty much in the dark about the whole problem. The world of academics, he said, had even fewer answers. He didn't leave out his own profession, saying that journalists were among the best and the worst of the lot – too many people in the media sacrificed sensitivity and truth in order to get the big story or the quotable quote.

His gentle comments and probing questions helped me to put Sheba Faye's demise in perspective. After the interview, conducted on the front steps of the teacherage, he asked me to accompany him to the site of Sheba Faye's suicide. I forced myself to return, for Sheba Faye's sake. Bill Bredner, thank goodness, had repaired the swing.

Under a slowly westering sun Delmond took a number of pictures of the schoolyard before he, Tall Wall and I returned to the teacherage. Reverend Framm was there to discuss the sermon for Sheba Faye's funeral, but after hearing about Delmond's articles, a debate broke out about suicide.

Tall Wall quoted Arthur Schopenhauer, a renowned nineteenth century German philosopher, who said, "They tell us that suicide is the greatest piece of cowardice . . . that suicide is wrong; when it is quite obvious that there is nothing in the world to which every man has a more unassailable title than to his own life and person." Was Sheba Faye a coward?

Reverend Framm, a bit flustered, argued that our lives are gifts from God – gifts of grace not to be destroyed by ourselves. In turn he quoted St. Augustine, who said, "Patricide is more wicked than homicide but suicide is most wicked of all."

From his suit jacket, Delmond Doby removed a folded piece of light blue paper which he identified as part of the research he had begun for his suicide articles. Leo Tolstoy, the Russian genius who lived from 1828 to 1910, had an even more cogent statement: "The possibility of killing one's self is a safety valve. Having it, man has no right to say life is unbearable."

I had nothing to add. While their arguments did not put suicide in a favorable light, at least they made the act appear less of a sin or a crime than I had been raised to believe. Something allowed me to reach back to my teachers' college philosophy class, and I spoke the words of the French positivist philosopher, Auguste Comte: obviously in the case of Sheba Faye, 'the dead govern the living.' My three companions stopped in their tracks. Tall Wall reached for a volume, flipped a few pages, and whispered, "Bright Boy, you've actually said something significant." Cleaning his glasses for the *n*th time that afternoon, he suggested that humankind has always been unsure about the issue of suicide. I had been told that my great grandfather's cousin, a suicide, was buried in Scotland outside the perimeter of the town's cemetery in nonsanctified ground.

Two days later we buried Sheba Faye Klanty beside Wilbur Adolph Stook. The congregation was small – only 19 people attended the service. School was out for the day, but not one of Sheba Faye's classmates came. We heard someone had arranged for the kids to go swimming in Riga. Margaret Jane Enders, her eyelids bruised with sorrow and fatigue, was the only relative who mourned the dead girl.

The funeral directors from the city were sincere, professional, and kind. Mrs. Bredner, accompanied by Mrs. Stone, sang the solos of my choice – "The Old Rugged Cross" and "Shall We Gather at the River?" while I wept. For all I know Mrs. Bredner might have hit some correct notes. The only person to offer me condolences was Casey, who was saved from drowning by Bill Bredner. Casey was now a grade 12 student and our second baseman. His look was direct and he hugged me long and hard. Was I or would I ever be as wise as "young Casey?"

Gradually the words that Reverend Framm intoned snapped me out of my sorrow and self-pity.

Our thoughts and inner hurt today rest with Sheba Faye Klanty. On the surface we are thinking of her – her life, her gifts, the beauty of her love for Stookie. Underneath we are wrestling with how she died. Can it really be true?

Jesus was wise when he linked truth with freedom. He understood that distortion and denial take truth away. He knew that dealing honestly with life, even when it was hard, was the better way. He knew that truth brings freedom, so He clearly taught that.

In these moments, as we give our attention to Sheba Faye and her life, it is right for us to acknowledge what is true. In the end, for her, life was too heavy, too despairing to endure, and when darkness was her only friend, Sheba Faye ended her time on this earth.

Suicide is something that happens in slow motion. The drive to live takes a long time to destroy. Her stepfather is not the only author of her distress. Some of us in this house of God added to her unhappiness – or else we ignored her. Inherently, life is too valuable to be easily squandered. And neither did Sheba Faye just wake up one morning and suddenly decide that "life isn't worth living any more, so I'm going to end it today." I believe that her most destructive and corrosive illness was loneliness.

Sheba Faye's life was a journey – a hard journey. It was one filled with pain, disdain, rejection and scorn. I can tell you that she deeply loved Wilbur Adolph Stook – the young man this community so recently lowered to his own place of rest.

Some religious thinkers contend that taking one's own life is an unforgivable sin. And in so doing, they logically conclude that people who decide to end their lives don't deserve to spend forever with their Creator. They reason that this ultimate act to deny life forfeits God's invitation to share life after death with Him.

On Sheba Faye's behalf and for our own reassurance, we have a strong basis to reject both the idea and the line of logic that would wrestle her out of God's care and eternal compassion. Life with God after we leave this earth is never deserved. It is not earned or merited. Life with God for those on this earth and after death is a mercy. It is a gift of grace.

Life wounded Sheba Faye. We know that. In the end, her wounds were more traumatic than her spirit could bear. Our solace on her behalf today – and also as we carry on facing the truth about our own woundedness – is to believe the scriptures as they speak to us in these moments. God walked with Sheba Faye during her scarred life. In her darkest night, when she could bear no more pain, God was with her. God's final rescue is from death itself. Today Sheba Faye has been rescued. All tragedies can be illuminating.

It seemed to me that Reverend Framm had said exactly the right things. He announced that I would make a short comment on Sheba Faye Klanty's behalf. I had thought about this "presentation" for a long time, and the best I could produce was the simple, beautiful "Prayer of St. Francis of Assisi:"

Lord, make me an instrument of thy peace. Where there is hatred, let me sow love; where there is injury, pardon; where there is doubt, faith; where there is despair, hope; where there is sadness, joy; where there is darkness, light.

O Divine Master, grant that I may not so much seek to be consoled, as to console; not so much to be understood, as to understand; not so much to be loved, as to love. For it is in giving that we receive, it is in pardoning that we are pardoned, it is in dying that we are born again to eternal life.

Five cars transported people to the cemetery. Sheba Faye's casket was identical to Stookie's. So were the pallbearers. Bill, Wallace and other friends filled in the grave. Now someone would have a second cross to build.

The June sun stays up late. Tall Wall and I took a long walk up and down the wood sidewalks of Baltic, purposely staying away from the railroad tracks and the cemetery bridge. A silent walk through a silent hamlet. When we returned home we sat on our front step and waited for the dark. Mrs. Stone's window was open and we could hear her phone ringing. From the porch we saw Maggie J answer the call. In a few moments, suitcase in hand, she hurried to her car, her heels making fast *tock-tock* sounds on the sidewalk. MJ left throwing up gravel from the heavy tires of the car. No goodbyes. Not a glance our way. Would I ever see her again?

When it was nearly pitch dark I heard a meadowlark whose throaty music no longer 'tasted' good.

With written permission from central office, I decided to leave Baltic as soon as possible. Since the two funerals, restlessness and creeping ennui had made me their victim. I had had enough of the unhappiness the place had provided. Mrs. Debrowski would finish the term for me and I would spend a few days in the hospital. Apparently my efforts with Sheba Faye's body had done considerable damage to my already injured left arm. When I told Tall Wall about my plans to leave he merely shrugged.

"So am I, Bright Boy, so am I. I sent in my letter of resignation four weeks ago."

Hurt he hadn't told me, I replied with considerable venom. "Thanks a lot, pal, for telling me your plans a month after you made them."

"Look, Bright Boy," he replied defensively, "I didn't invite you to be my acolyte, and I don't want or need your near-veneration, if that's the right word."

Wallace relented a little and told me that he and a friend, Henry Albert, were moving to New Orleans, where Wallace would play piano with a Rhythm and Blues quintet. He totally surprised me by telling me that over Christmas he had signed a contract with a major record company. (You just think you can keep up with Wallace Talleck.) Of course, I complimented him there and then, despite the fact he hadn't let on.

Tall Wall knew he was a terrific teacher and a superb communicator. In front of a crowd he anticipated and received immediate attention. I suppose the word is "charisma" or "magnetism." I expected that his gifts as a musician were of such calibre that a much wider "classroom" should be his: the North American public and beyond.

Then my bespectacled and learned colleague began to speak in a way I had never heard him speak before.

"When people are *really* your audience," said Tall Wall, "you discover the real meaning of power." He added that he agreed with Friedrich Nietzche about the will to power being that which drove modern man. All successful performers knew that to be true. Power was the greatest aphrodisiac under God's blue sky.

"Happiness," he said, and there was iron in his voice, "is getting what you want *now*." Had he forgotten what his mother had taught him? My opinion of the man was weakening by the moment.

Wall suggested we write short thank you notes to those who had helped with Sheba Faye's funeral. Maggie J was unable to perform that duty. She had left Baltic in such a hurry that night because her school principal had had a second heart attack. So Tall Wall and I sat and wrote the notes. For me it was an hour commingled with sadness, anger, gratitude and jealousy toward the tall man whose friendship I had seemingly overestimated.

Late that night I found my way to the two-holer, unaccompanied by meadowlark or robin music. No Stookie with long rubber gloves, 'honeywagon,' pails, and heavy overalls made an appearance. No coyotes said goodnight from beyond the cemetery. Mrs. Stone's night light shone harshly from her house.

I'm rather a slow thinker, on occasion, and it only occurred to me then to wonder who was Tall Wall's "Henry Albert."

On the way back Splat received my first-ever, good, successful foot in his guts, before I again twisted my ankle on those damn crooked planks which joined the teacherage to the throne.

Back in the teacherage it came to me. Mr. Greensuit, the school unit Secretary-Treasurer, was named Henry Albert. I confronted Wall with my knowledge and damn near fainted when he admitted that he and Albert were secret lovers. Tall Wall, shrinking before my eyes, told me about the numerous weekends he and Henry had spent in Wall's city apartment. They were together during that pre-Christmas weekend of shopping and loneliness I had spent in the city. Wall announced that he and Henry would be happy wherever they went. I left the porch and tried to make it to the throne again. Just about where last September the student minister got sick because of my hen's egg joke, my stomach turned. By naming his male lover, Wallace had given me an actual target for my disgust. My left arm screamed every time I dry heaved.

Picture Wallace Talleck, educator, friend, first baseman, bon vivant in bed with Green Suit! It is to cry. Or was I just behind the times? If so, let me stay there. Maybe it was childish of me but, damn it, Tall Wall's admission was just too real. Disappointment flooded me. Perhaps I hated him.

The next day, one arm in a sling, I paid my dues by calling on all my Baltic friends. Perhaps it was my imagination, but most of the goodbyes seemed perfunctory. Or were we all shell-shocked? Mrs. Bredner's naked baby wet on my new trousers – my thanks for helping him with his birth? Bill, meanwhile, was on his tractor somewhere. Mr. Horvath, with hair seemingly whiter than ever, sorted the mail while Mrs. Horvath, still in cahoots with her kitchen stove, prepared a second batch of rhubarb jelly. Iris Woolston, who needed a bath, told me to come back whenever I could make it. Chairman Reg, to whom I handed over all but one of Stookie's keys – the red key for the train station – told me he figured that I wasn't the worst teacher he had ever seen, and at least I had got a few things going. I walked north past the nuisance grounds to the Kleiner farm, did the barnyard polka around a few meadow muffins, and knocked on the kitchen door. "Can't stay and talk," said Jack, "because a farmer's work is never done." Janet Kleiner said she would never return to teaching, "no matter what." More cold handshakes. The Kleiner farmhouse had an atmosphere of brooding quiet.

I walked back on the famous Bannister mile to Baltic's resident clergyman and graciously (I hoped) declined Mrs. Framm's soggy apple pie. Reverend Framm, looking terribly tired, told me "theological college never prepared me for my Baltic episode." I told him sincerely he had done splendidly. "How does one do splendidly at a suicide's funeral?" was his unexpected response.

I spent a quiet time at the cemetery, where Casey, our shortstop, had added two new crosses to two new graves. So many of Baltic's citizens had been touched by war and other forms of violence. I hoped my farewells to Stookie and Sheba Faye were heard. There was an ashy taste in my mouth. I supposed it would be a long time before I forgave myself.

Before returning to the teacherage, I visited the railroad station one last time, letting myself in with the red key I had kept aside. There was something there that I wanted to take with me.

It was becoming clear to me that a few months just isn't enough time to become a significant part of a small community.

One has be there for a long time. Until then you are an outsider. It hurt. Were my so-called friends little more than acquaintances? I felt two parts melancholy and one part anger.

How in hell do you leave without really saying goodbye? Perhaps people were so stunned by recent events that normal courtesies were forgotten. But just before I was due to go, my students came by the teacherage and kindly presented me with a going-away present, a new baseball glove.

Wallace sat in his hard chair reading a book as I left the teacherage. He didn't even raise his eyes, let alone shake my hand. Both of us knew the cord of friendship had been severed. Splat had dumped again in the back porch but I left it for Wallace to enjoy for a change. The ugly cat could have my old chair for all I cared.

Because I could use only one arm, it took three trips to carry all my stuff out. Wallace sure didn't help. I sat by my suitcases and boxes on the wood sidewalk between the post office and Woolston's corner. As if to say goodbye to them, I glanced at the railroad station, the grain elevator, and the deserted, empty buildings where there had once been businesses.

I had picked up my mail at the post office and, sorting through the envelopes, recognized the handwriting on one. It was Maggie J's.

Her letter offered appreciation for my help with Sheba Faye's funeral. She thanked me stiffly for "the friendship given so freely by you to me" and added her apologies for blaming me for Sheba Faye's death. Was she sincere? She said that after she had lashed out that night in desperation, frustration and anger, she had looked deeply into my eyes and upon reflection she knew I had done my best.

The letter was signed Margaret Jane Enders. Not MJ or Maggie J – just Margaret Jane Enders. I felt totally deflated.

The bus arrived from the west. I waved it down and helped the bus driver load my stuff. At the last minute Mrs. Stone showed up on the nearly empty main street.

"Goodbye to you, my young friend." She tried to smile but all she could show was a rim of her small, white teeth. My legs felt somehow stilty, and I stumbled getting into the dusty bus to leave the place called Baltic. Two weeks later Delmond Doby sent me a copy of Mrs. Stone's obituary. She had been correct in her paranoid prediction that death came in threes. Echo: *Who is going to hold my hand when I die?*

As the bus bumped along the gravel highway, away from Baltic, I thought about how nearly everyone had used me as an audience: Stookie, Wallace, Klanty, Delmond, Maggie J, Mr. Horvath, Mrs. Stone, Iris and Reg Woolston, Mr. Clawson, Mr. Framm. There must have been a reason why they chose a young teacher to talk to and confide in. Perhaps it was to tell their story.

Mixed feelings came into my mind: teaching was no job for very young adults; a small, dying town was depressing. even if one were born and raised there, and then it was merely disappointing; one shouldn't place too high a bet on untested friendships; friendships can break because people are brittle. I felt as bewildered as I was unhappy.

Had I lost too much of my youth? For sure, I had lost both of Klanty's daughters.

26

Today

Memory is nothing' but experience. – T. C. Haliburton

Recently I found these notes and my old diary in the bottom of my wife's cedar chest. It seems right that after many years this small story should be told. As I reread the material, I'm a bit embarrassed by my mixture of brash conviction and self-absorption, shallow judgmentalism and awkward naivete.

Tired Baltic has almost disappeared. When I drove through last year there were only a dozen or so houses left. The only business left standing was the rebuilt service station. Gone were the elevator, railroad tracks, trestle and station, portable blues, reconstructed teacherage, ball diamond, skating rink, curling rink, town hall, post office, and locker plant. The schoolyard-ball diamond area had become a summer fallow field. Even the Riga River seemed shrunken.

A long time ago Klanty's empty house had mysteriously burned to the ground. The stone fence remains adorned with broken beer bottles and healthy weeds. The padlocked church stands apparently unused and the same wrought-iron sign announces the cemetery. Cemeteries always win, don't they?

I couldn't find Mrs. Stone's grave, but the Horvaths are buried close to Stookie and Sheba Faye. Someone provided them with four small headstones. Another headstone identified the resting place of Jack Klackston, 1928 - 1955, killed by a line drive at Riga's July 1st baseball tournament.

Nothing could have prepared me for the green emptiness of where the Kleiner farmstead used to be. No home. No barn. No trees. Nothing. There was only a barley crop recently pounded by hail. What has happened to our rural way of living? What has happened to our small towns? It's a sad story, indeed.

The retired Kleiners and Bredners live somewhere in the city. The Christmas baby the Bredners had is now a cabinet minister with steel-gray hair. As his father Bill once said, "my son has two cowlicks and that's a pretty good sign he will be clever." Reg and Iris Woolston divorced in 1955, sold out, and moved away from Baltic. I have no knowledge of Reverend Framm, although I heard him preach in the city in 1985 or so. He vaguely remembered me. Helen Fowler died last year. Her clever missionary daughter, Marsha, was murdered in Chile years ago. Clancy is the principal of Riga Collegiate. The Dobys and the Clawsons spend their winters in Arizona together.

After his trial, Wayne Klanty lasted eight months in the penitentiary before shop-made knives let the life out of his bloated frame. Would-be child rapists given to incest don't last long there. Echo: *I don't give a damn about death.*

Bill and Maggie J – Margaret Jane – Statiuk live happily in Vyborg. Three of their four children, plus 13 grandchildren, live within a few hours' drive. Margaret's arthritis forces her to walk with a cane, but she still has the figure of a mature 16-year-old. Bill, an old man, golfs regularly in the summer and daily invades the town's library during the winter months.

Wallace Justinian Talleck lives in a small room above a dive off Bourbon Street. If you hit the New Orleans music scene, as I recently have, you might see Wallace in one club or another. He is stooped, rather unclean, and looks very old. I'm not sure if there were needle marks on his arm or not. His fingers are still supple and fast. He plays Dixieland and blues only. Thousands of straight vodkas over thousands of nights have fried his brains. He ditched Albert a few months after they reached their destination. Wallace slurringly asked me for "a spare 20 bucks for an old pal," in a molasses drawl he has either affected or absorbed. I was surprised how easy it was for me to turn down his request.

A long time ago I became a Uni-Ed Egghead and am proud of it. Stookie's flattened coin is in my desk drawer in my study. Usually that tall, antique railroad clock – the clock I took from the train station on my departure from Baltic – ticks softy. But not all the time.